The Quiet Room

The Quiet Room

Rona Simmons

DEEDS PUBLISHING | ATLANTA

Published by Deeds Publishing
Marietta, GA
www.deedspublishing.com

Printed in The United States of America

Library of Congress Cataloging-in-Publications Data is available upon request.

ISBN 978-1-937565-91-6

Books are available in quantity for promotional or premium use. For information, write Deeds Publishing, PO Box 682212, Marietta, GA 30068 or info@deedspublishing.com.

First Edition, 2014

10 9 8 7 6 5 4 3 2 1

CONTENTS

For Marcella and Christine

Part One:
Father

Chapter 1

The Quiet Room

I've become comfortable in the room beside the kitchen. I've overcome my fear and hatred for the things that occurred there. I even enjoy the room now. I've known it in its many incarnations over the years, hating it, fearing it, then taking refuge in it. I wonder if I will die in it when it is my time.

Until I began spending my nights there, I was not aware of how the room absorbed and held the warmth of the kitchen long after the oven was extinguished or how the scent of cinnamon and sugar cookies, chicken and dumplings, apples and rosemary, cherry and rhubarb pies infused the cushions of the chairs and the pillow cases, even the clothes I stored in its closet.

No. My earliest memories of the room are of smells quite different. Clean smells, but of a cleanliness so stringent I could not breathe the air in the room. It reeked of floors scrubbed over and over, rugs beaten thin with a broom, furniture treated with linseed oil and rubbed to a high gloss. That was before it became my grandfather's room—when other smells invaded and other things occurred there.

* * *

My father's simple oak desk sat catty-cornered in the center of the room. I sat in a straight-backed chair facing the desk and orbited him in his chair along with the room's other objects, a floor lamp, a file cabinet, and a third chair. He sat hunched over the desk as he had for the last hour. The nib of his pen marred the quiet as it scratched against a page of parchment. My eyes were on my hands in my lap, not at him. My feet didn't reach the floor; they dangled in the air below the wooden seat. I wanted to swing them back and forth, to click my heels together, then my toes. But I didn't. I held my feet still, as still as our wash on the line in a breezeless summer afternoon, as still as the hands in my lap. I was being punished, or rather, made to reflect on my transgressions.

The scratching continued.

If it were a Tuesday or a Wednesday, my sentence lasted only an hour, the time it took him to write a member or two of his congregation he'd not visited that week—or that month. Many of them lived hours from town, in homes scattered across the valleys of lower Indiana where the Ohio River cuts through the dark fertile earth in long swooping S curves. I knew about the soil because we'd once lived on a farm. Most of the congregation, like us, were people of the earth, people who believed in the fundamental goodness of the earth, of salvation through hard work and unwavering faith, and of eternal damnation.

But this was Friday, the day he prepared his sermon. For disobeying my mother on Thursday evening, she'd sentenced me to spend Friday morning in his room, the quiet room, until he completed his work. My penance might last several hours.

In the sliver of the room visible through the corners of my eyes, left and right, though I dared not move my head, tiny specks of dust lit golden by the morning sun drifted in the air. They rose from below my line of sight, hovered for an instant, then flitted beyond my vision, only to be replaced by others. There were fewer today than normal as my mother dusted on Thursdays. The lemon-scented oil from her dust cloth surrounded me, punctured by a hint of lavender from the herbal soap my father used. Each time he exhaled, though he sat several arm lengths away, the floral aroma wafted toward me.

This was not the first time my parents had made me sit in the room. Nor, did I think it would be my last. No matter how carefully I tried to remember the rules, I invariably broke them.

"And what else?" my mother said. Each time I broke a rule, she made me recite them.

"Speaking when my father is working. Not watching when I carry my plate. Running instead of walking."

I committed the rules to memory, or at least I tried to; I'd invented a guide to my transgressions by working my way from my head to my feet. Each part of my body had the potential to offend. My head and mouth. I must think before I speak. I must choose my words carefully. I must not speak too loudly, especially when adults visit. And not at all when my father is working. My arms and hands. I must take care not to swing my arms, especially in the front room where the breakable things are, and not to look away when carrying my dinner plate to the kitchen for fear I will lose my balance and dash the plate to the ground. My legs and feet. I must walk properly, like a lady. Never run, or skip, or hop. Or, I thought, though not included on my mother's list, dance.

"That will do," she said when I'd finished or at least worn her patience thin with my triumph of memory. "You can go upstairs now and prepare for bed. And, in the morning, you can sit with your father." She levied the punishment in her measured voice, without anger, without sympathy, without feeling.

"Yes ma'am."

For solace, I imagined my mother as a child with the same rules to obey. I imagined she never broke them. In the chair, my head bowed, I pledged to try harder to be like her.

Four blocks of light had traveled across the floor toward me, and now they lapped at the leg of my chair. With the sun near its peak, the shapes had stretched into long, thin rectangles. He will be finished soon, I thought.

My father sighed. It was another clue. He sighed each time he reached the end of his sermon, satisfied, I thought, imagining his congregation enlightened by his message. Next, he would slip his pen into its holder and tap the edges of the pages of his sermon on the desk, to shape them into a neat bundle. *Tap, tap, tap.* Despite the tell-tale signs of freedom, I kept my head bowed. He had not yet given me permission to go.

"Liese, you may rise." I looked up. Although anxious to run from the room, from my prison without chains, I pushed forward slowly in the chair until my shoes touched the floor. I stood and waited to be dismissed. Those were the rules, too.

"How would you like to go with me to Mrs. Wiethorst's?" He bent his head forward and eyed me over his spectacles; the light bounced off the wire rim and sliced his eye in two equal halves.

"I'd like that very much, Father," I said to one of the halves. I would have much preferred to go into the garden behind the house, sit on the ground, and let the sun warm my face. It was October and few mild days remained. But I didn't complain. Complaining was another transgression. At least, I thought, accompanying my father on one of his visits meant I'd be outdoors for part of the afternoon. And, though the purpose of his visit was to offer condolences to Mrs. Wiethorst on her husband's death, I didn't mind. Death was an integral part of my father's life and, so I thought, of mine.

My father's responsibilities as pastor of Zion Evangelical Church included making frequent visits to members of his flock of Indiana Germans. He celebrated births, performed christenings and marriages, tended to the sick or lonely, and comforted survivors of those who had passed—parents, sisters, brothers, husbands, wives, or, far worse, children.

An unnamed illness plagued my mother. Often it prevented her from accompanying my father on his visits. On many of those occasions, he took me in her place—I wondered if he thought the presence of a young child brightened the otherwise somber atmosphere. To make myself useful, I tried imagining my mother's role during the visits. Would she take the children aside while he consoled the widow or widower. Would she offer her own words of comfort. But my father asked that I do nothing more than stand quietly nearby and not interrupt while he spoke or prayed with our hosts.

Mr. Wiethorst had died the week before. In the darkened parlor of his home, I stood beside my father. He leaned forward in the over-stuffed chair and wrapped his long, black-clad arm around the newly widowed woman's shoulder, then patted her son and daughter on the head, as I supposed Mr. Wiethorst might have done. He'd never done the same to me. When he spoke, though he listened more than he spoke, his words came soft, barely audible. Mrs. Wiethorst raised a lace-trimmed handkerchief to her nose and leaned close.

"Zachary has gone to a better place, Eleanor," he said with an expression as void of emotion as his tone. "He has no more pain."

I marveled at the effect my father's words had on Mrs. Wiethorst. She did not smile, but the muscles in her face and neck relaxed as if a gnawing pain had subsided, as if my father were a doctor and had applied a soothing balm to her open wound.

After the visit, to my surprise and disappointment, we did not turn east toward home. Instead, we walked north then made another stop. On arriving at the second home, we found Mr. and Mrs. Livermore weeping openly, shoulders rising and falling in great waves of grief.

The scene from the Wiethorst home replayed for a new audience. "Marianne has gone to a better place." This time, my father pulled a starched white handkerchief from the breast pocket of his jacket. He dabbed his eyes with a corner of the handkerchief then folded the cloth and replaced it in his pocket, without so much as a glance, fingers moving in a rhythmic, rehearsed manner.

I wondered if I should have carried a kerchief to dab my own eyes as he did. But, I didn't have a kerchief and I hadn't shed any tears.

We said our goodbyes, or rather, my father did while I nodded but said nothing, mindful of his request. Once outside, he paused and scribbled a few words in a small leather-bound book he carried. After replacing the book in his coat pocket, he reached for my hand and we turned the corner toward home.

He took longer and faster steps, which forced me to quicken my pace. I looked up to catch his attention, but his eyes gazed down the block ahead, his lips carried the trace of a smile. His tears from moments ago, forgotten, tucked away in the past.

I practiced writing the names of things I'd lost in a book I kept in my bedroom. Keeping a log of passings would, I reasoned, ease the pain. That was the secret I discovered on visits with my father and from spying on my mother. She'd written the names of my two dead brothers in the front of our family Bible.

From behind the half-open hallway door where I hid, I watched through the slit between the hinges as she crossed to the stand under the window in the parlor, opened the book, and ran her fingers down the page to a place near the bottom. After a moment, she raised her fingers to her lips then placed them on the page again. Then she walked away from the stand and up the stairs.

I tiptoed across the room to the Bible. She'd taught me to read that year, but my books contained short words in large, block letters. These pages held handwritten words scrawled along a slanted line, some of the letters squeezed together near the edge. I tried the shorter words, and sounded them out one by one, John, Henry, Lucas.

"Mar—"

"Margaret," mother said. Somehow, she'd come back into the room without my hearing. "And this one is Anneliese Margaret Bauer." She reached over me and ran the tip of her finger with its uneven and cracked nail underneath the many-lettered words. "That's your great grandmother's name. That's who you were named for."

She showed me where her mother and her mother's mother had inscribed the date for family births, christenings, marriages, and deaths on the first few pages of the Bible. There were many deaths.

"Here is where your father and I joined our families. And this is your name, here."

I ran my finger lightly over the inscription, as I had seen her do.

Anneliese Margaret Stephens b. January 1, 1900.

Above and below this entry were two others. "Who are these?" I asked, pointing to the two entries. She read them aloud.

Thomas Henry Stephens b. October 8, 1898. d. October 29, 1898.
Boy Stephens b. March 3, 1902. d. March 3, 1902.

"They died? Am I going to die, too?"

"That's enough for now, Liese," she said.

For weeks after my discovery, I waited for the right opportunity to ask about my dead siblings. I could not understand why neither my father or mother ever mentioned them. The only record I had of their presence on this earth were the scrawled inscriptions in the family Bible. When I died, I wondered if an inscription would be the only evidence of my life, a line in the family Bible with a beginning and an end.

If so, I decided, at least I could remember my brothers in the prayers I recited with my parents each evening before bed. I added them after my father's "Amen", silently, to myself. I raised my head and opened my eyes. Beside me, my mother's lips moved, forming the shapes of the same words I had whispered in my mind.

In the late winter of 1907, a kitten I'd adopted died. An ordinary gray and white striped ball of fur, he, or she, which gender it was I never knew, appeared behind the house on my birthday, the first day of the new year. I took a half step toward him, paused, then took another, inching my way across the garden. When I was within a few feet, he retreated beneath the shed where we kept garden tools and did not reemerge. That evening at dinner,

I secreted a few scraps of meat from the chicken bones on my plate and placed them in the pocket of my apron. After helping Mother wash the dishes and put away the pots, I hurried out into the garden toward the shed.

"Here kitty, here kitty," I whispered into the dark space below the shed. A feeble mew answered not from below the shed, but from beneath an overturned wheelbarrow by its side. Two pale blue eyes peered out at me. I mounded the scraps on the ground and backed a few feet away. The creature emerged and gobbled the meal, hardly pausing to swallow.

A few days later, Mother discovered my secret. As I crossed the kitchen with a bowl of milk in my hands, she said, "Liese, we don't need another mouth to feed around here. Besides, he might be sick." Somehow she knew.

"He's not sick. And he doesn't eat much, just a scrap or two. Can I keep him?"

She followed me to the shed and watched as I set the bowl on the ground. I placed a finger to my lips and took a step back. Mother hung close to me. The kitten reappeared and lapped the milk. When he was done, my mother crouched beside me and rubbed her fingers behind the kitten's ears. He closed his eyes and nuzzled against her hand.

"Don't let him in the house. And you'll have to look after him. Don't be asking me to do that."

"Oh thank you, Mother. Thank you. I won't." I clapped my hands together over and over. "I will. Luke won't be any trouble at all. Will you, Luke."

Luke lived for another six or seven weeks. One morning, he crawled from the shed. One of his hind legs dragged behind like an afterthought. It hung by a thin strip of flesh to the body. Dark blood matted his fur. I bundled him in a rag, held him in my lap, and stroked his head.

The next day, I found him dead behind the coal bin, his body cold and stiff. I cried as I had seen Mrs. Wiethorst, Mrs. Livermore, and countless other mothers do.

"You'll have to bury him," my mother said.

"Bury whom?" my father said. He rose from the breakfast table.

"My...cat," I said.

"A cat? What cat?"

"A kitten. I found him but now he's dead." My voice cracked. "He...Luke's outside under the shed." I didn't want my father to see me cry, but I could not hold back my tears.

"Come here, Liese."

I walked to my father, who pulled a square of white cotton from his pocket and dabbed my cheeks dry.

"Show me and we'll have a proper burial."

I walked my father to the shed. Together, we made a crude shroud for Luke from a rag. Then, we dug a shallow grave underneath a tree near the shed.

"He's gone to a better place, Liese. He doesn't hurt anymore," he said, his voice calm, unwavering.

I stood back as Father shoved dirt into the grave until it covered Luke's broken corpse. He was not in a better place. Not that I could see. He lay wrapped in a rag and covered in dirt.

On a piece of paper I took from my father's desk, I wrote Luke's name and the date. I folded the piece of paper until it fit in the palm of my hand. Then, I placed it inside my book of passings and returned the book to the back of my dresser drawer. I did not feel better. Once or twice over the next few days, I caught myself thinking of setting out a bowl of milk. But then, after several more days passed, as my father had promised Mrs. Wiethorst, Mrs. Livermore, the others, and now me, my sorrow vanished.

Part Two:
Adam

CHAPTER 2
Scheisse

Even now, fifty years later, people don't speak of certain things that happen inside a home, behind a closed door, even when they know they happened. True, there are occasional stories that make the headlines of the papers. There was the famous Charles Lindbergh case. That was in 1932. The Weinberger crime of 1956 was less sensational as it involved ordinary people, middle class people, like my family. Both involved ransoms for return of the children. Both ended tragically with the children brutally murdered. Both incidents involved third party perpetrators.

In my case, the perpetrator was a known entity, a member of the family. Its patriarch. A person who did not steal the child away in the night, but instead stole the childhood from the child. In broad daylight. These were crimes that went unreported and unspoken then and still do now. I can't say if my parents truly did not know or whether they knew and simply chose not to say or do anything. I am guilty, too, guilty of not saying anything, though I doubt anyone would have believed me.

Besides, the words to describe what occurred were not words I understood or words used in my father's house. I still have trouble finding the right word for what I experienced at the hands of my grandfather. Abused, beat, mistreated, tormented, tortured, or any of a dozen more. None quite seems to fit, or maybe they all do.

* * *

On one of the first warm days in the early spring of 1907, my mother's father, Adam Bauer, came to live with us. He moved into the quiet room.

Our home on First Avenue was a modest home, befitting the local preacher. It had only two bedrooms, mine and my parents, both upstairs overlooking the front walk. My father's ground floor study proved the only suitable place for my grandfather, who, because of his injury, could not navigate the stairs.

"It'll be fine, Maria," my father said to my mother. "I'll just move my desk into the front room. The light's better there anyway."

I welcomed the chaos that came with my grandfather; furniture sat in hallways, shuffled sometimes from room to room, dinners were delayed, and breakfasts haphazard. When he took up residence in the quiet room, I imagined the venue for penance would simply relocate with my father's desk to the parlor. But to my astonishment and delight, my parents, absorbed in looking after my grandfather and exhausted at the ends of their days, lost interest in meting out punishment. My pleasure was short lived. Soon, I would wish for a return to our prior life, to sitting out my sentence among the dust particles and the scents of oil and lavender.

Though I'd been with my parents when they'd found him, I didn't fully understand how my grandfather had broken his hip and leg. That day in April, we rode to the family home near Mt. Vernon, twenty miles outside Evansville. Every few miles, my father ranted about the sins of drink while my mother made a feeble attempt to defend her father's wayward ways.

"I can just imagine what he's eating," my mother said. She'd risen early that morning to bake two apple pies, one for the three of us and one for her father. Now, as we bounced along the rutted road, she balanced the extra pie in a basket in her lap for fear it might be crushed if left on the floor between two boxes of food, one of preserves and the other an assortment of canned goods.

"Ever since Mother died," she continued, "he's been alone in that drafty old house."

"Well, if he wasn't drinking himself to death," my father said, "he would have more time to eat."

"Tom, I'm sure he's not drinking that much."

"Any amount is too much."

"You haven't seen him touch a drop, not in over a year."

"That's only because now that he knows I've found out, he's hiding it. And, as a member of our Women's Temperance Committee, you might want to remind him that he should follow your example."

"I have. I've tried to tell him what drink will do. But he just doesn't want to listen."

I sat on the bench between my parents for the two-hour drive, dizzy with the buggy rocking from side to side and the conversation volleying back and forth above my head. I understood only enough to know that something my grandfather did was sinful and that, like me, he would be punished. The occasional whiff of apples, cinnamon, and sugar helped me endure. There'd be a treat for me at the end.

Usually, when we arrived, we'd find my grandfather in a chair on the front porch. From high on the hill where the house sat, he could see our buggy make the last half mile of the journey. But that day Adam Bauer was not on the porch or anywhere else in sight.

"Father?" My mother called out as she stepped from the buggy and made her way to the front door. "Father, we're here."

I followed her into the house and remained inches from the folds of her skirt as she trod up the main hall, then back, opening and closing doors to dark and dank rooms as she went. When we returned to the front room, she stood in the center, hands on her hips, and surveyed the scene: newspapers piled high next to a chair, mounds of cold ash in the fireplace, and over the sideboard, an open window. Dust had blown across the room; it coated the surface of the few pieces of furniture with a dull brown film. She ran a finger across the top of the sideboard, shook her head, then took up her search again.

"Tom," she called to my father who was climbing the front stairs, the basket and box of preserves in one hand, the canned goods in the other. "Tom, have a look around outside, please. He's not in here."

On a second check of the interior, Mother noticed the half-door to the cellar was unlatched. She fingered the latch for a moment, then yanked the door open. Stale air from the cellar swarmed into the hallway. Mother put her hand over her mouth and nose and headed down. I hesitated, not knowing which would be worse, to follow her down the steps into the rank air or remain alone upstairs. Taking one step at a time, my hand against the wall, I descended into the underground cellar. A heavy scent of yeast grew more pungent with every step.

The sound of our feet on the stairs must have wakened the old man. A whimper, as if from a wounded animal, rose from the darkness below. It reminded me of Luke, the way the kitten had whimpered as he'd crawled to me with his severed leg.

"Oh my dear Lord," Mother said. "What has happened to you?" She sped to the bottom of the stairs. I remained midway down, afraid to go any further. The only light, a mere sliver of gray, came from between the louvers set in a vent on the opposite wall. Outlined in the dim light, a man's body lay on the earthen floor.

"Liese, run upstairs. Go find your father and tell him to come here right away. Quick, now girl. Go!"

I scrambled up the stairs as fast as I could. When I reached the hallway, my father, having given up his search outside, was coming through the back door.

"He's down in the cellar." I shouted. "Grandfather's down in the cellar. Mother says—"

He pushed past me and down the stairs before I could finish.

"I'm here, Maria. I'm here. Where is he?"

Alone again, I crept toward the cellar door and then down two of the stairs. Below, in the semi-darkness, my parents knelt together, hunched over the old man's body.

"Tom, he's fallen. I think he's unconscious." My mother turned to her father, "Father, can you hear me?" She held one of his hands in hers and, with her free hand, patted his bearded cheek.

My father raised his head and looked around at the rough-hewn shelves attached to the earthen walls. A mound of planks, straps, ropes, and other debris littered the cellar floor. "He must have been at this for years," he said. "I can't imagine how he got all of this—"

"Oh, I don't know. But it looks like he's been hurt pretty bad-ly."

"Looks like one of his contraptions fell on him. Look at all this glass."

"I think he's cut himself and his leg may be broken, too. Everything is soaked in—"

"Drink. I told you he would come to no good."

Alcohol, or "drink" as my father referred to it, was the source of the overwhelming stench. The spilled liquid had soaked everything it touched—the scraps of wood, the earthen floor, and the old man's clothes. It had even seeped into the fabric of my mother's skirt as she knelt beside her father.

My grandfather moaned but otherwise showed no reaction to his daughter's words. She shook his arm, which had no effect except to push his moan another octave deeper. "We'll have to get him out of here. And to a doctor. If we can get him to move at all."

My father removed what remained of the broken vat, most of it scattered across the old man's lower torso and left leg. He tossed pieces of the wreckage aside and with the back of his hand brushed away small fragments of glass that dotted the old man's trousers like crystals of coarse salt. Once he'd cleared most of the debris, he had a better view of the man and his injuries. Even from where I sat, I could see the stains on my grandfather's pants. They were dark. Blood, I thought, not alcohol.

"I think you're right, Maria. He is badly hurt."

"Oh, dear me," she said. "I'll go get some water." She lowered her father's head to the ground. As she climbed to my perch midway up the stairs, I retreated up and into the hall and the fresh air. Mother returned in a moment with a glass of water in her hand then disappeared into the basement again. I resumed my position on the stairs. My grandfather, conscious and in obvious pain, groaned as he spoke. "Get away. Let me be. My leg. *Ach*, my leg." He flailed the air with one arm to fend off my father's attempt to help.

"Yes, yes," mother said. "We know." She dropped to his side again, despite the vileness of the damp ground.

"I've been thinking," Father said to her, "maybe it's best if I go back to town for a doctor."

"Oh, no, Tom. Please, don't leave us here alone."

I wanted to add my pleas to my mother's. My father would be gone for hours, perhaps all night. I did not want to stay behind with the broken body in the cellar.

"Well, then, let's try one more time," he said. "Let's see if we can get him up and out to the porch together—wait a minute—I have an idea. Wait here. Keep him still until I get back."

My father climbed up, skirted around me, and vanished down the hall. His steps faded. The back door opened then closed with a bang. He returned in a minute with a few scraps of wood and a roll of twine in his hands.

Together, my parents fashioned a crude splint from the scraps and strapped it to my grandfather's leg. "Adam," my father said, "let's see if you can walk over to the steps." They managed him to an upright position. Then, flanking the old man, they steered him to the stairway and climbed the steps one at a time.

"Go get a chair, Liese," my father called as they neared the top of the stairs. I found one in the kitchen and pushed it in front of me the length of the hallway, meeting them as they emerged through the cellar door. My grandfather lowered himself to the edge of the chair, his left leg, stained in blood, smelling of alcohol and now, bound by the splint, stretched across the hall.

"Adam, how long have you been down there?" my father asked.

"*Die ganze nacht, denke ich.* I don't know," he said. "What day is it?"

"Well, never mind," mother said. "We're going to take you with us. Into town. And to a doctor." She leaned over her father and wiped his face with a damp cloth.

"Doctor, yes, doctor," he repeated. "*Scheisse,* my leg, *scheisse*" he said as he gripped his thigh between his bony hands. "*Scheisse.*"

Mother cringed and avoided looking up at my father who stood behind the chair and glared at the old man.

I'd never heard the word before but gathered it was a word not said in polite company and that I should not ask its meaning. The word, however, eased my grandfather's pain. The tension in his jaw slackened each time he uttered the profanity. But he never walked again without a cane and even then, he hobbled as he walked. He never lived on his own again. Like me, he became a prisoner in our quiet house. Unlike me, he would not be a silent prisoner.

Scheisse! I became accustomed to the sound of the word echoing in the hallway or escaping through a cracked window, or open door. *Scheisse!* My grandfather would shout the word from his room day or night. He would shout it when he was hungry. He would shout it when he was angry, and he was often angry.

When my father asked him to refrain from using profanity in the house, my grandfather merely grunted in reply, neither agreeing or disagreeing. For years after, whether my father was home or not, my grandfather shouted, piercing the quiet, and casting his misery into the far reaches of the house, and my soul.

CHAPTER 3
Liniment and Balm

"Liese, where have you been? I've been calling you for the last fifteen minutes."

I'd heard Mother call but ignored her, hoping she'd give up and take the dinner tray to my grandfather. She called several more times. Though I'd retreated from view of the house, her voice found me.

"I was outside in the garden. I picked you a bouquet." I brandished half a dozen daisies in front of her face at the sink, my most obedient and innocent daughter smile on my lips. "See?"

"Put them on the counter. Then, when you've delivered the tray to your grandfather, you can help me arrange them in a vase."

I'd not fooled her. Not for a minute. "Yes, ma'am." I turned toward the tray of food, dragging my feet as if quicksand sucked at my shoes.

"Liese!"

"Yes, I'm going." I curled my fingers through the handles of the tray and carried it down the hall to Grandfather Bauer's room. Mother had passed the responsibility to me on my thirteenth birthday, nearly six months ago, though it seemed much longer. I was supposed to be grateful for being given an adult role in the household and the opportunity to help with the daily chores. Instead, I'd suggested I could pick and wash vegetables, peel potatoes, even cook dinner, leaving her free to serve Grandfather.

The vegetable peeler had flicked back and forth over a carrot she rotated in her left hand. She'd tilted her head down, turned, still flicking the peeler, and looked at me full on. It was her look. The one that meant the discussion was over.

Grandfather's door was down the hall on the right, fourteen paces. I scuffed the heels of my shoes against the hardwood floor to announce my arrival, seven scuffs on the right, seven on the left. I wanted him to hear me approach and cover himself. He often sat with his injured leg and hip exposed, whether to bathe it in sunlight or to remind him of his earlier carelessness, his drunkenness, I didn't know. Once, only weeks after I'd started serving him dinner, I caught him half naked in his chair, his eyes locked on the blue-black scar that zigzagged the length of his thigh. Hoping he hadn't seen me, I'd darted back into the hall. If he had, he'd said nothing, but ever since, I counted and scuffed my way to him.

Today I found the old man propped upright in a chair by the window, his eyes fixed on some object outside that I could not see, his twisted leg elevated on a needlework pillow atop a stool. He had to know I was at his door, nevertheless, he sat motionless and stared at the vacant strip of visible sky. I took a last deep breath of fresh air from the hallway, then entered the room. The air reeked of white liniment, camphor, ammonia, and an assortment of other salves.

Sparsely furnished, his room contained a rocker with an embroidered seat cushion, a table where he took most of his meals, a nightstand, a stool, his bed, a four-drawer dresser and two identical wooden chairs, one in which my grandfather now sat.

Atop the dresser, two photographs stood, unframed, still in their original photographer's tri-fold paper envelope. In one, several generations of the Bauer family posed in front of their home in Mt. Vernon; in the other a stern-faced woman, my grandmother, Henrietta Boerner Bauer, squinted as if she might have been nearsighted and never quite sure of what passed before her. I never knew my grandmother, but from her pinched expression,

I doubted I would have found her to my liking; after all, she'd married my grandfather.

A cane rested against the dresser. Grandfather seldom walked any great distance, but used the cane to maneuver his broken body between the bed and the chair and to hobble to the closet-like bathroom another few paces down the hall. My father had placed a Bible on the nightstand, and my grandfather's spectacles lay folded alongside the book as if moments ago he had read a passage. Even so, I'd never once come into the room and found the book open or him reading from it.

The bed was cast iron. Its headboard bore a heart fashioned into the metal, and if anything could have made me smile, it was the sight of that metal heart in this room. I supposed the bed had once belonged to a young girl.

Folded at the foot of the bed was one of my mother's basket-themed quilts, the only brightly colored item in the room. I avoided looking at the quilt. If I stared at it too long, the squares of oranges, reds, greens, and blues shifted. They tumbled like pieces of colored glass in a kaleidoscope, hovered for a moment, and then dropped and vanished in its center. I kept my eyes on the bowl of soup in the middle of the tray. I breathed the aroma of chicken and dumplings in a broth yellow with butter. I'd invented a game of naming the ingredients—chicken, I'd say, then chicken and flour, then chicken and flour and butter. I'd recite the list in my head and add a new ingredient on each repetition. Yesterday, it was beef stew, and I'd memorized twelve ingredients.

"I have your dinner," I said to draw his attention from the window. "Mother's bringing your coffee," I added to give him notice we'd not be alone for long.

"*Danke.* Put the tray here on the table."

I balanced the tray against my hip and pushed aside a glass of water that Mother had brought earlier. I placed the tray on the side nearest him and turned it so that the spoon lay within his reach. I hesitated, took a half step back.

"Will you help me? I'm not feeling well, *liebling*. I'm not up to it today."

I jumped at a sound at the door. My mother stood in the doorway, a cup of coffee in her hands. "Oh dear, don't tell me," she said. "Are you still under the weather?"

"Yes. I think I'm worse today than yesterday. Could Liese help me, please?"

"Of course. Liese, please help your grandfather eat. I'll finish putting supper on the table." She set the cup on the table and turned to go.

"Yes, Mother." I watched as she went out the door. I watched until the hem of her skirt disappeared around the doorframe.

"We'll wait for you," her words faded in the empty hall.

With no other option, I turned to my grandfather, reached across the table, and picked up the cloth napkin. I shook it open and with the tips of my fingers, placed it across the old man's chest then tucked it under his chin, spreading the corners over his shoulders as best I could. All the while, his hands remained in his lap, clasped together, unmoving. Beneath their thin, taut skin, his knuckles bulged, heavy and gnarled as knots of twine. The nails on his fingers, the color of ochre, were clouded and thick with age.

I looked away, back to the bowl. I picked up the spoon, dipped it in the broth and scooped both a bit of chicken and a piece of dumpling.

"Please, sit down."

I lowered the spoon back into the bowl. He'd won. I dragged the spare wooden chair to the table. I filled the spoon again and followed it to his coarse lips, cracked with flecks of dried skin along the crevices. He had not shaved, or rather been shaved, since Monday. A stubble of gray hairs littered his chin.

My heart screamed. Its cry rang in my ears. He turned his head toward me. I wondered if he'd heard it, too.

I tilted the spoon between his teeth and drained the liquid into his mouth. The morsels of chicken and dumpling dropped to his tongue. His slack-skinned, stubble-strewn jaw rolled up and down as he chewed. I traced the pattern of pink flowers along the edge of the soup bowl with my eyes. Chicken and flour and butter and salt. Four ingredients. I waited for the sound of him swallowing before I spooned more soup.

"*Brotchen.*"

I tore a piece of bread from the *brotchen*, a round, fist-sized roll that accompanied many of our family's meals. I lathered the bread with sweet butter and lifted it to his mouth; as always, keeping my fingers as far from his lips as possible. Another spoonful of soup. And then another, until at last the bottom of the bowl came into view. Except for his requests for another bite of bread or spoon of soup, no conversation passed between us.

"Enough. I'll have my coffee now." He dismissed a last spoonful of soup with the back of his hand.

Trying not to rush, I placed the spoon back on the tray and stacked the soup bowl on top of the bread plate. With two hands, one on the delicate finger loop, one on the base, I guided the full cup to his lips. His hand found mine. The fingertips, hot as red cinders, burned the back of my hand. I jerked my hand away. Coffee spilled from his mouth and dripped to his chest leaving a brown stain the length of the napkin and down the front of his shirt, ending where the shirt met the waist of his trousers.

"*Ach!* Look what you have done, you clumsy child. Take it away. Bring me another cup."

I tore the napkin from his neck and shoulders, threw it on the tray with the dishes, and sped out the door. When I returned with a fresh cup and napkin, he said, "Leave it on the table. I can drink it myself."

I set the cup and napkin within easy reach on the table and hurried to the door.

"Child," he called after me, as I passed through the doorway. "Close the door or you'll have me catch cold."

I stepped back to the doorway. He had already turned himself away from the table to stare out the window. The fresh cup of coffee sat untouched where I had placed it. I drew the door closed then stood motionless outside the door, my left hand clenched around the doorknob. His phlegm-laden breaths, each capped with a wheeze, were audible through the closed door.

In the hallway, I doubled over and waited for the colors that swam behind my closed eyelids to vanish. The memories from earlier days in his room rushed into my head.

I was seven years old again. I'd shared the house with my grandfather for six months.

"Father," my mother said, "I'm going to leave Liese here to keep you company while I take my pies to the church. Is that all right? *Ist das gut?*" My mother resorted to German when she thought her father had drifted and lost himself in his one-room world.

His leg had healed but not mended. The doctor who attended him after we'd brought him to town said he would need a cane to walk, if he ever walked again. I understood only that he was injured. Bitterness and hatred were concepts I did not comprehend. Not then. Fear I learned first. Hatred came later.

What worried me most at that long ago moment in his room was Mother leaving the house, leaving me alone with my grandfather in his room. I peered up at her, but she was looking at him, waiting for a sign he'd understood. He turned his head toward her, glanced at me, then back at her. He nodded.

"I won't be gone long. Less than an hour." When I would not let go of her, she reached down and peeled my hand from hers. She walked over to her father and pecked him on the cheek. Then, she tucked the crocheted afghan around his hips and patted it gently. Turning finally to me, she said, "You behave while I'm gone. Mind your grandfather. I'll be back soon."

My mother crossed in front of me and disappeared out the door, taking the fragrant cloud of baked apples and cinnamon with her.

We were alone.

I stood where she had left me, leaning against the cold metal frame of my grandfather's cast iron bed. Not wanting to look at him, I kept my eyes on the quilt folded at the foot of his bed and fingered the colored shapes. I traced the outline of several squares before hazarding a glance at him only to see that he had turned in his chair toward me. I shifted my glance and turned my full attention to the yarn doll in my hand. I picked at its miniature pink apron.

After a few minutes of the standoff, he said, "Come here, *liebling.*"

I did not hesitate. I minded him. He was my elder. He was my grandfather. I closed the short distance between us, heel to toe, heel to toe, each tiny step deliberate. When I came within an arm's distance, he bent over, picked me up, and maneuvered me onto his lap, balancing me on the thigh of his right leg, his good leg. His awkward fumbling caused me to lose hold of my doll. He did not see the doll fall to the floor or hear the tiny thump when it landed on the floor beside his chair. I squirmed in the old man's grasp and wiggled in his lap until I could see my doll on the floor. She lay face up, her blue button eyes stared unblinking at the ceiling. Her hair made from strands of yellow yarn knotted around the head lay sprawled on the floor. I opened and closed the fingers of my right hand, straining to reach the doll but grasped only empty air. My grandfather took no notice.

"Let me see," he said, to himself more than to me. I did not turn toward him. My eyes remained focused on the doll on the floor. But I felt his fingers on me. He pushed aside my skirt and took my left leg in his hand, twisting it to examine both sides of my shoe. He did nothing for a moment but made a gurgling sound then moaned once. Startled, I shifted my gaze away from the doll and back to the old man. The shoelaces that criss-crossed to just above the ankle must have confused him as it took him some minutes before he loosened the laces, removed the shoe, and cradled it in his hand. He explored the shoe's still warm inner surface with his forefinger then placed the shoe in his lap. With the open palm of his left hand, he cupped my foot in its black woolen sock. His fingers moved from the toe to the heel, to the ankle, and to the length of sock that covered my leg to the middle of my pudgy thigh. He inserted the tips of his fingers into the cuff of the sock, and rolled it down to the ankle.

His hand was coarse against my soft flesh I stared at his hand and followed it as he caressed my foot softly at first, then more firmly.

He repositioned me on his lap, turning to face away from him. My left leg fell across his damaged left thigh. Words tumbled from his lips and filled the air in the room. Words I did not know. With both hands, he pressed my leg hard against his, tilted his head back, and cried out in pain.

A gasping sound brought me out of the fog of memory. The sound was me, struggling for air in the semi-darkness of the hallway. I never allowed myself to follow that memory to its end. With a determined shake of my head, the basket shapes vanished, the feel of his hands on my body evaporated. I waited until I could count three even breaths then released my hand on the doorknob, and stepped away from the door. As I walked back down the hall toward the kitchen, I did not scuff my heels or make a sound.

Part Three:
Will

CHAPTER 4
Hogs and Boys

When I look out the windows from the second floor of my house, a floor I no longer inhabit, I cannot see the river. A slice of it used to be visible to the south, between the Alderman and Wilkin homes across the street. I can't see the riverside park now either. Even the tops of the trees that once peeked above the houses to the east are today obscured by three- and four-story buildings. I've grown accustomed to the changes, and at times have trouble remembering what it was like before.

The city has been my home for close to fifty years though I was born in the countryside surrounded by fertile black earth and fields of hay. Now and then, I drive to the country, avoiding the parts southwest of town where the railroad crosses the river and the area to the north where the hills afford a view of Illinois on a clear day. I stay mostly on the flat land where crops cover the earth.

If I leave the car window down, the smells of the country blow in and waken my city-dampened senses. Once, I enjoyed the scent of new mown hay left in the sun to dry, of the hides of cows in the barn, and the smoke of fragrant wood heating kettles for our annual hog butchering. Later, those smells lost their magic. They bore only the memory of a boy who stole a piece of my heart.

* * *

In November 1916, we crowded into the buggy for the three-hour ride to my uncle's farm east of Mt. Vernon. I sat on the front seat between my parents. My grandfather sat alone in the back where he could stretch his leg across the length of the bench. We were the last to arrive for the family's annual hog butchering as our route from town had taken us past the home of a church member who'd taken ill. By the time we reached Uncle Paul's farm, preparations were well underway.

A chorus of greetings erupted from those already gathered.

"Pastor Tom, at last!" a neighbor called out when he spied my father.

We've saved some of the heavy work for you," one of the men shouted.

"And the blessing, of course," Edward Kline, another neighbor, said.

"Hello there, Maria! Tell me you've brought some of your delicious pies."

"Well, well, and here's Liese," Uncle Paul said, after we'd climbed down from our buggy. "You are sure a young lady now. And, I dare say you're looking more and more like your mother every day."

I glanced down at my feet. If anyone noticed the shade of pink on my cheeks, I hoped they'd attribute it to the brisk ride in the cool November air.

At sixteen, I was nearly as tall as my mother. I shared her slight build, her olive coloring, and dark hair. The rest of the assembled party, for the most part, tended to have fair complexions, more typical of our German heritage. Working outdoors had darkened many of the men's faces, necks, and forearms, even those with the lightest skin. Some of the younger boys who often worked without a hat had streaks of sun-bleached strands massed on the tops of their heads.

Paul was the host. He owned both the farm and the land where the hogs roamed, but everyone who came to help received a share of the bounty. This year, besides the three Stephens families, four other families and a few of the local farmhands attended the butchering.

My parents fell into their accepted roles at once; my father joined the other men near three large footed kettles of boiling water, my mother the other women. With the work not yet in full swing, I sat on an improvised bench, a flat area carved from a fallen log. Children scampered nearby, running after one another or in pursuit of imaginary delights, games unfamiliar to me. Occasionally they upended a chair or table and caused a minor disturbance followed by a chorus of scolding from the mothers.

Once or twice, I looked back to the women's table, each time meeting my mother's glance. I searched the crowd to find my cousin Hannah, my closest friend. Perhaps my only friend. When I spotted her across the yard, engrossed in conversation with a few young boys, I raised my arm to catch her eye. She nodded at me and smiled.

While I waited for Hannah, I scanned the crowd for Will Hammer. I spied him sprinting between the kettles and a far table. Will was my cousin by marriage. His father, a widower with two sons from his first marriage, had married my mother's youngest sister, Henrietta.

Will was one of the older boys, seventeen, and I supposed nearly a man. His forearms, visible below the rolled sleeves of his woolen shirt, were as well formed as the muscled arms of the older men. His arms, like theirs, bore a deep tan from working outside.

Hannah finally extracted herself from the group of boys and came over to me. She sat down beside me on the log and put her arm around my shoulders.

"Liese, I'm so glad you're here. I was wondering if you were ever going to make it."

"Hello, Hannah," I said, returning her hug. "We had to visit Mr. Heit on the way. He's been sick and—"

"Oh forget about old Mr. Heit. I don't care. Let's talk about something more interesting, or someone."

"And who would that be?" I said. Hannah had a weak spot for Arthur, another of my cousins, but I pretended not to know. "Arthur? Where is he?"

"Down there, with Will." She nodded toward the vats. "I was talking to them earlier. Before things got too busy."

Hannah amazed me. She could carry on a conversation with any one of the boys on almost any topic. She was as much at ease with talk of snakes and frogs and horses as she was with things that interested me. I, on the other hand, became tongue-tied if one of the boys so much as looked at me. Most of them had little to say to me and even made conscious attempts to avoid me altogether, or so I thought. I attributed their standoffishness to their respect for my father's role as a preacher rather than that I had little to say of interest to them.

But Will had been different last year. He'd been friendly toward me. We'd sat together at Saturday's supper, though the arrangement had been an accident. Hannah had promised to keep a place for me, but when I reached the table, only one empty seat remained. One next to Will. Each time he shifted in his chair, his hip or elbow brushed against me.

I wanted to say something to him, but could not bring a single word to mind. While I ate, I tried to think of what Hannah might say. I'd paid close attention to her conversations with Arthur and some of the other boys, to her choice of words, turn of phrase, topics of interest. I'd even practiced saying some of the same words at home at night. I spoke the words to my pillow propped against the headboard. But Hannah's words were not what I wanted to say.

Thankfully, to my great relief, Will started the conversation, such as it was.

"Is that all you're having to eat," he asked after glancing at the small piece of meat and a few vegetables dotting my plate.

"I'm not hungry," I said. In actuality, I'd lost my appetite.

"More for me, I guess then," he said and laughed. He reached over my plate with his fork and stabbed the remaining slice of meat, then raised it to his mouth. As he chewed, he smiled at me and, I'll always believe, he winked.

It was over in moments. When I looked up again, he'd finished and left the table to join his friends.

These fond memories were interrupted by a creaking noise from the left of where Hannah and I sat. I turned my head to look and remembered where I was, not safe inside the warm protective walls of my home, but in the middle of an open field beside my uncle's farmhouse.

Three men were bringing a cart up the hill. The cart's wheels creaked as they turned under the weight of two hog carcasses. The sound grew louder as they approached. The men swung the cart around. Four muddy hooves dangled over the back and flopped lifelessly with the motion of the cart until they reached the clear, level patch of ground where the kettles sat.

Clouds of steam billowed into the air from the kettles full of boiling water. A handful of other men held their hands in the steam and warmed them against the chill. From time to time, one of them tossed a new piece of firewood from a stack mounded behind the kettles. When the wind blew in my direction, the warm, moist air and the scent of charcoal filled my lungs.

Hannah and I watched the men work. Tyler Miller, I'd forgotten what relation he was to me, and my normally fastidious father with his sleeves rolled above his elbows, blew puffs of air from their mouths as they struggled with a third carcass on another cart. Two farmhands came to the rescue. They dragged the hog to the edge of the cart then hoisted it into position on a waiting tripod.

Hannah laughed. "What's so funny?" I asked.

She was watching Tyler and Edward. "Look at them." Hannah stood up, held her arms in the air and stepped once to the right, then again, mimicking their motions. "They look like they're dancing."

I looked at the men. They moved in unison from opposite sides, circling the hog, going around and around the carcass. They worked swiftly up and down the length of the carcass, scraping the hair from the hide in practiced, familiar motions.

"Do it with me, Liese."

"Don't be silly, Hannah. You'll make a spectacle of yourself."

"Liese, you sound just like your mother."

"I do not."

I looked away, back toward the women grouped around the table. Their voices hummed and occasionally snippets of conversations laden with familiar women's words bubbled up only to fall away again, roiling then subsiding like the water in the kettles.

"...a new baby. It's a girl," Uncle Paul's wife, Dora's voice.

"Of course we'll make dumplings later. Lizzy, you'll be in charge," Maria's voice.

"...she's taken ill. Gone to bed so I hear from Henry," Aunt Lillian's voice.

Hannah resumed her seat and droned on about something I did not quite grasp. I drifted with my own thoughts. Then a glint of light ricocheted from where the men were working. Paul held a long bladed knife in his hand. He'd drawn it in a jagged motion across the first hog's throat, severing the head from its body. Another blinding flash from the sun. I raised my hand to shield my eyes.

Will took the knife from Uncle Paul. As he bobbled the thick handle in his hand, his shoulders drew back, an unconscious motion I thought. I wondered if this were his first time to take part in the actual butchering. As Will drew the knife across the hog's neck, I winced, looked away, then found myself turning back to watch. Will had failed to sever the hog's head. Paul pointed to a place above Will's first cut. Will made a second slash across the hog's neck. The head dangled now by little more than a thread. When he took a final swipe, Will jumped back to let the hog's head fall to the ground. Will grinned as Paul nodded and clapped him on the shoulder.

Hannah poked me below my ribs. "Liese, your mother is calling you."

We hurried over to the table and left Will, Arthur, and the headless hogs behind.

CHAPTER 5

Muffled Steps

The men worked through the early evening until they'd split and propped the hog carcasses wide open.

After storing away items they wouldn't need again, the adults turned to walk up the hill to the main house. The women led the way. Nathan, Edward, and my father stopped half-way up and crossed to a fence at the edge of a cornfield. The earth, turned last fall and pounded by recent rains, lay before them in one long swath of brown. As the sun set over the fields, they stood in a row; each man rested one foot on the lower rung of the fence. Nathan took a pipe from the pocket of his wool vest and lit it to smoke.

In the waning minutes of the day, the children made the most of the last few rays of light and scampered back and forth between the farm equipment and stacks of firewood. Hannah and I, charged by our mothers with minding the younger ones, ambled behind them. Hannah threaded her arm through mine and pulled me close. I turned to her and smiled. I wished she were my sister.

She was the same age as I, but she'd not lost the childlike fullness of her face and figure. Her features were soft, the lines of the nose and cheekbones smooth under a translucent fair skin. She kept her light brown hair tied behind her head, though strands inevitably escaped and fell in loose curls around her ears. Like her mother, Lillian, Hannah was always in motion. She never sat for more than a minute between chores, and she maintained a constant stream of chatter on any topic. Were it not for Hannah's gregariousness, I would have been ignored, the quiet girl, head always down, voice rarely heard, an inconspicuous child. Hannah forced me into the center of her antics, pressing me into service as a stage prop or supporting character for one of her stories. I knew I could never be like her.

Hannah bent her head toward mine and whispered, "Arthur and Will are behind us."

I turned to look.

"No, don't look back. Don't let them think we're interested."

"What do you mean?"

Will and Arthur trailed a few steps behind us, engaged in their own conversation. The boys were close in age and spent most of their time together at school, on the farm, or wherever they had the opportunity. Will stood a full head taller than Arthur, but in most other ways the two were indistinguishable. Both had heads of thick hair the color of parched hay, strands darting at odd angles above their ears. Both had long, lanky legs. Long legs were, according to my mother, a sign someone would be tall when fully grown.

The boys followed behind us, but we had no illusions about their lending a hand with the young ones, or even striking up a conversation with us. Their voices grew faint. They'd slowed, deliberately to distance themselves from us further. Hannah's curiosity grew and she turned her head back to check. I looked back as well. The boys had stopped and now stood shoulder-to-shoulder, heads cocked toward each other.

Out of the corner of my eye, I saw Arthur gesture to Will. He extended one arm parallel to the ground in front of him, supported at the elbow by his other arm. He swung his extended arm as if it were a shotgun, to the right, then up into the air, then aiming back to the left. He repeated the action several times.

Once we reached the barn, Hannah and I found a place to sit while we minded the children. Will and Arthur caught up to us. Will propped himself against the barn. He shot a glance our way every few minutes while Arthur kicked the dirt and loosened rocks with the toe of his boot.

"Going hunting tomorrow?" Hannah asked.

"Shush," Will said, raising a finger to his lips. He moved closer to us and continued in a hushed voice, "We are. But don't you dare say anything in front of Dreas or Toby. If they find out, they'll bellyache. Then Ma will make us take them along."

"The last thing we need," Arthur added, "is those two, or anyone else."

"Where are you going?" I asked.

"Promise you won't tell?"

"Yes, yes," Hannah said at once. I nodded.

"There's a pond," Will said, "down past the Boerner farm. Some geese were headed that way on Monday. I think they're nesting down there, somewhere in the high grass around the pond."

"You sure you wouldn't like some company," Hannah said.

"You're not serious, Hannah?" I said, shifting in my seat to look her squarely in the eye.

"Hmm. I don't know. It might be fun. I've never been, but...."

Arthur must have known what Hannah was thinking. Before she could continue, he jumped in to put an end to any ideas she might have about going with them. "You wouldn't like it," Arthur said. Then, for added insurance, "Besides, you don't know how to shoot. You don't even have a gun. And besides, besides...," he paused for a moment. "You'd probably get your skirts all tangled up. We can't be stopping every ten minutes to wait for you."

"I'll wear my brother's pants," Hannah said.

"You will not," Arthur said. "Girls talk too much, anyway. You'd scare off the birds. That's why we don't want Andreas or Toby, or anyone else along."

"Well, I don't want to get up that early anyway," Hannah said. Satisfied that she'd goaded Arthur long enough, Hannah lost interest and turned her attention to the young ones. "Careful, careful," Hannah shouted to Toby. He walked heel to toe across a fallen log as if on a tightrope. Halfway across, he flailed his arms and groped for an invisible handhold. Hannah bolted from her seat and ran the few feet to where Toby teetered, and caught him before he fell to the ground. She returned with a firm hold on both Toby's and Dreas' collars.

"I'm taking you two up to the house,' she said. "Coming, Liese?"

"Yes." Then, surprising myself, I added, "In a minute."

Arthur started up the hill behind Hannah.

Out of earshot of Hannah and Arthur and the children, I said, "I could shoot a gun if you, or...if someone showed me how." As soon as the words were out of my mouth, I looked away. I wondered for a moment whether I had actually spoken the words aloud.

"I'll show you," Will said. He scanned the ground, skipped over to a tree nearby and picked up a fallen branch. Forcing it over his knee, he snapped it in two. Then, he circled around behind me and placed one end of the branch against my shoulder. He took my right elbow in the cup of his hand and nudged my arm upward to take hold of the branch. With his other arm, he reached around me. I felt his shirt brush against my back and the warmth of his arm alongside mine. Will guided my left hand to the side of the imaginary barrel. I glanced around expecting to see my mother, but no one was there. Just Will. And me.

"Don't squirm. You have to stand still. There, now, lean your head so that you can see down the length of the branch."

I repeated his instruction, making certain I'd caught each detail. "Lean, like this?" My cheek was resting on the branch.

"Yes, like that. Just do it."

I planted my cheek against the branch. Will was now so close his chin brushed against the top of my head. His breath washed against my hair. I caught the scent of him and breathed in deeply while wondering what scent he'd catch of me.

"Liese, pay attention. Now, imagine a flock of geese rising from the right, over there, just behind the barn. Yes, point it there."

I aimed the end of the branch to my right.

"That's it. Now, follow the birds to the left. You have to think like you're one of them. Think ahead. Think where they're going. Now, let the gun go there, too. Follow them, follow them. Get out in front, just a touch."

"Okay, got it?"

"I think so."

"Okay, now, fire."

"Watch out," Will said. "Pow." He jerked the branch upward, mimicking the recoil of a shotgun. Will chuckled. "Oops, looks like you missed. Better luck next time. I think you'll have to practice before you can come with us."

I turned to look at Will who still held the branch with one hand, his other around my shoulder. I paused for a minute, then stepped back.

Will, too, took a step away.

I realized I'd thrown away the opportunity, for what I wasn't certain. But the moment was over, gone, lost.

"You'll be back in time for supper?"

He looked away. "Of course. I wouldn't miss supper for anything." He tossed the branch toward the stack of firewood.

"Liese, Hannah, children? Time for supper," a voice from the house ended our conversation and we turned to climb the hill to the house.

The three Stephens families crowded around the table. After a blessing from my father, little more conversation disrupted the meal, but chairs scraped the floor as children came and went, iron lids clanged against their pots as Dora ladled soup or served vegetables, and forks and knives scoured the dinner plates. After dinner, Hannah, Molly, and I helped my mother and Aunt Dora put away the leftover food and utensils. Soon, the children went to bed and in another hour, the rest of us.

Hannah and I shared one of the bedrooms upstairs; the twins slept with their parents in the front room on makeshift beds. Arthur and Will were together in a second room upstairs. My parents and the Struhls had gone to stay with the Boerner family at their adjacent farm. Everyone would reassemble on Saturday morning to finish carving the meat. It would be a long day of work capped by supper, which promised to be a festive event.

As we lay side by side in the big cot, Hannah chattered away.

"Did you hear what I said? Are you listening, Liese?" Hannah said, trying to keep her voice low.

I lay on my side facing away from her.

"Yes, yes, I heard you. You're going to marry Arthur." I had not actually heard as much, but I guessed at Hannah's favorite topic.

"And, go on. What else, did I say?"

"I don't know."

"I said I will marry Arthur and you will marry Will."

"Hannah, hush. Don't be stupid. I'm not going to marry anyone. Now, go to sleep before you wake everyone."

"Oh, alright, but you're wrong. You'll just have to wait and see."

Minutes later, Hannah's breathing softened. All I could hear was the light breeze of night air, no more than a rustle across a distant patch of high grass. The whole house fell silent. I lay in the warm bed, my head resting on the pillow angled toward the window through which I could see the first glimmer of stars. My thoughts sped ahead to Saturday's early supper when I would see Will again. I picked a single star from the sky and made a wish. Then, I said my prayers, as my parents would have wanted.

If Will and Arthur were true to their word, they would start their adventure early, before anyone else rose. Despite what they had said about girls and hunting, I wanted to go with them. Dreading I'd not wake when they did, I did not sleep, only dozing off and on throughout the night. In the wee hours of the morning, I woke to the faraway hoot of an owl and cracked one eye open. Without raising my head from the pillow, I peered out the window. A thin cloud, little more than a wispy gray line, crept across the sky, its tendrils warped by the uneven panes of glass. Other sounds made their way to the second floor of the farmhouse and into the room—close by a horse snorted in its stall and out in the field hooves stamped the ground. The cattle were eager for the day to begin.

Then I heard a noise, this time from inside the house, a creaking noise. I held my breath. Down the hall in another room, a bed creaked. A rustling noise followed and then someone spoke. I heard a shushing sound. It was them. They moved about quietly, dressing, I assumed, without further conversation so as not to wake the rest of the house. The younger boys would beg to go along if they woke.

I followed them through the house with my ears. The landing creaked. They were on the stairs. I held my breath again. They had halted and I guessed were listening for sounds of anyone else stirring. Then several quick but muffled steps followed. I imagined two pairs of sock-covered feet on tiptoes padding through the hallway into the kitchen.

They stopped for a while in the kitchen then left by the back door, no doubt edging the door closed to prevent it from banging against the frame. I listened for Hannah's breathing. She stirred and turned onto her back. Her breath was heavy but regular. She'd heard nothing. Slowly, I rolled from the bed and pulled on two sweaters I'd placed beside the bed the night before. I grabbed my shoes and shuffled in my stockings to the stairs. I leaned on the handrail to quiet my steps and avoid the loose board on the landing, the one that I knew creaked.

In the kitchen I discovered the boys had raided the bowl of Aunt Dora's biscuits on the counter where she'd set it after dinner. I snatched a biscuit from the bowl and tucked the remaining biscuits back under the red and white checkered linen cloth the boys had tossed carelessly on the counter.

Will and Arthur stood only a few steps outside the kitchen door. From the grunts and thumps, I guessed they were putting on their shoes. I leaned against the kitchen wall for support and did the same, shutting my eyes to concentrate. A murmur of words floated in the air. Then, a clatter erupted as the boys retrieved their guns from where they had been propped against the back of the house. I chuckled quietly at their clumsiness, my hand against my mouth to avoid making a sound. A few soft crunches followed—the soles of the boys' boots on the gravel that covered the well-worn path from the back of the house to the fields beyond. They would follow it, then cross through the Hammer's cornfields, circle the Boerner's farm, then turn east to the lake. I listened intently but silence cloaked the house and the path behind.

When I was sure they were several yards away, I ventured outside. Careful not to make a sound, I too edged the kitchen door open then closed it behind me. They were already well down the path but not out of sight. As I started after them, I looked up. The thin, gray streak I'd noticed earlier was lighter, bleeding life into the darker patches. Still, sunrise would not be for an hour or more.

I followed Will and Arthur at a safe distance. It was surprisingly easy. Once out of everyone's hearing, they made a considerable amount of noise. By the tone of their voices and the occasional chuckle, I guessed they were teasing each other. I envied them their easy camaraderie.

As I scampered along, doing my best to make no noise, I wondered what they might say when they found me and if they would let me go with them. As the light came up, my fear they would discover me rose. I slowed to put more distance between us.

The terrain was more uneven now. Up ahead, with Will leading the way, the boys clambered through the brush, over fallen logs, and across numerous rock-studded streams. I thought I'd lose them. After another hundred yards, I stopped. They were nowhere in sight. No words drifted back to me. No thump of boots sounded on the trail. I guessed they had veered to the right, where I believed the lake lay, perhaps another mile ahead. When I ducked under a low-hanging limb, my skirt caught on a briar. I stooped to free it but, before I could finish, the shrubs on both sides of the path exploded with the sound of breaking limbs. Thinking I had disturbed a wild hog, I screamed, "Scat, scat."

Roars of laughter from Arthur and Will erupted as the two jumped into the path, one in front of me, one behind.

"What are you doing here, Liese?" Arthur asked.

"I want to go hunting with you."

"Hunting?" Arthur laughed. "You're hardly prepared to hunt. Where's your gun?"

Will said nothing. He stood to the side, the butt of his shotgun threaded through the crook of his arm.

"I don't have one."

"Well you can't come with us. See, I told you yesterday. You'd just get tangled up." Arthur bent down and removed the briar snagged in my skirt. "You'll scare off everything."

"I won't. I promise I won't. I'll be very quiet."

"No, Liese," Will said. "Go back."

Before turning, I examined Will's face, hoping to see a sign. Of what I wasn't sure. Perhaps, concern for my safety, or regret that I could not join him and that, because of Arthur's persistence, he had no choice but to tell me to go. But, his expression was blank. He left me nothing.

CHAPTER 6

A Glass Half Full

I returned home as the house came alive. Families weaved in and out of the kitchen in shifts for breakfast. After I'd eaten a second biscuit, lathered with honey this time, I carried a pail of water down to the barn where the vats waited. The three splayed and headless hogs hung from the gambrel sticks, two hooves aimed skyward, two stretched toward the ground, as if with luck they might free themselves and scamper away.

A few of the adults tended the kettles. Tyler crouched next to the hogs. He ran a bare hand over one of the carcasses; he paused at different spots to check that the heat had gone out over the course of the chilly evening. He nodded at the rest of the men who'd assembled in a semi-circle beside him. They were ready to carve; it would take the better part of the morning. Once they began, the men handed off sections of hog to the women who carved and separated the meat into smaller portions. They fed some of the meat into a grinder and cranked its shaft. Later, when the cutting and grinding were complete, they would divide the meat into shares for the families and farmhands who had come to help.

I knew a few of the farmhands by sight: Edgar Stutz who worked the Stephen's farm, Jack Linger an Irishman who worked on Nathan's farm, and Milton Dahl. Milton lived in the vicinity with his own plot to tend but he also worked the Boerner's place.

Others I might have seen before, but had forgotten their names if I'd ever known them. The hands were most often single men with families somewhere back East. They'd come to the area to find work.

To an outsider, they were indistinguishable from the farm owners in the sense of dress or stature—all had weathered skin on their necks and muscular build from the demands of farm work. All had coarse hands with deep creases that radiated across their palms, like the fields they tended. Though treated like family, they mostly kept to themselves. They huddled together at the periphery of the gathering during any break in the work.

The men worked without stopping for several hours. I worked alongside my mother at the women's table.

Finally, Uncle Paul stood up from where he had been squatting. He pressed his hands on his hips, arched his back, and winced. "Thirsty, anyone?" he asked. I looked up and saw several of the men nod. The women took advantage of the break in activity as well. They stepped from the table, wiped the blood and fat from their hands, and sat, huddled in their own groups. I sat with my mother.

Uncle Paul drew his shirtsleeve against his forehead. "Mina!" he called out to his daughter, "could you get us some fresh water?"

Mina scampered over to him. "Yes, sir," Mina said. She grabbed Hannah by the hand. The two climbed to the well near the house. In a few minutes, they returned, Hannah lugging two pitchers of water down the hill and Mina following with glasses and cups. Hannah poured a glass full and offered the water to her father. He shook his head and motioned her to serve the others, their guests, first. Hannah turned to make the rounds of the other men.

I left my mother's side to help Hannah and Mina.

"*Danke*, thank you, there Liese," Uncle Paul said as he took the glass from my outstretched hand. "Aren't you growing up fast!"

I blushed. "Uncle Paul, you said that already." I scuttled away to serve someone else.

Mumbles of thanks echoed all around. When everyone had had their fill, we collected the glasses and turned to go. Just then, Jack Linger, one of Nathan's farmhands called out. "One more here," he said, beckoning us back.

I walked the few steps back toward Jack to take the last glass.

"*Danke*," he used the German word for thank you as he'd heard the others use. He raised his half-full glass and bent back his head to take what remained in one long drink. Though I was tall for my age, Jack stood another foot over me. His clean-shaven chin moved up and down as he drained the glass. An unfamiliar, musky scent, a mixture of earth, sweat, and perhaps tobacco hung in the air around him. Jack finished, licked his lips, then held out the glass for me to take. I reached for it but instead of letting loose, he kept hold of the glass. For a moment, both of our hands were on the glass, the tips of our fingers met. The hesitation was almost imperceptible, but sufficient to cause me to raise my head up toward him a second time. His eyes glanced over me from head to toe. I lowered my eyes and looked away, as if my looking away would cause him not to see. Finally, he released his grip on the glass.

"*Bitte*, you're welcome," I said. Then, I turned around and picked up the last pail filled with empty glasses from beside the table. I started up the hill to join Hannah and Mina who were by now halfway to the house. I glanced back to where Jack stood. He had not moved or gone back to work. He'd remained where I had left him, his eyes fixed on me. I let my back take the full brunt of his gaze though my blouse burned against my skin, as if scorched by his stare. I climbed on to put distance between us, but I didn't hurry.

"Liese," Hannah said when I caught up to her and Mina, "are you okay? You look like you could use some water."

"I'm fine. I'm just catching my breath."

"Who's that man?" Mina asked.

"What man?"

"The one down there by the fence," Mina said, "the one staring at you."

"Hush, Mina," I said. "Hannah, don't look. I'm sure I don't know who you mean and I'm sure he's not staring at me."

"It's that Irishman. I think his name's Jack. He's staring at you." Hannah had the advantage; she stood facing down the hill toward where Jack was.

I took a few more steps up the hill and circled Hannah. "It doesn't matter anyway."

"Nonsense," Hannah said, turning to join me.

She was right, though I would not admit to her or anyone else that I wanted the young man to notice me and think me attractive. For some reason, the thought of Will popped into my head. The faces of the two young men danced in front of me, first one then the other, back and forth. Will's young, unblemished face hardened and lengthened and took on Jack's darker, coarser features.

"Come on," I said, shaking my head to discard the images.

We were only steps from the house when a motion at the edge of the woods caught my eye. A figure ran toward us. At first, I thought it was another farmhand, late to the butchering. As the figure came closer, I could tell it was a boy but not whom. He waved his arms over his head. In one hand, he wielded a long dark shape, a shotgun.

I had not expected Will or Arthur to return until at least noon.

When the boy emerged from the shadows, I recognized him as Arthur; he waved his arms again. Then, he yelled something unintelligible across the expanse, unintelligible but with a tone of panic in his voice. His concern grew more urgent as he closed the distance between us. When he had reached the top of the crest, only fifty yards or so away, his words were clear.

Arthur called out again, "Liese, Hannah, get my father! Get Mr. Hammer! Liese!"

I squinted to see behind Arthur to see a second figure, but only shadows flickered in the path to the woods.

Hannah ran past me toward the adults who mingled near the kettles and what remained of the carcasses. I tried to take a step forward to meet Arthur, but I was unable to breathe, unable to go any closer to Arthur, to what I feared. When I halted, the pail of empty glasses swung awkwardly and flew from the pail, they shattered on the ground around my feet. Shards of broken glass littered the path. They caught the rays of the setting sun and hundreds of tiny rainbows glinted upward. I tore my eyes away, dropped the pail, and ran toward Arthur. I was willing to endure a lifetime of the quiet room in punishment for running, for coveting, for loving.

"Help! Help!"

When Arthur reached the farmhouse, he bent over to catch his breath. Hearing the commotion, a few of them men came up from the carving area to where we stood. We formed a tight circle around Arthur.

"Mr. Hammer—" he opened his mouth, but no other words emerged. We could do nothing more than wait and watch. Nathan craned his neck, as I had done earlier; he peered over Arthur's shoulder. He looked for his son. I followed his line of sight to the edge of the woods.

"What happened?" Nathan said.

"Will's hurt. The gun went off. I ran as fast as I could."

Arthur's obvious distress infected everyone. Several of the adults in the circle peppered Arthur with questions.

"What happened?"

"Where's Will"

"How badly hurt is he?"

Nathan Hammer stood unmoving beside the young boy. He placed his hand on Arthur's shoulder while the boy tried to catch his breath. He said nothing but his eyes betrayed his concern; they were riveted on the dark stains striping the front of Arthur's shirt and trousers.

"Slow down," Nathan said. Take a deep breath."

Arthur nodded and doubled over again, his hands propped on his knees for support. He took two deep breaths and then rose upright. He stared down the hill at the kettles, then at the nearly depleted stack of firewood, then at the ground. Arthur did not look at his friends, or his father, or at anyone in the group.

"Now, what do you mean, he's hurt?" Nathan said at last. His voice was flat. His words slow.

"We were going to the lake where we thought, where we thought there might be a flock of birds. We'd crossed over a ditch. I—I was on the log, and I slipped. My gun went off. It was an accident. I—"

"Okay, Arthur. John," Nathan turned to my uncle who stood among the men in the circle, "can you round up Milton and Edgar? Be quick about it."

"Sure thing."

"Now, how bad is he hurt, Arthur?"

"Real bad I think. He didn't move. He didn't answer me. I think he's dead."

The blood drained from Nathan's face. My legs grew weak. I prayed that I would not faint, then I added a prayer for Will.

John disappeared into the house. The rest of us waited for him to return, we said nothing. Nathan wiped his forehead, brushed his hair with his fingers, and combed it back from his forehead. When a high-pitched scream from inside the house reached us, I shuddered and guessed that Uncle Paul had told the family members inside the farmhouse what had happened. Then a door banged. John and a few others sprinted out of the house toward us while setting their hats on their heads and stuffing their arms inside their jackets. They were ready to join Nathan, Paul, and Arthur. Ready to rescue Will, I thought.

As much as I wanted to go with them, I knew they would not allow me to go. Instead, I watched until the men disappeared down the same track Will had taken that morning, down the same path I had followed.

On Sunday morning, as the sun crested the treetops, I stood outside the farmhouse and watched the sky lose its golden, early morning hue. I kept my back to the crowded but silent farmhouse, a tomb with only the light of a few candles flickering on the walls. Most of the families had stayed after the somber dinner, and through the night, far beyond the time they had originally planned.

My father and mother had left at first light this morning. Despite the tragedy, my father needed to hold services this morning, Sunday. They'd left me in the care of my aunt and uncle who would deliver me to town later today or Monday after they'd done what they could to help the Hammer's transport Will's body home, across the valley, and bury him.

The men had brought Will out of the woods. He'd come the last half-mile aboard the same cart that had carried the hogs on Friday. They had made a place for him in the front room of the farmhouse. This morning, before anyone else had risen, I crept downstairs and into the room to be with him. He lay on the table, on his back, arms at his side, legs extended, but the toes of his boots were splayed apart and aimed at opposite corners of the room. I stole one glance at his head. Since yesterday evening, someone had cleaned the blood from his neck and wrapped the side of his head the shot had torn away.

I could not find the courage to look again and went outside. I walked a few yards down the hill and squatted where the broken glass still littered the ground. Taking care not to catch my fingers on any of the sharp edges, I gathered the shards and dropped them one by one into the hollow of my apron. Intent on the chore, glad for something to occupy my thoughts, I didn't notice Arthur by my side until he knelt and picked up a shard.

I turned to look at Arthur. His eyes were red, the skin around them swollen. Together, without a word, we cleared the remaining pieces of glass from the ground.

"Arthur," I said when we were done, breaking the silence, "I want to see where Will died."

Part Four: Jack

CHAPTER 7
Piano Music

I learned to bake and to play piano in the same year, the one by choice, the other because my father said I would. Both, it seems, were in my blood.

I learned to bake by watching my mother, the mechanics of baking, if not the art. She provided no instruction and rarely asked for my help. But I followed her around the kitchen even at an early age. I observed her: the way she passed a knife over a measuring cup , as if shaving it to make a clean full cup of flour, returning the excess flour into its bag, never allowing a speck to escape, the way she touched a finger to a cake or loaf of bread, leaving a fairy's footprint, one that vanished if I looked away and back again.

I learned the piano by rote repetition and practice, not discovering my affinity for it until I'd been allowed to experiment on my own.

Baking, that quiet, mostly solitary pastime, never left me. But I no longer play the piano. The music inside me died.

* * *

I did not have a say in the matter. After breakfast on my seventeenth birthday, January 1917, my father announced that Sylvia Bracher, the church pianist, would begin my formal piano instruction the next day. I supposed he meant the lessons and the implication that I would assume the role of church pianist as a gift. For as long as I could remember, Ms. Bracher had accompanied the church choir—or rather the congregation, as everyone in attendance during services comprised the choir. Sylvia was in her seventies and in the last few years suffered from prolonged coughing spells. Sometimes, her hacking exploded during prayers, or in the middle of a hymn, or my father's sermon. Often the bouts drowned out his words.

I took lessons at Sylvia's home. I learned Sylvia earned a few dollars each Sunday, funds my father siphoned from the offering plate. By having me play, I realized, he would have the benefit of the entirety of the congregation's contributions. I wondered if my father had given any consideration as to whether or not I had any musical talent.

I had difficulty picturing myself at the piano, at the front of the church, in full view of the assembled congregation. To my surprise, with another month of lessons, and considerable practice, I became reasonably proficient—Sylvia proclaimed me a natural. Still, she complained that I did not practice enough and that I did not use the exercises she designed for me. They were tedious, endless repetitions. If she stepped away from the room where we practiced, I abandoned the sheet music propped in front of me to play by feel. I relished the freedom, though it lasted only minutes, until she returned, stood beside me, and glared at my fingers on the keys.

In March, at the end of one of our weekly sessions, Sylvia pronounced me ready to play for the congregation. She suggested I take her place in May, then sighed heavily. Whether she felt relieved or whether it pained her to turn over the responsibility to me, I could not say. We moved the venue for our next few lessons to the church. And, for the last few weeks of the month, I sat beside her at the piano during services.

My father never once asked how my lessons progressed. He showed no interest. I supposed he trusted that the Lord would provide.

Our church, representing a small congregation of modest means, was a simple unpretentious wooden clapboard structure under several coats of white paint, none of them recent. The main room held five rows of pews on either side of its central aisle. My father had elected to build a simple one room wooden structure. Initially he'd balked at the idea of including two sets of large, multi-paned windows on both sides of the church. He relented and in the end was happy that he had. Except on the darkest days, the congregation could rely on the natural light during services. The slanting rays of morning sunlight drenched the wooden floors, the straight-backed pews, and the congregation, it bathed them in light, heavenly or not.

Each day of the week prior to my first solo performance, I practiced by myself in the church. The day before, on Saturday, I entered through the church's side door. The piano sat across the wooden floor, past the pulpit on the opposite wall. As I crossed the room, the heels of my hard-soled shoes reverberated into the void of the vacant room. I glanced toward the pews and imagined them filled with worshipers. To save myself the angst of crossing in front of the assembly and feeling all eyes on me, I planned to arrive early.

Careful not to scratch the floor—Sylvia's admonishment rang in my ears—I pulled back the piano bench and took my seat, then peered into the envelope I'd brought. I extracted a few sheets of music and placed them in front of me on the wooden rest. With my eyes closed, I straightened my spine, lifted my head and drank in the fresh scent of the heart-pine floors and the recently oiled pews.

Free of Sylvia's domination, I had discovered that I could play reasonably well, maybe even better than reasonably well. At least better than Sylvia, I thought. My only regret was the limited selection of music. My father usually cycled through the same tired hymns over and over again.

"I don't know these, Father," I said one week when he handed me new sheets of music.

"You'll learn them. These are difficult times and I think we need to reassure the faithful. I only hope they'll stop to consider the message."

A growing uneasiness had spread across our close-knit community. A few weeks earlier, President Wilson had asked Congress to declare war on Germany. No one knew quite what to make of the announcement. Everyone indulged in speculation and rumor.

I'd caught snippets of news at the grocer, after church services, from passersby in the street, and at a benefit recital I attended. During a break in the performance, I approached Belinda Fedders to thank her for organizing the event. Henry Krug, who played the coronet, was relaying news he had heard to the other musicians. "They're saying that we'll have to register with local authorities. All of the German-born males, that is."

"It's worse than that," Adda Roth said. Adda was the quartet's violinist. She held her hand over her mouth and looked around before she continued with her dire news. "My sister who lives in Indianapolis wrote me to say three people she knew had been arrested."

"For what?" Henry asked.

"For nothing. For being German, I suppose. She said they'd set up a camp there for holding people suspected of aiding the enemy. She said some people might even be deported."

"Nonsense," Belinda said. "Those are just rumors, as you said. People are exaggerating. That would never happen."

"Well, they'll have a hard time if they come to Evansville," Henry said. "Half the community here emigrated from Germany. What are they going to do, arrest us all?"

"Well, I for one," Adda said, "hope we stay out of it altogether. America should remain neutral."

"Please, please, ladies, gentlemen," Belinda said. She put a finger to her lips. "No more talk of this. You'll just cause everyone to panic."

I relayed the rumors to my parents. They said nothing, but I saw a look pass between them that implied they knew more.

"This is a topic not to be discussed outside this house," my father said.

"No Father, I didn't. It's just, Henry said—"

"Some people, the authorities, might misconstrue your words. I've told Paul and John to be careful, too, and not to discuss their views in public. Neither should you, Maria. Or you, Liese."

I wondered whom he thought I would have the opportunity to pass the information on to.

"And, no more German in public. Maria, you are going to have to watch Adam carefully. Keep him from lapsing into German."

"What about your sermons?" Mother asked. While most of father's services were in English, he'd always included at least one prayer in German for the older members.

"I'll be doing them only in English from now on."

My mother raised her eyebrows, but made no further comment. It was not a surprise to me. I'd noticed more English spoken on the streets and in the shops, even the *guten tach's* and *auf wiedersehen's* had become hello's and goodbye's. Now, my father had yielded to the pressure.

That Friday, the *Evansville Courier* reported Congress had made a formal declaration of war. My father spent the rest of the day locked upstairs in his bedroom where he revised his sermon and chose the new hymns.

Every week, once he'd written the sermon, he spent several hours laboring over the choice of hymns. Sylvia had encouraged me to think of the hymns as extensions of the sermon—and though I played more for the joy of the music, I understood their significance. They were an integral part of the evangelical Christian service, as much a part of the message as the sermon. This week, they would be particularly important, if he were to succeed in allaying his congregation's fears.

I glanced at the sheet music for the first hymn. While I had hoped he might have chosen a light, joyful tune, to buoy their spirits, his tact was the opposite. He'd selected a hymn that acknowledged their concern. It extolled the congregation to turn to prayer for comfort. It offered no other solution.

Are we weak and heavy-laden,
Cumbered with a load of care?
Precious Savior, still our refuge—
Take it to the Lord in prayer.
Do thy friends despise, forsake thee?
Take it to the Lord in prayer!
In His arms He'll take and shield thee,
Thou wilt find a solace there.

I raced through the music; I skipped notes, played pieces of stanzas, and searched for a bar or two of the mournful tune that I might lighten. After the hurried first pass, I returned to the beginning, and picked my way note by note, chord by chord through to the end. Engrossed in the music, I did not hear the main door to the church open or the soft steps of a visitor who entered and took a seat in the last pew. Not until I inhaled the scent of tobacco smoke mingled with the scent of the oak and poplar did I realize I was not alone.

In mid-stanza, I stopped and sniffed the air to take in more of the aroma. Above me, a light haze filled the hollow space beneath the apex of the roof. Puzzled as to the source, I spun around on my seat. The light from the side windows had crept forward, leaving the last pew in shadow. Nevertheless, I could make out the figure of a man seated there. I squinted. A shock of thick hay-blond hair caught the light as he leaned forward. I did not recognize him as a member of the congregation.

He wore a clerk's attire, a starched white shirt, a dark tie, and matching wool vest. He'd removed his suit jacket. It lay folded over the back of the pew in front of him. In his right hand, he held a pipe. A waft of velvety gray smoke emerged from the bowl, danced as it passed through a ray of light, and dissipated as it rose into the air above.

"Ahem," he cleared his throat. "Please, continue. I'm sorry if I startled you," he said, his voice hoarse. "I heard the music as I was passing by on my way home and thought I'd come in to listen."

"Do I know you?" I had barely whispered the words, but to my surprise, they reverberated in the open hall.

"My apologies. I've come to services here before. I can't say as it was on a regular basis though." The man cleared his throat again. "My name is Oscar. Oscar Wolf."

"I—I thought I recognized you. I'm Anneliese Stephens."

"Ah, so you would be Pastor Stephens's daughter."

"Yes."

"Please do go on."

"Well, I'm almost finished. You're welcome to stay if you want." I'd lied. It was a small lie, but a lie nonetheless. I wanted him to leave. I did not think I could go on playing. I rearranged my skirt, tucked my left foot behind my right, and settled back on the bench.

Oscar settled back into his pew. He made no move to leave. I swiveled slowly back to the keyboard and took several deep breaths. It was one thing for me to imagine playing for the congregation or, in the future, the church's numerous social groups; but, playing for a one-person audience, a stranger, a man even, was another matter altogether. I scanned the sheet in front of me and found my place again. I paused, to give him one more second. Still no sounds of his retreat reached me.

I raced through the hymn, uncomfortable, conscious of my audience. My concentration broken, I shifted twice on the bench. I imagined his eyes tracing a line down the back of my neck, down the length of my arms. I imagined them following the movement of my fingers on the keyboard, overlooking nothing, enveloping me as the smoke had. My right hand cramped. I missed a note. Then another. Once I reached the end of the piece, I pulled the sheet music together and tapped it on the stand, as if I were ready to go.

"Oh, please don't stop on my account. I was just leaving," Oscar called from the back of the church.

I turned, but he had already left through the main door, the smoke cloud hurrying after him. I turned back to face the piano and placed another hymn on the stand. I took several, slow deep breaths to clear my head. This was a familiar tune, but again I missed several notes. I let my wrists fall freely at my side and shook both my arms to remove the tension. I began the hymn again; this time I played slowly, deliberately. Then, in mid-stanza, I halted. It was no use; I did not know where I was. The Lord would have to provide for me on Sunday.

I stuffed the sheet music back into the envelope, rose from the bench, and crossed the room. I tapped my way across the wooden floor back to the side door and cracked it open. There was no one lurking nearby or in the street. Satisfied he had gone, I made my way out the door, checked again at the corner, then hurried home across the open ground.

CHAPTER 8

Hymns and Rags

Stallman's General Store was the center of much of the local social life in town. Though the store sold primarily produce, meats, and sundries, it also hosted a small restaurant, and in the back, a bar—the reason many also dubbed the store "Stallman's Saloon". My mother shopped there, but made it a point not to visit the back of the store.

Men who lived in town would pass by on their way home to discuss the news, and on holidays or special occasions, they stayed for a beer. On the weekends, younger adults, men and women, frequented the saloon. At least that is what Hannah had told me.

Lucas Stallman, one of the two owners, served his own home brewed ale for those who imbibed, as well as lemonade or other soft drinks for those who did not. Hannah and her sister, Molly, and a mutual friend, Emma Bohn, occasionally brought cakes or other treats to sell to Stallman's patrons.

"It's for a good cause," Hannah said. "Our proceeds go to one of the church's charities."

"Still, it's in a saloon. You shouldn't be seen there. My mother would die if I were to come within a block of it," I said.

"But she shops there."

"I know, but that's different. She keeps to the grocery and dry goods area."

"You should at least come once," Hannah said. Lucas is very nice. He's said we're welcome to bring our baked goods to sell anytime."

"I'm sure he is, but I couldn't."

"Why ever not?" Emma chimed in. She'd just come into the room but picked up quickly on the conversation. Over the last several weeks, she'd been the more vocal of the two about my accompanying her and Hannah. "It's not like you're doing anything wrong. In fact, it will benefit your father's church. Surely, he'd appreciate that."

I shook my head.

"Besides, I want you to meet, George. Hannah's met him already, but I want you to meet him."

I refrained from saying what was on my mind. Emma, I thought, wanted to go to the saloon far more to see George than to raise money, regardless of the cause. George, I gathered, frequented Stallman's on a regular basis. Under the guise of selling her baked goods, Emma had created an opportunity to see him. And, accompanied by her friends, I assumed, she had assuaged her parents' concern and the curiosity or possible suspicions of impropriety from others in the community.

"They have a new piano, too," Hannah said.

"So? You don't think—"

"Yes, I do. Lucas told me if we could find someone to play, it might bring in more guests. If more people came, we'd raise even more for the church."

"You see," Hannah added, "it makes sense."

"Everyone knows how well you play, Liese," Emma said.

"Everyone knows I play for the church."

"You can play anything," Hannah said. "That's what I told Lucas. I said you know lots of tunes, all the popular ones."

My two friends had obviously rehearsed this conversation. "How long have the two of you been planning this?"

"Just once, Liese," Hannah said. "Just come with us once, then if you don't like it you don't have to come again. Besides, your date bars are everyone's favorite treat. You know they are.

You're likely to sell everything you bring. Just come to sell your date bars, nothing else."

On Friday evening, after I'd placed the last layer of powdered-sugar dusted date bars in a tin and snapped on the lid, I heard my friends' excited voices. They chimed their greetings to my father. They spoke rapidly, one voice weaving over the other in the hallway. Hannah, Emma, Molly, and I had agreed earlier in the week, if asked, we would say only we were taking cookies to a benefit sale. We would avoid any mention of Stallman's. I grabbed the tin and hurried to the door. I did not want the group to tarry too long and be pressed to divulge more than our agreed upon story. Fortunately, they had had only time to say their hello's.

"I won't be long," I said over my shoulder as we hurried from the porch. Despite his acquiescence to my stated plan, I think my father would have preferred I not venture out. I did not look back. I did not want to see the frown on his face.

We maintained a suitable decorum, at least until we were out of sight of my house. When we reached the end of the block, our pace picked up. Our conversation grew more lively. We walked two abreast, arm in arm. Hannah with me. Molly with Emma. Our free arms held tight to our baskets of baked goods.

We were dressed as we would for any ordinary church social club meeting, dark mid-calf length skirts topped with white blouses. It was the fashion, almost a uniform, though each of us had added a particular accessory, a touch of color whether in the hand-embroidery on my collar, or the fabric flower broach on Hannah's bodice, or the mauve eyelet-edged handkerchief in Molly's pocket. We each wore a hat. Mine bore a pale, powder blue satin bow above its brim.

Hannah and I led the way. She kept up her normal chatter the entire distance. I looked back only once, when we'd gone several blocks. I expected to find my father or mother there, running to catch us and drag me back to the house. Only Molly and Emma were there, walking arm in arm. They smiled and nodded as they chatted, their heads together, the rims of their hats nearly touching. The thought occurred to me they were there not only to prevent my mother or father from grabbing me unexpectedly but also to deter me from changing my mind and dashing back on my own.

Once we rounded another corner, Hannah breathed a sigh of relief, or perhaps it was just an innocent pause. She resumed her chatter, the volume rising, the tone more lively.

During the twenty minutes it took us to walk to the store, Emma had more than enough time to confide her ulterior motives for visiting Stallman's this particular evening. As I had suspected, they involved her latest beau.

"George came to call this week." She paused, for emphasis I thought. "Again." A smile lit up her eyes.

"Tell me again, about him," I said, as if I did not already know.

"His name is George Hausman. He's twenty and works as a clerk at the railroad office."

"How did you meet him?" I goaded her, though she needed no encouragement.

"I met him about a month ago. No, make that four weeks and five days. At a church social. But I've only managed to see him twice during all that time."

"This will make it the third time in three weeks, right?" asked Molly. "It sounds like this is serious."

"Well, perhaps. Well, yes, I hope so. He shared some great news this week. He's taking on more responsibility from Mr. Davies at the railroad. He thinks he'll soon have a chance to earn more. Last week he told me he'd bought a carriage from old Mr. Swanson, or at least, I should say, his father did. Anyway, next week, he made me promise to go for a ride with him."

"What fun," Hannah said. "We'll be expecting a full report, of course."

"Well, of course. He's the most kind, and generous, and, dare I say, most handsome young man around. Don't you agree?" She looked at Hannah and then at Molly, who had met George on one occasion at Stallman's. "He's very respectable and has a great future. I think he may just run the whole office one day."

"Has he kissed you?" asked Molly. She blushed after asking her question. At fifteen, three years younger than the rest of us, her parents had not allowed her to have gentlemen call or to leave home except in the company of her sister or another older relative.

"Not yet," Emma said. "But, maybe, just maybe, next week on our little adventure."

"Here we are, ladies," Hannah said. "Let's go in." She let loose of my arm and skipped up the two steps to grab the door.

"Quick, quick, do I look alright?" Emma asked. "Is my hair straight?"

"Yes, yes," Hannah said. "Stop making such a fuss. Come on."

Boisterous voices, laughter, shouts, and the tinkling of glass spilled though the open door. I stopped for a moment. I hesitated, reconsidering whether to go forward or turn and go home. I looked back down the empty sidewalk. Back toward home. In a second, Hannah's fingers closed around my arm. With me in tow, she charged through the crowd toward an open table. The patrons, tables, chairs, and the bar passed by me in a blur.

"Hannah, you sit here, Molly there, and Liese, you sit here," Emma said, shouting to make herself heard over the din. She pointed to the seats she assigned to each of us.

Hannah said as quietly as she could in my ear, "George is across the room. He's in the far corner. I think Emma wants to make sure she has a clear line of sight to him."

Once we had taken our seats, Stallman appeared at our table.

"A very good day to you, ladies. What can I offer you to drink?"

"Four lemonades, I think," Emma said. She arched an eyebrow and glanced around to check. I nodded. Stallman disappeared, melting back into the crowd along the bar.

"Is he—?" Molly started.

"Shush," Emma said, not allowing Molly to finish. "Yes, he's here, over there in the far corner, facing this way. Please don't turn around. Act like we don't know he's even here. Don't stare, Molly."

A few minutes later, George appeared at our table, a tray with four lemonades in his hand. "Ladies, please allow me to serve you," he said as he placed the glasses on the edge of the table, then passed them around.

I could not help but notice his slim, long boned fingers, as pale as the lemonade. They could have belonged to any one of us.

"Oh, do come join our little party, George" Emma said, though George had already reached for one of the empty chairs nearby. He pulled it toward the table while Emma introduced him around. George touched his forehead and nodded at each of us in turn. When he took his seat, Emma chattered away, speaking far too fast and far too loud. She left no opportunity for anyone, even George, to utter a word. The hum of the crowd ebbed and flowed around our table. Occasionally, a particularly loud guffaw or the clink of glasses from one of the nearby tables drowned even Emma's conversation.

Distracted by the sights and sounds of people enjoying their Friday evening, I realized several minutes had passed without my doubts about being here concerning me. I hadn't relaxed, but at least the tightness in my chest had disappeared.

A few minutes later, Stallman sauntered back to our table. "Ladies, I'm longing to add some music to this little gathering. Would any of you be so kind as to oblige me and play my new piano?" No one at the table said a word. Lucas continued, "Liese, I hear you have a knack for the piano. Hannah, here, tells me you know a tune or two my guests might enjoy. Not your Sunday hymns, of course." He added the last with a smile, but I thought a tinge of worry, too.

I shot a glance at Hannah and wondered whether she had been truthful about what she had said to Lucas, but Hannah was speaking with someone who sat behind her at an adjacent table. Curiously, I realized, Emma and Molly were focused on something else in the room as well. Lucas had not moved. He stood beside me and waited for an answer.

I opened my mouth to say no. Thinking, surely he could find someone else in the crowd to play. I wondered whether I could even make a sound, much less speak. My throat felt as if it had withered like a stalk of corn in October.

"Well, well I do play, but I could never—"

"Of course you could my dear, just a piece or two. There are some sheets of music on the piano. Pick anything you like. I'm sure you'll find something everyone will enjoy."

I glanced to where Stallman pointed. Though we must have passed the piano when we'd entered the room, until that moment, I'd not noticed it set against the far wall, the stool in front vacant, waiting.

Stallman reached for my hand, still clasped around my lemonade. He lifted it gently and raised it higher and higher, forcing me to follow, to stand. Emma had turned to whisper something to George.

"Oh, Liese, please," Hannah said, clapping her hands together. "This will be wonderful."

I shook my head from side to side, but saw no way to escape from my predicament. Already some of the saloon guests at the other tables had interrupted their conversations and turned to watch Stallman coax me from my seat. Lucas pressed the tips of the fingers of his free hand on my far shoulder and guided me through the narrow aisle between the tables.

I sat on the edge of the round stool in front of the piano. I blinked, not believing I was actually at Stallman's and that I was about to play the piano for an audience of raucous men, few of whom I imagined had ever sung a hymn. I paged through the sheets of music propped against the backboard of the upright. A few of the tunes were patriotic songs, popular tunes often broadcast on the radio in the spirit of America's growing commitment to the war. Many were rags I'd never dared play during my practice sessions with Sylvia or even when I practiced alone in the church. I paged by those and chose instead a simple melody, "If You Were the Only Girl in the World". I was thinking of Emma.

"Please, please, go ahead. That's a good one," Stallman said. "Play it for us."

"Yes, indeed," echoed Axel Martin. Axel, owner of the local bakery, sat at the table nearest the piano. I'd met him while shopping at the bakery with my mother. "Let's hear a tune, Liese."

Though my fingers were stiff with fright, the encouraging smiles on the faces in the crowd lessened my anxiety. I turned to the piece and played.

> *Sometimes when I feel low and things look blue*
> *I wish a girl I had...say one like you.*
> *Someone within my heart to build her throne,*
> *Someone who'd never part, to call my own.*

I was appalled at the hesitancy with which I played, embarrassed. For a moment, I wondered if Lucas regretted asking the church pianist to entertain his patrons. Then, after a few more bars, Stallman's and Axel's voices joined in, loud, boisterous, and definitely off key. I kept playing. Somehow, I managed to say a prayer between notes.

"More, more," Axel said when I reached the end. "Find another we can sing along with. Let's brighten up this dull group."

I hesitated but saw no alternative. Giving in to the clamor, I flipped to a new tune, "Bugle Call Rag". My fingers tingled with excitement. They seemed to dance over the familiar keys.

> *You're bound to fall for the bugle call*
> *You're gonna brag 'bout the Bugle Call Rag.*
> *Hold me baby; Let's syncopate to that blue melody;*
> *Just hesitate while a break they take Shh!*
> *While we're dancing please hold me tight; step lively don't lag.*

This time, more of the revelers joined. They sang or tapped their feet in time with the music. I picked up the pace. At the end of the tune, everyone clapped. Axel and another man at his table hurrahed. "Next. Next," he said. I searched across the room for a sign from Molly, Hannah, or Emma. They were leaning forward in their chairs with their heads tipped toward each other. Emma's face was hidden from view; the others bore smiles from ear to ear. They clapped their hands along with the crowd, encouraging me to continue. I prayed again, this time not for the ability to play, but that word of my performance would not reach my father or mother.

Once I'd played all of Stallman's songs twice, I nodded to the group, acknowledging their applause, but I shook my head in protest when they continued to clap. As I threaded my way through the haphazardly set tables, the patrons at each nodded or murmured their thanks. Conscious of being the center of attention, I hoped the dim lighting concealed what I could only imagine was a splash of deep crimson on my throat and cheeks. A few feet remained of the distance I had to cross. As I squeezed between one last throng of people alongside the bar and several tables opposite, a hand emerged from among a wall of arms, elbows, and torsos. The hand, tanned from exposure to the sun, prevented me from proceeding. I stopped, followed the hand, to a wrist, to the sleeve of a jacket, along a shoulder, and into Jack Linger's face.

"Hello, Liese," he said. You have talents I wasn't aware of. A welcome change from Lucas' clumsy plunking. Thank you for entertaining us."

"I'm afraid I played rather poorly. The songs were not ones I know," I said. "But, thank you all the same."

"*Bitte*," Jack replied. He grinned, I supposed, at his use of the German word, then tipped his glass toward me, nodded his head, and smiled.

When I reached my table, George stood and reached over to hold my chair. I sank into it gratefully, unable to explain the sensation I experienced, whether from approval of the audience or of the single farmhand, I didn't know. My heart raced as if it still kept time with the rag. I reached for the glass of lemonade I had barely touched and took a long sip, followed by another even longer. I placed my fingertips, cooled from the glass, against my cheeks.

After several minutes, the noise of the crowd swelled once again, filling the room. Assuming the conversation had moved on to other things than me, I took a deep breath and dared glance around the room, searching the crowd at the edge of the bar but failing to find even a trace of Jack. Across the room, in one of the far smoke lit corners, I recognized another young man. Oscar Wolf sat rocking back and forth in a chair tipped on its hind legs. He stared at me and, when I guess he was certain he had caught my eye, he nodded toward me.

In the coming weeks, I played the piano several times at Stallman's. I'd waited long enough after the first time to ensure word had not reached my mother or father, or that, if it had, they approved, which I doubted, or they simply chose not to mention what they had heard. Almost every week, Jack stood among the assortment of young men, farmhands, grocers, clerks, and store-owners, leaning against the bar, one elbow propped on the edge. Oscar appeared again only once.

Each time I played for the saloon audience, I became more confident. From time to time, the heat rose in my neck and spread to my cheeks, but not every time and not as deep, except when it concerned Jack. Still, I dared not say anything about him to Hannah or Emma. I needed more time to understand my feelings and find a way to express them. I did understand, even if only partly, Emma's enthusiasm for visiting Stallman's establishment. Playing afforded me the opportunity to observe Jack more closely, to discover who his friends were, to note what he wore, his mannerisms, especially the way he ran his fingers, rough from a day's work no doubt, through his hair, combing it away from his forehead. Often, too, he pinched the back of his neck, relieving some of the day's pain.

Invariably, I left Stallman's in good humor, Emma noting how quickly I skipped on our walk home. Until my father mentioned it, I'd been unaware of how the rags, love songs, and patriotic tunes had woven their way into the hymns I played on Sundays. The notes, of course, were the same, but my manner of playing had changed.

"Your playing has improved measurably, Liese," he said one Sunday after services. "I don't know quite how to describe the difference. Perhaps it is more inspired. Are you hearing the call of the Lord?"

I brushed a speck of lint from my sleeve, avoiding his eyes. "Perhaps. I think I just have had more experience." I looked up again. Neither my mother or father looked my way.

One evening after a performance at the saloon as my friends and I prepared to leave, I noticed Jack turn and cross the room from the bar to a spot near the door. As we approached, he reached for the handle, and opened it, stepping aside to allow us to pass. He nodded.

"Liese, may I walk you home?"

He'd purposefully kept his voice low, intending only me to hear, but Emma and Hannah both turned their heads in the direction of his voice. I prayed that neither of them could see the flush on my cheeks. I could only nod.

Jack stepped to my side. I stared straight ahead, deliberately avoiding making eye contact with anyone. I didn't have to look at Hannah and Emma to know they were smiling, but they spared me any comment, turned, and joined arms as they started down the walk. They stayed a few steps ahead, though not so many as to miss what passed for conversation between Jack and me. I had mentioned his name only once over the last few weeks, asking if either Hannah or Emma knew him.

"He's a farmhand at Nathan's," Emma said.

"I think his family lives near Plainfield. They're quite poor. And, I think his mother's a widow," Hannah added.

"He's been at Nathan's for gosh, let me see...over five years now" Emma said. "Yes, it would be five years."

"Emma," I said, "how do you know these things?"

"I make it my business to know what's going on, especially among the young men," she said, grinning. "Anyway, I remember someone saying that the same day he came to work at Nathan's, his father died. He had to go back to Plainfield straight away."

Jack walked beside me, clumsily at first as he adjusted his long-legged gait to mine. For a while, we walked in silence and let the evening air fill with the bits of louder than normal chatter that flowed back from my friends. Finally, Jack said, "I enjoy listening to you play. The last time we spoke, I remember you said you don't play very well. I suppose that means I have a bad ear for music."

"Thank you." No other words came to my mind. The silence returned. It hung in the air between us, like a thick fog. I coughed and tried to summon a few words from somewhere. "I ... I didn't mean to offend you. By making that remark, I mean. I enjoy playing, but I'm still learning. I only started a few months ago." Suddenly I was prattling on and on, unable to stop talking, out of control. Threads of possible conversation spun in my head. For reasons I could not explain, I wanted to put him at ease.

"I play for my father's church every week. Hymns. So, it's rare that I have the opportunity to play music that everyone recognizes."

I willed myself to stop, to leave room for Jack to say something, anything. He let a few steps pass before he spoke. "I don't attend church much. When I can, I go to St. Joseph's in Heusler. It's closer to the farm. Nathan's farm. I think you know him, that is, I think you're related to Nathan."

"Yes, he's married to my Aunt Henrietta."

More steps passed in silence.

"Well, some Sunday, the next time you're able, you could come to my father's church," I said. I blinked. I'd surprised myself with the invitation and wondered if it were proper. Ahead, Emma and Hannah's heads were closer now, almost touching. They spoke more softly, their words fading before trickling back to us.

"I would like to do that. I accept your invitation," Jack said. "Soon, perhaps," he added.

Hannah and Emma had reached the front gate to my home. They stopped there and turned around as Jack and I approached.

"Well, here I am. This is my home. I'll say good-bye now."

"Could I call on you again?" Jack asked. He'd taken his hat off his head and held it in his hand by his side. With his free hand, he combed his hair from his forehead.

"Yes, of course." I said. I tried to sound as if I'd encouraged other callers a hundred times before. "Perhaps next week? On Saturday after supper?" I did not wait for his answer. I stepped aside to say good-bye to Hannah and Emma.

"Next Saturday then," Jack said. He nodded at Hannah and Emma and then at me. Donning his hat, Jack sauntered back the way we had come moments earlier.

"My, my," Hannah said as soon as Jack wandered out of ear-shot. "What will Pastor Stephens, think, Liese?"

"Shush, none of your nonsense. It doesn't mean anything."

Hannah and Emma laughed aloud. "No? We'll see," Emma said. She chuckled. "We should be going now, too. Will we see you tomorrow, Liese?"

"No," I said. "I have some chores I must do for Mother."

I did not have as much time as Hannah or Emma to visit friends or "gallivant about" to use my mother's phrase. She'd lost much of her strength in the last few years and needed help to manage even the lightest of chores; including the one I dread-ed most, caring for my grandfather. The mere thought of my responsibilities weighed me down. My steps slowed to a crawl. My hands were heavy, as if I carried a pail full of water in each. I paused at the door. For a moment, my mind raced ahead to Saturday. What would I say to Father if Jack did call.

On Monday, I thought I'd mention to my mother that a young man might call on me on Saturday. I wanted to tell her first. Her reaction would be a preview of what my father might have to say.

We were in the kitchen preparing dinner, alone. "Mother?"

"Yes, Liese?"

"I wanted to tell you there might be..." I swallowed. What should I say, a man, a friend, or just his name. Why had I not thought this through ahead of time.

"Liese, could you finish here for me? I think I need to sit down for a few minutes."

She left the room.

I tried again on Tuesday and then on Wednesday with no success. By Friday, I was desperate. I'd waited too long and run out of time. I would have to tell them both, at once.

I ate dinner slowly. I took one bite then returned my fork to the table, paused, picked it up again, and then stabbed another morsel of chicken. My mother finished her meal and placed her napkin on the table. She tucked it under her plate.

"Jack Linger may call on me tomorrow."

There, I'd said it. I'd blurted it out. I returned to my meal and attacked my food with my fork and knife. I chewed one piece of meat for a long time. I dared not swallow or make eye contact until they responded.

I imagined they had glanced at each other, my mother at my father for a clue of what to say. They said nothing, no word of approval or disapproval. Nothing. My father sliced a bite from his roast, placed it on a piece of bread and drove it around the plate to sop the gravy. He finished in silence.

As soon as I finished and placed my napkin on the table, everyone rose. My mother followed my father, as usual, to the parlor. I cleared the dishes. In the kitchen, alone, I ran cool water over my hands and splashed a few drops on my forehead. I walked to the door that separated the kitchen from the front of the house. Snippets of conversation floated down the hall to the kitchen. I leaned closer, my ear to the hinged side of the door.

"She's not even eighteen yet. "

"...of the church."

"...he's twice her age."

Their voices grew fainter. They whispered, the words faint then gone when they reached the hallway.

Later that evening, as I lay in my bedroom adjacent to my parent's room, they resumed their discussion. Their words penetrated the thin wall between us.

"Tom, there are many girls who are married at her age. I was seventeen when we met and eighteen when we married. Remember?"

My father grunted in response. A few moments later, he said, "He's not one of us. He's not of the church."

"Well, maybe he won't come after all," my mother said. "Stop worrying and go to sleep."

The bed creaked. One of them had rolled away from the other. I heard nothing further.

I could hardly eat the food I'd prepared for supper on Saturday. Throughout the meal, though I knew he would not come until well after we'd eaten, I listened for any telltale sound, the whistle of someone approaching, the fall of a foot on the porch. I wanted to greet him at the door. Twice, while my mother and I put away the dishes, something, somewhere in the house creaked or thumped. At the sound, I dropped my towel and hurried toward the front room. My mother pretended not to notice and chatted idly as we worked.

Finally, there was a knock at the door. Two dull thumps.

I wiped my hands and untied my apron. "Mother, leave the rest, I'll finish up later," I said as I hung the apron on the back of the pantry door.

My father had beaten me to the door.

"Jack, come in," he said. He stepped slightly to the side.

Jack squeezed around him and into the entryway. I glanced in the hall mirror, patted the curls around my forehead into place, smoothed my skirt, and made my way to where the two men stood facing each other. My father held his paper in one hand, Jack his hat, arms at his side.

"Father, I think you know Jack Linger," I said to fill the awkward silence. Tom nodded and reached out to shake Jack's hand.

"Jack, let's sit on the porch." I took a crocheted shawl from its peg on the hall tree and swung the wrap over my shoulders. Though warm during the day, the late Indiana summer was giving way to fall. Evenings already brought a hint of the cooler weather ahead. Jack followed me out the door. I glanced over my shoulder and caught a glimpse of Jack as he nodded to my father.

A pair of wooden chairs sat on each side of our porch. I chose the pair on the western-most side, furthest from the door. Here, I often caught the last light and scents of the day. A passionflower vine, one I'd planted years ago, flourished there. It had wound its way to the top of one of the porch columns. It held a dozen or more faded blooms, but their sweet fragrance remained.

Jack waited for me to take my seat. Then, he sat beside me. He folded his long legs, first one way then another to fit himself into the too-small chair.

"It's a lovely evening," Jack said. His words broke the brief, uncomfortable silence.

I let a hint of a smile betray my thoughts.

"I think that is the first time I've ever used that word. Lovely. But it is."

"Yes, it is lovely."

We sat in silence for a minute and let the sounds of the evening speak for us.

The front door latch clicked as it closed. My father's steps echoed as I pictured him returning to his desk or to the back of the house. Jack placed his hat on the nearby table. He sank deeper into his seat.

CHAPTER 9

Harvest Lessons

Jack called at my home intermittently from that fall. After the harvest, there was less work to do at Nathan's farm. Jack escaped to town more frequently and arrived each Saturday morning before noon.

He was a frugal man. A quality I thought my father would admire. Jack had worked for a number of years at Nathan's farm and some days at other farms when the days were long enough. A hard worker, another quality I thought spoke in his favor, one that might help my father see past Jack's Irish heritage. Two years ago, with money he had saved from his wages, together with money his mother had given him, he had bought a piece of property alongside one of the larger farms in Marrs Township. He'd asked me several times to travel with him to see the plot of land he'd purchased. I had promised to go with him, later.

Toward the end of October, as the days grew shorter, I knew I would have to agree now or wait until next spring. It would take Jack several hours to come to town, drive back to his farm, spend a few hours there with me and then repeat the journey, all in good daylight. I consented to make the trip the following Saturday. My parents had been accustomed to his visits and to my long walks with Jack. I never mentioned where we had been or what we talked of. They were not curious, or at least they did not ask. Nevertheless, I couldn't imagine they'd approve of an all day journey alone with him to his home.

When he arrived earlier than usual on Saturday, I surprised Jack and greeted him at the door. His face brightened when he saw me. For once, I'd spared him the annoyance of the pastor's head to toe examination and then the awkward silence that hung in the air until I rescued them. It had become a ritual of sorts, even if uncomfortable for both men. Jack said he could never think of anything to say to the pastor. My father never uttered more than a hello or a good morning. Though Jack never admitted the cold greeting bothered him, I'd seen him shift from one foot to the other. His unease was obvious.

"I've come by buggy," he said. "I hope you don't mind. I wanted to bring Mr. Norris's automobile." Edward Norris, a landowner near the Nathan farm, occasionally sought Jack's help. When automobiles became available in Evansville, Edward had purchased one of the new Fords, making his frequent trips to town less difficult. Now, while common to have a car in the city, they were still a rarity in the country. On occasion, Edward had allowed Jack to borrow the car and shortened the twenty-mile, two-hour drive by about an hour each way.

"I don't mind at all." Well, perhaps I did, but I didn't want to hurt Jack's feelings. "Before we moved to town, my mother and I used to make the trip to Mt. Vernon every few weeks," I said. "I'll confess though, it has been quite a while."

My family owned a car as well, but my father reserved it for special occasions or longer outings, he preferred to walk for most of his errands. Besides, his customary route, from home, to the church or to any one of several church members' homes, or the main stores in the heart of the city was an easy walk.

I remembered little of my earliest days on the family farm, for the most part, the temperature extremes, the sweltering summers, and frigid, snowy winters. One particular December had been so cold my mother had delayed a trip to town several times. At last, when the temperatures broke, Mother decided to brave the elements. We dressed warmly, me layered in nearly every item of clothing I owned. Bundled tightly, I could not lower my stubby arms to my side. I waddled outside to the buggy while my father watched from the front porch. He said I looked like a tiny scarecrow that had come to life. My father laughed at the sight, one of the rare moments I had heard him laugh. Perhaps that is why I remembered the scene.

Once seated in the buggy next to my mother, I watched as she pulled back the corner of a dark woolen blanket that lay in a mound on the floor of the carriage. She spread it across her legs and tucked it around mine for added warmth.

"What's moving under there," I said, startled when something bumped against my feet.

"Chickens, Liese. They'll keep us warmer than just this old blanket. Don't worry, they'll settle down in a bit. Just don't kick your legs."

Curious, I lifted the edge of the blanket. A burlap sack, tied at the neck with twine, lay below the blanket on the floor. The lumpy sack heaved from time to time. The lumps were four chickens my father must have gathered from the coop. Whenever my mother or I shifted our feet, the irritated creatures clucked and scuttled aside before coming to rest again on the floor. My feet were delightfully warm the entire trip, nevertheless, I could not rid my head of the image of chickens scampering about, tumbling from the buggy with each bump in the road, one by one abandoning us to the cold.

On this surprisingly warm fall day, I had no need for chickens. As I climbed on board, the memory flooded back. I made a quick check of the floor of the buggy.

Jack craned his neck to peer inside the large basket I'd placed beside me on the floor. A blue and white checked cloth covered the contents, blocked his view. Noticing his curiosity, I smiled. "I've brought a lunch for us for later, Mr. Curious."

Jack smiled back. I thought he sighed from relief. "Wonderful. I was worried about that. I don't have much to offer at my cabin." He said he ate most his weekday meals at the Nathan farm with the other hands. His own store of food was basic. As I learned later that morning, the entire contents of his pantry lined one shelf; a tin of coffee, which he took black, some dried pork jerky, and a jar of preserves, together with what remained of a loaf of bread that Henrietta Hammer had given him earlier in the week.

I sensed the real purpose of the trip was to see how I would react to his way of living. He knew I'd been born in the country, in Mt. Vernon. Though I'd spent my first years there, most of my life had been in town.

"You are such a lady," he'd said a few weeks ago as we rocked in the chairs on my front porch. I blushed and was glad for the distraction my embroidery afforded. Each stitch demanded my attention while we talked.

He continued. "If we got married, you'd have to give this up for a simpler life. A life on the farm."

"Ouch!" I had jabbed the end of my finger with my needle. "What did you say?"

"You heard me. Don't pretend you didn't."

"Marriage is a long way off. I'm not ready to even think about something like that."

"Well, we'll see. But, if we did, I want you to know, I can't promise you much. Not yet anyway. I want to expand my place. Enough to support a family."

I pulled the thread through to the other side and tied it off.

We rode the ten or twelve miles to Jack's place near Heusler and along the way encountered a dozen vehicles headed in the opposite direction. Their riders waved, called out a greeting as we both slowed our buggies and veered to the edge of the narrow roadway to pass. Many of the families from the countryside were bound for town.

"They're going to the parade, I suppose."

"Looks that way."

"Hannah said it was going to be Evansville's largest yet."

"You probably would have preferred going to see the festivities, but, I'm glad you agreed to come. This might be the last free day I have for awhile. Mr. Norris has asked me to help carve out some new fields."

Along our route, Jack pointed to the farms that bordered the road. He asked or announced the names of the owners as we passed. "Do you know who lives here?"

"The Blumfelds," I said. "And the farm over there," I nodded to the left, "belongs to the Martins."

"Are they relatives?" he asked. "It seems everywhere I turn, someone I meet is related to Tom or Maria," Jack said. "I mean the Pastor Tom and Maria."

I did know many of the families from the surrounding countryside, at least those that attended Zion Evangelical on the Sundays they came to town.

"Alright, what crop is that?" he asked. Defeated, he changed the topic. He let loose of the reins of the buggy and pointed to an expanse of green vines on our right.

"Soybeans."

"And, that's corn," I said as we passed the next field lined with tall stalks. "I might be a city girl now, but remember, I was born out here in the country. We lived here for a five or six years before we moved to town. And, I've visited many of the families here with my father."

"I don't think I'm cut out for town," he said.

After close to two hours, we climbed a small hill. Jack turned off the road onto an even narrower trail, one I hadn't noticed until he'd almost completed the turn. The buggy wobbled to one side as it crossed the well-worn ruts in the roadway. I grabbed the side of the carriage; I feared we'd tip without warning. I did not let loose until we were safely back in the middle of the trail.

"You're safe, Liese," Jack said, looking down to where my fingers were, clenched around his arm. He laughed. "I've done this a thousand times. You'll get used to it."

I chose to ignore his insinuation that I would be making the trip on a regular basis.

Numerous plots, some hardly worthy of being designated a farm, ran along each side of the trail. The original owners had carved out these parcels and fenced them. Some they sold or rented to supplement their income. Jack had purchased one of the smaller plots. Because no fence identified where his property started or stopped, I wondered how he knew where the boundaries to his property lay.

"I don't need a fence to tell me. I walked the boundaries with Mr. Norris. We drove a marker into the ground at each of the corners of my few acres. Besides, you can tell just by looking."

"How?"

"Look at the rows there. Squint your eyes. Notice the pattern." Jack pointed at the rows of corn that ran the length of the hill to my right. His forearm hovered above my shoulder. His hand brushed my cheek as he motioned up the hill. "Those are mine."

His rows ran perpendicular to those on the next field. Mr. Norris' farm, I guessed. Jack's were set just a few feet closer to each other too, with tighter turns at the ends of the rows to make room for one or two more plants, one or two more bushels at harvest time. Once he'd pointed out the difference, I could see it myself.

"Here we are," Jack said as he stopped the buggy next to a wooden fence on the left side of the trail. The fence prevented two goats from scampering away to forage in other fields. Jack jumped down from the buggy and glanced quickly at me.

I looked across the terrain in front of me. A dirt path abutted the fenced enclosure and continued over a rise to a clapboard structure. One story. A single window on the side of the house that faced me. A stone chimney on the right. A porch halfway across the front of the house. It lacked a rail.

"Before, you come to any conclusions," he said, "let me show you around."

"I haven't 'come to any conclusions', Jack." My second lie of the day, I thought. "Besides, it's just as you described it. It's exactly what I imagined." I'd pray for forgiveness tonight.

I remembered my family home in Mt. Vernon. It had been larger and in far better condition and adorned like some of the more established and well-to-do with architectural or ornamental touches, a triangle of scrollwork softening the plain upright supports of the porch, a balustrade that edged the porch, or scrollwork around the roof or window caps. Most small farm families lived in clapboard sided homes of a similar style.

Jack opened the gate, walked the buggy through with me still aboard, then circled behind the carriage and secured the gate. He passed to the opposite side to help me down.

"I'm fine. You can take the basket though."

Jack reached over, grabbed the handle of the basket from the back of the buggy. He set it down at our feet.

"Let me introduce you to Biddie and Marta." He headed toward the fence, nothing more than a few posts with wire strung between them that defined an oblong enclosure along the right side of the path to the cabin's door. The spotted goats eyed us. Strands of grass hung from their muzzles. They ambled to the fence, curious to see who had come and whether or not we had food to offer.

"That's Marta. The larger one," Jack said. "I've had her for about a year. Mr. Norris gave her to me. She looked lonely though, here all alone, so I bought her a friend to keep her company. I got Biddie here from another landowner. The Norwoods. They had to sell their livestock to move to town. Biddie was the last one left. She was small. A runt I suppose. They were happy I would take her." Biddie nudged the fence. Her fur was soft as she nuzzled against my outstretched hand. With no apparent prospect of food, though, the two were soon bored and left us to graze.

"Are you ever going to show me your house, Jack?"

"Of course, but I warn you it's not much to see."

The simple house consisted of three rooms, though I could have easily mistaken the main room and the room where Jack slept for a single room. He had built a cabinet that he had fastened to one wall to divide the room in two. The third room was the kitchen. He did not count the tiny water closet as a fourth room. A previous owner had added it to the back of the house just before Jack acquired the property. Other than that addition, he had said, he'd lived with the house the way he had found it. As the only occupant, he needed little else.

I glanced around the sparse rooms. I noted their tidiness and the scant furnishings.

"As I said, nothing much to see here. What I really wanted you to see is outside at the top of the hill over there. It's the best part. Let's take lunch with us."

Jack led the way out and around the house, into the surrounding field. We paralleled the furrows of black dirt. I watched my step and tried not to sink to my ankles in the mounds. I was determined to keep pace with Jack who moved deftly along the rows though he never looked down. The corn stalks towered above my head, thanks to the plentiful rains we'd enjoyed over the summer. The leaves were deep green, striped with yellow and brown. Ears of corn studded the thick stalks.

Jack pointed to a rise in the land behind the cabin.

"Let's go up the hill toward that tree. It's a great place for a picnic lunch."

As we climbed, the slope grew steeper. Jack took my hand. I had no need to watch my feet further. I glided alongside him.

When we reached the crest, to my dismay, he dropped my hand and led the way across the last few rows of corn to a large oak.

"This is the edge of the property," Jack said. He spread his arms in front of an immense oak. A stand of younger trees stood beyond the single oak. Someone, I supposed it had been Jack, had nailed a smooth board across the stump of a long dead oak to fashion a bench. Here, the trees cast a pool of precious shade, a welcome relief I imagined during the height of summer.

I marveled at the view from the top of the hill. The spot sat on the furthest boundary of Jack's farm. The fields that spread over the hills immediately below, though, were not his. They belonged to Mr. Norris.

Until that moment, I'd not been aware of how high we had climbed during our journey from town. The last few miles had carried us far above the Ohio River flood plain. The rise where I stood was the highest point for miles. It afforded an uninterrupted view to the north.

Below my feet, the plowed rows rolled away across a series of low hills until they disappeared over the horizon. Here and there, I could make out a house or barn surrounded by dark patches of trees, similar to the patch where we stood. Fields in squares and rectangles dotted the landscape, as if a patchwork quilt lay draped over the hills, the shades of gold in the cornfields yielded to the verdant green of the bean fields, or farther away, a vacant patch of black, newly fallowed earth.

"You were right, Jack. The view is lovely." I breathed in the scent of clear air, fresh earth, and sunshine.

"I hoped you'd like it. I think Mr. Norris decided this section was too rocky to farm. And, since it was so far from the rest of his fields, he was happy to leave it untouched."

"It's beautiful. It's such a welcome change from the view in town. Every day it seems another brick building appears. The river used to be visible from my window. But not anymore."

We ate our lunch on the rise, under the tree and lingered to admire the view. We didn't speak for a long while. Then, mindful of how little time we had before we would need to return to town, I rose. Jack followed my lead. He helped me gather the plates, cups, and tins I'd brought and returned them to the basket.

"Before we go back down, I want to check a few of the rows. I think some of the corn's ready to harvest," Jack said. Cooler weather had blown in the week before. Many of the corn stalks had dried in the wind. "Why don't you wait here in the shade? I'll come back for you in a minute. I won't be long."

"I'll go with you," I said. Jack opened his mouth as if to say no. Before he could say anything, I took a step around him toward the first row of corn.

"Alright," he said, "but at least, let me show you how. I warn you, it's hard work." He held out his hand. I placed my hand in his, a calloused and coarse palm. "As I suspected, you've not been doing a lot of farming of late."

We walked to the nearest row. He showed me how to check the stalks, how to mark weedy patches he needed to return to later. Jack explained how to identify ripe ears and use the husking knives he had with him.

"Hold it this way for the ears growing upright," he said, slicing off the nearest cob as he spoke. "Then, for the others, cut down and across, like this." Jack handed me one of the knives and pointed to an ear on the nearest stalk. I made several cuts under his supervision.

"That's it," Jack said. "You've got it." I moved down the row to another stalk. "I should have brought you some gloves."

"Oh, go on," I said. "We're not going to do the whole field are we?"

"No, of course not, just a row or two."

"I garden almost every day. Of course, my little plot is nothing like this."

"There's a basket at the end of the row. You can just toss any ears you cut there."

We worked our way along several rows over the course of an hour. Jack walked down one row and I another. On reaching the end of a row, Jack leapfrogged me to the next. Periodically, Jack stopped to glance at me through the stalks. The third or fourth time, I stopped, looked over, put both hands on my hips, and stared back. "Jack you're falling behind. If you don't stop checking on me and finish what you're doing, we'll never get done." With that, he smiled and completed his row without another pause. I watched as he raced to finish and work back down the next to meet me again at the end of my row.

We arrived back in town later than planned, but still before sundown. The instant Jack stopped the buggy in front of my gate he hopped down and hurried around to the other side to help me down. He held my hand longer than necessary, he did not let go even as I tugged at his arm and turned to open the gate.

"Stop your teasing," I said. "Let go of me."

In a furtive glance toward the house, I caught a glimpse of a figure at the window, but it had moved away the next time I looked. I didn't care what my father or mother thought, I turned back toward Jack. I hoped he'd not noticed my parents spying on us. With my head angled away so that the brim of my hat shielded my face from view out the window, I said goodbye.

I smiled and squeezed his hand gently, then withdrew and passed through the gate without another word.

I closed the front door behind me and stood for a moment in the vacant, or now vacant, front room. I stood where I thought someone had been earlier and pulled aside the curtains. In the street, Jack turned the buggy. He tipped his hat toward the window before he urged the horse on toward Heusler, alone. I hurried to the kitchen and poked my head around the door to ask if my mother needed help.

My parents were in their usual positions—Mother at the sink and Father bent over the table. A draft of what I assumed was this week's sermon lay on the table in front of him.

"Ah, you're home. Good. As soon as you change, you can help with Grandpa's dinner," my mother said without looking up.

"Of course, I'll be right back." I think the cheerfulness in my voice must have surprised my mother. She glanced in my direction. My father, however, sat, unmoving, silent, stone-like. I wished they had bothered to ask after my day, I thought as I changed my clothes. Had they asked, I would have let them know I'd agreed to help Jack at his farm again next week and, for that matter, any other time he asked.

As far as I could tell, no conversation passed between them after I left the room.

CHAPTER 10
Silk Threads

Jack's visits to town became more frequent. His excuses more flimsy. He skipped several days of work on his own farm, good weather or bad. More often now, too, on Sundays, he drove to town to attend Sunday services. I'd watch for him from my place at the piano. When the church filled, to avoid any undue attention, he'd scuttle to a seat in one of the pews at the back. From the end of the row where he sat, if he chose the right side and leaned just so, he had an unobstructed view of the church piano. He would be able to watch me.

When the services ended, Jack leapt from his seat. He exited through the large double doors and held them open for others to follow. I usually preceded my father and mother out the door and stood by while Jack made a point of greeting my parents. He spoke to no one else, though, not even to me, until most of the congregation had dispersed.

I guessed that my father held no illusions about Jack's recent interest in the church. Each Sunday, he would acknowledge Jack and thank him for attending the service, but he would quickly turn his attention to the other members of his congregation who wished to engage him in conversation.

Even though they did not approve of my relationship with Jack, I presumed my parents were relieved that, preoccupied with him, I had less time, if any, to spend at Stallman's. I believed they had discovered I'd frequented the establishment, but they continued their reign of silence on that matter. Hannah, however, had relayed an encounter she had with Adola Roder, self-appointed head of the Zion Church Women's Temperance Society. Hannah was on her way to shop at Stallman's when Adola Roder exited. Adola cornered Hannah outside the store, nearly accosting her, in Hannah's rendition of the encounter. Adola had shaken her finger inches from Hannah's face. She'd berated her for frequenting a place where alcohol was served. Hannah said Adola went on and on, and threatened, no, confirmed that she had spoken of the girls' behavior to the assembled members of the society and to Pastor Tom himself.

I imagined, relieved as they were about that circumstance, they were now as concerned about the unsupervised time I spent in the country with Jack, whether in his carriage or borrowed automobile, whether I returned before or after dark. Perhaps they had thought either Jack or I would grow tired of each other's company. Though I had never given them cause to believe I would resist their counsel or be tempted to engage with Jack to spite them, I believe they feared the subject.

In truth, they had a right to be concerned. They had no idea how deep our relationship was and how intimate we had become.

Jack had managed to weave mention of marriage into every visit. At first, I chided him for his presumption, then I ignored him, and finally I took it as a matter of course. I couldn't say yet that I had fallen in love. I didn't know what falling in love was. Over the weeks and months, I had become used to his presence, to his manner, even to his small home, primitive as it was.

I had not become accustomed to his intimacies. Our meetings in town, at my parents' home were innocent enough, but once out of sight of home, Jack became more demonstrative. We'd progressed, if that is the right word, from a shy embrace or a light kiss.

As one of our visits in late December ended, Jack grabbed me around the waist and took me inside his home. On that overstuffed and lumpy muslin covered mattress, he held me close to him and kissed me passionately. Then, with one hand, he pulled my head back and with the other, lowered me to the bed.

"Jack, Jack," I said. "I—"

"Liese, don't worry. I'll show you."

"But—"

"This is what people in love do."

I let him make love to me. Though my cheek was red from where his beard had pushed against my face, he had been gentle and kissed me lightly on the lips when he had finished. I could not bear to look him in the eyes, not as I combed my hair back in place, not on the drive home, and not even as I said goodbye at my gate.

For days afterwards, I could not convince myself that what I had done was not obvious. I expected my parents to rise up when I entered the house, that they would see the change in me, smell the smell of him, of him and me. I thought Hannah or Emma would know by the way I held my head or walked or by what I might say of Jack. But no one did.

The next time, I found myself in his home and in his bed, I brought up the topic of marriage. "I must break the news to my parents. We'll need to give them some time to get used to the idea."

"Liese, you are a grown woman. Eighteen in just another week. You can make your own decisions."

"I know, but, you don't know them. I think it would be best if we give it some time. ."

"Some time?" Jack sat up.

"Not long, Jack. We could get married next summer, maybe."

Winter passed. Spring arrived. I'd still not found the courage to tell my parents my plans, despite Jack's pressing me. We went on as before and I spent more and more time with him at his farm. One day in late May, from the rise, Jack and I watched the color in the fields change hues with the light. The dust-colored furrows of fallow acres grew a deep chocolate brown while bean and corn-fields turned richer with the lowering light, an emerald green and gold. We stood side by side and stared out to the horizon. We stood apart but close enough to sense the warmth of each other's bodies as the sun slipped in the sky. It fell, first below the jagged lines of the treetops in the distance, then below the horizon.

Jack reached for my hand. He held it in both of his and lifted it to his chest, pulling me toward him. My gaze remained fixed on the horizon where I could avoid looking into his eyes. I knew.

"I've decided to go," he said. The words spilled out and hung in the void between us.

For the last two weeks, each time the subject arose, Jack had changed the topic and by so doing he'd aroused my suspicions and my fears instead of calming them. I had guessed that he would go. I had hoped somehow that he would not. Each day the number of men who'd enlisted in the Army grew. They left countless women, mothers, daughters, and wives behind to face an uncertain future and to manage alone for an undetermined time.

Even the mere idea of war had intoxicated many of the young men in the community, whether old enough to enlist or not. I imagined they dreamed dreams of war—they'd defend the country, vanquish the enemy, and return triumphant. Fresh from the enlistment office, papers in hand, they would pass me on the sidewalk. Their faces were radiant. They beamed with pride, sure of themselves, full of bravado. They were Americans now, not just German-Americans like their parents or grandparents. The older adults' initial hesitation had given way once the country had entered the war, though they had no illusions as to the difficult times that lay ahead. The young men were the foolhardy ones.

We had discussed his enlisting once, earlier this month. "Everyone is going, Liese. Edgar, Peter, Milton. Everyone I know."

"I don't care what 'everyone' is doing," I said.

Indeed, many of the local youth had joined much earlier in the year, completed their training, and departed for Europe. May, though, was still just the beginning of America's participation in the war. America's young men lacked the experience of significant battles. Few had yet to see the front lines or witness anything more than scattered casualties. Reports of the dead did not fill newspaper columns as they would in the weeks and months to come.

I stared at the black earth underneath my feet. I looked at my feet, only to see the tips of our shoes, pointed toward each other, dotted with clods of soil that clung to the sides of the shoes. Under my left foot, I glimpsed the rotten remains of a cornhusk.

Jack kept hold of my hand, our fingers interlaced. Where our wrists met, my pulse tapped through my veins and beat against his. With his free hand, he touched my chin and forced me to raise my head. He bent and kissed me gently. "You shouldn't worry. I'll be fine. It won't be long. I know it. I promise."

"But, what about us getting married?" For once, I championed the idea.

"We will. We can. As soon as I return."

I could not find the right words to say. I could not have said them if I had. The air had gone from my lungs. I managed only to shake my head before I fixed my eyes again on the horizon, now just a dark shape behind which the sun had set. The tinges of orange, pink, and yellow had given way to deeper hues of blue and gray, precursors of the ink-filled night sky.

"I had best be getting back to town," I said, when I could find my voice. "How much time do we have?"

"Till dark?"

"Till you," I paused, "leave."

"My Company is scheduled to go tomorrow," he said. He turned away. Though I had tried to hide it, I gasped aloud. I wanted to hide my emotions, but I could not.

"How long have you known?"

"I decided two weeks ago. I didn't want to tell you earlier. I didn't want the news hanging over us all week and keep us from enjoying every moment we have."

"You should have told me at once. Even before you enlisted."

"Why? So you could try to change my mind?"

"Yes." I choked back a few tears. I did not want him to see me cry. "How can you leave me? You're all I have."

"Nonsense. You have your friends and your family. They'll be here with you until I come back."

I didn't want my friends and my family at that moment. I wanted Jack. I realized at that moment, I had formed the vision of my future around him.

"Will you see me off at the depot? At ten?"

I wasn't sure that I wanted to, that I could bear it, but I nodded. Perhaps I had time to dissuade him.

The sky had darkened, now a deep gray. I turned to walk down the rise back to the house and the waiting buggy. I halted and then retraced my steps to where Jack stood. I stopped in front of him and rose onto the tips of my shoes. He bent down to me. We kissed a second time. This time deeply and passionately, as if this were our last moment together.

Afterwards, we walked to the buggy hand in hand. I climbed onto the bench and slid across to make room for him. We rode back to town, the *clop clop* of the horse's hooves and the occasional snap of the reins on its hide the only sounds.

At eight the next morning, I walked to the depot. Drained both physically and emotionally from a long, sleepless night, it took every ounce of effort I had to put one foot in front of the other. I left the house before breakfast. I ignored Grandfather Bauer's meal that Mother had set out on a tray in the kitchen. I said only that I was going out and that I would return by noon. As I closed the front door behind me, I imagined my mother and father, still staring after me, startled, as if they bobbed in the wake of a craft that had passed them too quickly in the river.

Still a small Midwestern town in 1918, Evansville's station was accustomed to only a few passengers coming or going at any one time. Today, however, as I saw when I arrived, the depot had difficulty accommodating even half the travelers and their families and friends who had gathered to see them off. Dozens of men stood about the platform, some with smooth cheeks, too young for war, some with thin wisps of gray hair, too old, all dressed in new woolen uniforms, despite the warmth of the season. Most of the men busied themselves with arranging their tickets, stowing their luggage, and saying their goodbyes.

I rose on to the tips of my toes to see over the heads of the throng in the waiting room but failed to catch sight of Jack anywhere. I pushed my way outside, onto the equally if not more crowded platform. After searching along the platform several times, I spotted him in the shadows of the awning where he chatted with a young man in uniform. I had difficulty referring to them, even imagining them, as soldiers. Although I called his name as loudly as I dared, the din nearly swallowed my voice. I tried a second time. This time, both men turned their heads. Jack's face brightened. He left his belongings where he had dropped them, as many others had, and made his way toward me. He had to push aside one or two people and thread his way through the jumble of trunks scattered across the platform. I had dressed, despite my concerns and sense of impending loss, in my brightest, lilac-blossom covered print skirt underneath a white lace-trimmed blouse. A matching lilac blossom embroidered in my most careful exacting stitch on the collar.

"You look lovely, today." He smiled. I wondered if it were because he'd used the word "lovely" again. "Thank you for coming." He reached for my hands and held them in his against his heart, never taking his eyes off me.

I found it difficult to speak and impossible to match my mood to my cheerful outfit. Try as he might, through talk of the weather—what a fine day it was—or of the throngs of people around us—over there, that's Billy, you remember him—Jack could not offer me the solace I wanted. He could not promise to return safely. He could not promise to return at all. I pushed these thoughts aside and forced myself to smile. I wanted him to remember me dressed for another spring in the country, confident, and happy.

"I've got something for you," Jack said. He reached inside his jacket to retrieve a folded bit of fabric that he offered to me in the palm of his hand. I unfolded the square of gossamer cloth edged in a fine, pearl-colored lace. With one corner in each of my hands, I raised it to hold it in front of me. The sunlight streamed through the platform's portico and obscured the scene embossed across the center. I lowered the handkerchief and held the silk against one hand to see it better. The words "The Farewell" were emblazoned across the top of a banner caught in the beak of an eagle in flight. On the right side, below the banner, a cannon aimed toward an unseen enemy. On the left, a soldier with gun drawn lay propped against the wall of a trench. Between the two scenes, an American flag served as a backdrop for a young couple in a last or future embrace—I did not know which.

Where, I wanted to say, where were the scenes of soldiers lying dead on the ground, of the tears that broken families would shed, the rubble of homes, villages, and lives destroyed? I fought hard to keep the tears from coming. I bowed my head while I composed myself; I folded the kerchief again, until it formed a neat square. I placed it in the pocket of my blouse, the lace trim spilled over the edge as if it were a corsage.

Jack surveyed the platform for a place to sit for the few minutes left us. Two young men in uniform who sat together on a nearby bench caught his gaze. They rose out of courtesy and yielded their place on the bench to us, to a couple in love.

We said little. We found it hard to talk of trivial day-to-day matters and wanted to avoid any mention of what lay ahead. Jack assured me he would keep his wits about him. He vowed to return the moment they had done what they needed to do. The blare of the stationmaster's voice startled everyone on the platform.

"Boarding in five minutes. Boarding in five minutes," he shouted as he walked up and down the platform. I could barely hear his voice over the noise of the assembled families and friends and the locomotive as it hissed and sputtered. More clatter came from the street where new groups of young men stepped from cars and buses every minute.

Jack rose and took my hand. We crossed the platform back to where he had left his belongings. I stayed close to him, I feared the press of the crowd would separate and deny us even the precious few seconds that remained. Just as we reached the open door of the car, Jack turned and kissed me on the lips. Then, he bounded up the stairs and disappeared.

I stood where he had left me, stunned, frozen to the platform. He was gone. I had not convinced him to stay.

The train lurched forward then paused, as if it were taking a breath, my breath. Then, it pulled away. I turned to leave. The crowd massed around the door in front and behind me, it pushed me on my way, it widened the distance between Jack and me. I heard my name and turned back in time to catch sight of Jack leaning through an open window. I waved. He called again then raised his hand to comb his hair away from his forehead With the crowd converged on the area near the train car, hats, heads, and knapsacks blocked my view of him. I pulled the silk square of cloth from my pocket and held it aloft where it caught the light. Whether he saw it or not, he raised his arm and waved.

Outside the depot, a whistle screamed into the clear air. As it gained speed, the train's wheels clattered against the rails, then faded as the train drew away from the station. I waited until the sounds died out, then turned toward home. I walked several blocks out of my way from the station. I took the longest route possible. Once home, though, I hurried up the stairs to my room without a hello to my mother in the kitchen. The click of the latch on the front door would have alerted her I'd returned.

In my room, I removed the silk handkerchief from my pocket. I folded it then placed it in the top drawer of my bureau. I would not look at it again, not read the inscription, not see the eagle, the flag, the cannon, the soldier, or the lovers for six months, not until November 7, 1918, when the war had nearly ended.

I baked a blueberry pie that night. Baking cleared my head. Flour and butter and cream and sugar. I caught myself reciting ingredients. I rolled the dough for the piecrust on the counter and pushed away my darkest thoughts. I whipped cream to dollop on top, beating it into frothy peaks and let my fears go.

CHAPTER 11

Form Letters

To everyone except me, it was as if Jack had never existed. My life returned to the way it had been before he had first called. During the week, I helped Mother around the home and looked after Grandfather. These chores occupied most of my morning. In the early afternoon, I'd prepare dinner. I served it at six o'clock after Father finished his sermon or returned home from ministering to a member of his congregation. In the evenings, I crocheted or embroidered under the light of the floor lamp in the front room while we listened to the radio for news of world affairs. On weekends, I stayed home. I made no more forays into the countryside. My sojourns away now were limited to visits with my father.

Each time Hannah and Emma passed by on their way to Stallman's they would plead for me to go along. I'd agreed once, just after Jack had left, but had regretted the decision immediately. Now, no matter how long or how earnestly they pleaded for my company I would not go. With Jack in grave danger every moment he breathed, I could not fake happiness, not even for Hannah and Emma's sake.

I hadn't received any news from Jack, nevertheless, whether from what I heard on the radio, or read in the newspapers, or gleaned from conversations during rounds with my father, I'd grown concerned.

At the start of the war, I'd consulted reports in both the *Evansville Courier* and the German community newspaper, *The Demokrat,* until the latter shut its doors. Its editor had found the mandate to file official translations of the news with the local postmaster before printing was a cost he could not afford. My grandfather, like many of his generation, subscribed to the paper until the end. He clung to the last few issues, grumbling and cursing as he read them over and over. He refused even to glance at the headlines in the *Courier.*

"This is an outrage. *Wir sollten nicht zulassen.* We should not allow this to happen. We should not allow this," he said to anyone who would listen, or to no one.

"Father, please," my mother said, "you should not say such things."

"I'll say whatever I please."

"Certainly not outside this house," my father said.

I suppose they were thankful that my grandfather's condition confined him to the home where he could voice his opinion openly. Were he to venture outside, less sympathetic ears might have overheard him. Recently, they'd kept him home even during Sunday services so as not to subject the congregation to his harangues less someone construe that the Stephens or the membership at large shared his view. No one wanted to garner attention in the uneasy times, especially anyone of German descent.

It had been two months since Jack had departed. I had no idea how long he might be away. No one hazarded a guess how long the war would last. I allowed myself only to think in terms of months, setting my mind on six months, nine at the outside. Still, I fretted over the lack of correspondence from him. He was not one to write, nevertheless almost everyone I knew had received letters from their sons, or brothers, or husbands, or yes, sweethearts. During a visit with my mother to Alma Dause, an elderly church member, Alma had shared three letters she'd received from her son, Max. He'd left at the same time as Jack. I remembered that I had seen Max on the platform that same day, another man in uniform. Max had stood with his shoulders back, his head high, but his hands fidgeted with the buttons on his jacket, the hem of his sleeves, and whatever he had in his pockets.

Then, in early August, I received a letter from Jack.

My mother carried the letter to me in the kitchen. "Liese, the postman brought a letter for you."

I glanced at the envelope in her hand. My heart quickened. I wiped my hands and took the envelope from her. The letter had arrived though well crumpled and with a tear across one corner. It had clearly suffered on its trip from France to Evansville. I placed the letter in the pocket of my apron and rolled out the remaining ball of dough.

"Aren't you going to read it, Liese? Is it from that man?"

"I will as soon as I finish here, Mother," I replied. My fingers are too messy right now." She said nothing more but I doubted she missed how quickly I began working the dough; the rolling pin nearly banged the wall as it flew across the counter. As soon as I had helped her clean the pans and bowls, still in my apron, I walked through the house to the front door and out to the porch. I slid the envelope from my pocket, trying not to inflict further damage on the fragile paper. I placed it on the balustrade; face up, where I could see my name written in his hand. I untied the apron and wiped my hands to remove traces of flour and the oily residue from the lard. I took a seat in the nearest wooden rocker.

From the muffled steps on the wood floor, I knew my mother had tiptoed into the living room and stood behind me at the window. From there, concealed by the lace curtains, she could watch and see my reaction. I would not give her that satisfaction. I wanted the moment for myself. I rocked slowly, for several minutes. The still unopened letter lay in my lap.

Mother's steps faded back into the house, retreated to the kitchen. I stopped rocking, took the letter in my hands, turned it over, and pried up the ragged edge of the flap with the tip of my finger. I extracted a single page.

To my surprise, I discovered Jack had written an earlier letter, one I'd never received. In this letter, he described none of the terrors he had witnessed or the fear I imagined he'd come to know. Instead, he wrote only of his hope and prayers for the future.

Dearest Liese:

It has been two weeks since I last wrote. I'm sorry I'm not better at writing. I have not heard from you but am hoping that I do soon. There is little that I can tell you now that we are in the midst of things. Our training is over and mostly we've been walking every day. Some of the fellows who are not so used to walking had sore feet, but not me. I'm doing very well. We're about to go closer to the front lines. But please don't worry. I am safe. I worry more about your well-being than my own. I get plenty to eat here and have lots of company in the fellows around me. We all miss our families. Mostly our sweethearts. May I call you that?

The land and farms of France, at least the parts I've seen, remind me of Indiana.

I have had no news of home except what I learned from some others through their letters. Luckily, I came over with two friends. George Dumas. You might remember I spoke of him. And Richard Kroener. I met him at the recruiting station. He's a bank clerk in Evansville. Lucky for us, we've been able to stay together and look after each other. A new friend from Kentucky received a cake from his mother last week! He shared it around as far as it would go. Perhaps, you could send one of your favorites. Wrap it well and be sure to make it a big one! Everyone here misses meals from home, and me, even my own cooking.

I would count the days until we see each other again, but I can't even guess how long this war or my Company's deployment will be. Several months at least, I suppose. When I do come back, I promise you, I will never let anything separate us again!

I suppose I had best be ending now. Goodbye till next
time, with all my love,

-Jack

I paused for a moment at the first line, where I discovered Jack had written me previously. I read the letter several times. I tried, yet feared, to picture Jack in France. I had read every report from the war that I could find in the *Evansville Courier*. Though the news had been favorable, the list of casualties grew each week. Already, Martin Lauder had come home gravely wounded. He had survived but lost both legs. I dreaded the thought of what such an injury might do to Jack and how it would affect our future. Martin lived with his parents as he had before, but he could not work to sustain himself, let alone a family. There had been one thousand forty-two deaths of sons of Indiana reported. I had kept a running total.

The letter lacked a date and the postmark was illegible. I knew it had to be at least two or three weeks old. I had no way to know when I read the letter whether Jack was still safe, still unharmed, or even still alive.

The newspapers took care not to print the names, ages, or hometowns of local residents wounded or killed in action until they could confirm the details and that the Army had notified the family. Even so, the deadly statistics filled column after column of the paper alongside other news of the war, troop movements, and significant battles.

I had nightmares. I believed Jack was dead. I would see men, young men, men in uniform, some too young to be soldiers, the sleeves of their uniforms hung below the tips of their small hands. Despite their age, they followed the others out of the trenches. The older men carried rifles and sticks, and shovels. One of them brandished a hoe. He aimed it forward toward an unseen enemy. Fog filled the air. Moisture in the air dampened the ground. As they moved forward, they left behind a trail of steps in the soft earth. The trails were perfect as if they walked in each other's footsteps, carving deep furrows as they went. Furrows to plant their crops in the spring.

One young man became disoriented and lost sight of the others, his feet could not find the trail. He could not go back, he could not stop, he moved on, forward, or what he fathomed was forward. He put one foot in front of the other in the same direction he thought he had been headed. The fog thickened as he went. His uniform was soaked, wet on the outside from the fog, on the inside from sweat. Wet, too, from fear. He stopped several times to wipe his forehead with his sleeve. He accomplished little more than to spread the dampness around before he continued forward, enveloped in a cocoon of smoke and heavy mist that moved with him step for step.

The sound of shells, gunfire, tanks, and men tromping across the earth eased, sealed by his cocoon. He strained to see through the mist. Rows of corn stood all around him, tall corn, ready to harvest. He shook his head and looked again but this time he could see nothing more than a few dark shapes, rising and falling as they advanced in the same direction. They, too, walked cloaked in their own cocoons, backlit by haloes of light.

In the next instant, the landscape transformed again. The new world was now nothing but sound, a world comprised of one single deafening, unending roar.

He opened his eyes but could only see from his left eye. Someone's foot, then a leg, passed through his line of sight. The figure seemed to scale an impossibly vertical slope. But it was he who had fallen. It was he who lay on the ground with the right side of his face buried in the mud. It was he who watched his fellow soldiers pass. He saw now that his left hand extended from his body at an odd, unnatural angle. His fingers encircled and held tightly to a clod of thick damp soil from the furrows of a field in France.

CHAPTER 12

Miss Miller and the Midwife

When another two weeks had passed, now three months since Jack had left, I could no longer deny my condition. I was certain. I needed to confide in someone, someone who might know what to do.

"I'll be back before dinner," I said to my mother as I rushed out the door, purposefully. I left no time for her to protest or ask me to run an errand. I had no time to spare, not for her or anyone else that day.

Emma was working on a piece of embroidery when I found her on the patio behind her house.

"Hello, Emma, your mother said I could find you here."

"Liese," she said, a lilt in her voice, "what a wonderful surprise." Emma turned and squinted up, a hand against her forehead to deflect the glare of the sun.

When I sat down next to her, the smile on her lips faded. She realized at the sight of my face, the slight pinch at the corners of my mouth, the slope of the worry lines on my forehead, this was anything but a cheerful visit. A tiny sob, more like a child's whimper escaped. I had tried so hard not to cry.

"What's wrong, Liese? You look terrible." Emma put her needlework aside and shifted to the edge of her seat, closer to me.

I slid a handkerchief from my sleeve and dabbed at my eyes and nose. "I don't know where to begin. I don't think I can talk about it, even with you."

"Nothing can be that bad."

I took two deep breaths, my chest rose and fell like bellows. Emma said nothing. She waited for me to regain my composure. Before I spoke, I glanced around to make certain we were alone. The back door was closed, as I had left it, the windows vacant.

"Promise me, if I tell you something, you won't say a word to anyone. Not a word. I mean it."

"Liese, I promise. Tell me what's wrong."

"I'm so worried. I don't know what to do. I...I...I think I'm pregnant." It took three tries but I had said the words. I had blurted them out, forced them into the world.

Emma gasped, her eyes widened. Her hands went to her face then back to her lap. "Pregnant? How could you be pregnant?" A long pause. "Well, I guess, I shouldn't say that exactly. But... but, you...you and Jack?" Emma's voice trailed off. She looked away but I could tell her thoughts raced as she considered the possibilities. "Surely, you didn't—" She stopped. She realized she needn't speculate further.

"Yes, I did."

"How long...how far along—" The right words, if there were right words eluded her.

"I don't know exactly. I can only guess..."

"Does he know? I mean...did he know?"

"I hadn't written to tell him. I wanted to wait until I knew for sure. Then, I thought I shouldn't tell him anything. That it would only add to his worries."

"We'll have to think about this," Emma said. "We have to think how best to handle this."

We sat in silence for a few minutes and stared into the garden. We avoided looking at each other—I out of shame and I supposed Emma still wrestling with the facts of my situation.

"What am I going to do? It would devastate my parents if they knew. They'd have to ask me to leave the house."

"Nonsense."

"Emma, I'm the daughter of a preacher."

"Liese, it might not be that bad."

"It would. Trust me. I could never bring myself to tell them. I have a cousin in Indianapolis. I was thinking of maybe going to live with her. I'd have to swear her to silence though."

Emma frowned; her eyebrows knit together. Several creases formed on her forehead. "Liese, there are places, I don't know exactly where, but places where...where women go. They have their children there and then come home to their families.

"I could never come home. Not unwed with a baby.

"Have you told anyone else?"

"No. You're the first. I came straight here. I was going to tell Hannah, too." I leaned forward and held my head between my hands. "They will all find out about it soon enough I suppose."

"We'll need help," Emma said. She patted my arm to console me, but her fingers flickered up and down, rapidly, nervously.

"No. No one else can know. Don't even think of telling Edgar, promise me." Edgar was Emma's latest male friend, George having come and gone. "I don't want anyone else to know about this. I couldn't bear him knowing." I grabbed the fingers that still pulsed against my arm. Emma winced and I realized I had nearly crushed her fingers in mine. "Promise me you won't say a word."

"I've already promised. But," she began, trying to sound hopeful, "this is not the end of the world."

"No, I mean it, Emma. Hannah, but no one else."

"We need to think."

"I've already been thinking. I've been thinking and thinking and thinking until, there's nothing more to think."

"You could tell your parents you married Jack before he left."

"I don't think so. They'd ask too many questions. They'd never believe me, nor would anyone else in town. I'm going to see Mrs. Becker tomorrow. Will you come with me?"

"Mrs. Becker? Why Mrs. Becker? She's a midwife. I don't think you're going to need her for months?"

I dropped my head and rocked back and forth. I put my head in my hands again. "Mrs. Becker is a midwife," I said. I spoke the words into my fist. "She's a midwife, but...she also takes care of... things. Things like this. So I've heard."

Emma pulled away abruptly. "You mean, do away with the child?"

"Yes. That's exactly what I am thinking. I don't have any other alternative. Will you at least come with me to see her?"

On Tuesday, Emma and Hannah drove me to Mrs. Becker's home and place of business. As we often shopped or went as a group to meetings of one or the other of the young women's benefit societies, we had little trouble arranging to be out together, even all day.

Mrs. Becker lived across town on Forest Avenue, an area of town I seldom visited. Her home had the same black roof, white clapboard, and black shutters as the other modest houses on the street. All sat a few feet above the street behind a low wall made of rough stone set in place when the city had carved the road through the uneven terrain. Like its neighbors, a flagstone path led to the front door.

We climbed the short flight of steps cut through the wall and across the path to a point a few steps shy of the front door. I had lost all my earlier courage. Emma supported one of my elbows, Hannah the other. They propelled me the last three paces to the door. Hannah knocked. I couldn't even lift my hand to accomplish that simple task. I stared at the black iron numerals beside the door. They confirmed the street address, one, one, seven. Three long, dagger-like figures nailed to the wall.

When the door opened abruptly and without a sound, Hannah nearly stumbled headlong into the foyer and into the ample bosom of the heavy-set woman who held the door. She stood at least a head taller than any one of us. A single, uninterrupted stiff swath of white fabric, a starched apron, covered her gray cotton dress from the waist to a few inches above the hem. A uniform, I thought. Not a doctor's or a nurse's uniform, though. More like a baker's outfit with an apron to absorb grease spatters and conceal flour dust.

Gray streaks ran through her hair, cropped at the chin. She was perhaps in her late fifties or even early sixties, as old as my mother. "Yes?" she said. Her eyes narrowed. She needed the spectacles on a chain around her neck, but she ignored them. Despite her apparent nearsightedness, her eyes bore holes in mine and, I suspected, Emma's and Hannah's. She did not discriminate in her directness. None of us moved or opened our mouths to speak.

Exasperated but not likely surprised at our silence, she spoke again. "Elizabeth Miller?"

"Yes ma'am. That's me. Are you Mrs. Becker?" Out of the corner of my eyes, I saw both Hannah and Emma's heads swivel toward me. I'd forgotten to tell them I'd given Ms. Becker another name.

"Come in," she said after she'd sized us up. She moved aside and we filed into the foyer.

I'd been vague, even secretive when I scheduled the appointment. Nevertheless, she had agreed to the meeting, never asking the purpose. I was no doubt not the first of my kind. I presumed that now, as I stood in front of her with no detectable signs of pregnancy, no puckered waistband, no tell-tale bulge beneath my skirt, and no gentleman in tow, she understood the situation.

Edith Becker had been a midwife for close to thirty years. Though she never discussed the range of her services, there were always rumors, little more than whispers, hints that she attended to unwanted pregnancies. With abortions infrequent occurrences among the German immigrant population, and the details not shared with the preacher or his family, I'd been able to discover only the sketchiest information. But I'd heard the gossip.

We shuffled behind Mrs. Becker, with shorter than normal steps, into a windowless room that served multiple purposes, an office, a sitting room, a waiting room, or, as in our case, a hand-wringing room. Mrs. Becker held the back of a chair opposite her desk for me. Hannah searched for a seat next to me but the midwife waved her hand in the direction of two empty chairs that stood apart against the wall. Emma followed and took the chair furthest from Mrs. Becker. In another moment, though, Hannah defied Mrs. Becker's dismissive wave, she rose came back across the room, and stepped behind my chair. She placed a hand on my shoulder, a welcome gesture of reassurance.

Mrs. Becker, I couldn't think of her as Edith, shuffled a few papers on her desk, found a pen, and without another glance at us jotted a few notes on the page of a ledger. "How long have you known of your pregnancy, Miss Miller?" Mrs. Becker asked. She pronounced the words "Miss" and "Miller" in a flat tone, without emphasizing or de-emphasizing my marital status. With her deliberate inflection, however, she announced to everyone in the room she understood the situation—that I was pregnant, that I wanted an abortion, and that Miller was not my real name. She had made no introductions, offered no pleasantries, and now lost no time as she delved into the details of my condition.

"Two months, maybe two and a half," I said. I forced the words from my mouth.

"Excuse me, can you speak up?"

Even Hannah, behind me, had leaned forward to catch my answer.

"Three months."

In less than thirty minutes, I had secured an appointment for the following week, Tuesday at eight in the morning. Mrs. Becker never suggested I consider any other option than the one I requested. She gave verbal instructions for preparations I would need to make and confirmed that my friends would accompany me again next week.

"You will need a car to take Miss Miller home," she said to Hannah. Again the flattened title, the monotone voice. "She'll need to rest here for the better part of the day. She will not be comfortable walking any great distance afterward." She did not elaborate on what would transpire before.

Over the course of the week, Emma and Hannah spent as much time as they could with me. Emma consoled me if I talked of the risks. Hannah discussed alternatives, where I could go, who I could stay with, what I could do there, when I could return. I shook my head at each suggestion. I refused to consider any of her ideas. They were ideas I had explored in the first few weeks after I had known my condition.

All three of us knew what we were doing, or more precisely, what I was doing, was illegal. I'd asked around, as delicately and surreptitiously as I could and learned that once, before 1900, abortions were allowed if performed in the first twenty weeks, before the fetus moved in the womb. But, shortly after the turn of the century, activists had pressured lawmakers to outlaw abortions at any stage. The number of abortions declined, so accounts in the newspapers claimed; but they were not eliminated. Mrs. Becker was, I assumed, aware of the risks she took. She had to know, if she left women like me to our own devices, we would find other, even more dangerous ways to end our pregnancies.

As the date approached, I ate almost nothing. I feared my parents would ask if I were ill, but I could not put food in my mouth, I could not chew or swallow. I had no appetite. I'd glanced in the mirror and wondered if they could tell my condition or my deception from my face. My skin had lost its normal luster and looked almost transparent against my cheekbone. I looked closer and thought I could see tiny veins criss-crossing my temples, like the blue network that pulsed below a newborn's flesh. Even the light powder Hannah gave me to dab on my cheeks failed to lessen my ashen complexion.

On Tuesday, Hannah borrowed her brother's car. We agreed that if anyone asked, we would say we were on our way to visit one of the Struhl relatives in Heusler and would be gone the entire day. After Hannah pulled the car to a stop, outside Mrs. Becker's home, we looked at each other for reassurance, then stepped from the car and climbed to the front porch of 117 Forest Avenue. Once again, Mrs. Becker met us at the front door, escorted us inside, and motioned Emma and Hannah to the two seats against the wall in the front room.

"Miss Miller, come with me. Your friends will remain here until I call for them." I balked and glanced toward Hannah and Emma. I had expected to have my friends by my side, but Mrs. Becker did not impress me as someone with whom I could barter. The midwife had already stepped into the hallway. She held open the door to a second room. Hannah and Emma embraced me then turned and took their assigned seats.

When I was near consciousness again, Mrs. Becker's dry voice penetrated my delirium. She was speaking to Hannah and Emma. "Miss Miller is resting now. She may sleep for a few hours. When she wakes, you can see her. You can wait here or you can leave and come back, but you must return by five."

If they answered, I didn't know. I returned into the void, into the soft light and warmth.

The sun, still high in the sky, flooded the room. It bleached the already white furniture, the white bedclothes, and the white skin on my arm. The light hurt my eyes. Mrs. Becker stood over me. I closed my eyes and looked away from her, at Hannah and Emma who stood to one side, a safe distance from her. They clasped their hands in front of them, expectant, uncertain.

"You may help Miss Miller dress. When you're finished, you may escort her home."

"Emma. Hannah. It's over. I've done it," I said. I paused after every other word to take a breath.

Hannah rushed to the side of the cot and grabbed my hand. "You look terribly pale. Are you strong enough to sit up?" She touched my forehead with her free hand and let it rest there a minute. She nodded at Emma.

Authoritative as usual, Hannah barked instructions to Emma. "Get Liese's things from the dresser. Over there. Help me get her dressed." When Emma hesitated, Hannah added, "Now! Go! Let's get out of here as quick as we can."

Emma gathered my things, my undergarments, stockings, petticoat, blouse, and skirt. She laid them on the cot where, with

Hannah's help, I sat upright. "I think I can do this myself," I said as I inched one leg out from the covers.

After dressing, I stood and as I did, the room moved in front of my eyes. I flailed at the air to find a solid, unmoving object. I found Emma's shoulder. She and Hannah guided me to the doorway. Before we exited, I looked around the room. I expected to see some indication of the life that had passed, but there was nothing out of the ordinary, the table, the cot, a cabinet, and a screen behind which I'd disrobed earlier. All in bright, spotless, empty white.

Arm in arm, we made our way to the front room and to the front door of Mrs. Becker's home. I was thankful the midwife did not reappear.

Weak and still slightly groggy from the sedative Mrs. Becker had administered, I allowed my friends to decide what to do next. Hannah suggested we take a short drive down to the riverfront. We could sit there and not attract too much attention while I gained some strength. "I think it might be best if you stay with me tonight," Hannah said, "just in case you need something."

No, I'll go home. If Mother asks, I'll just say I'm not feeling well."

Fortunately, the weather was mild on this fall day. We sat together on one of the wooden benches scattered at irregular intervals along the boardwalk, Hannah on one side of me, Emma on the other, like bookends. I sat erect, my head up so that I could not glimpse my midsection where a life had been ripped away, where I had ordered a life be ripped away. I could not help but contrast the moment with the recent happier times, those I'd spent walking on the boardwalk with Jack. It seemed a world away.

A number of commercial barges trundled goods from one side of the river to the other. We watched the welcome distraction. Every so often, as a ship passed, Hannah read the name of the vessel aloud, commented on its speed, and attempted to identify the cargo. She spoke in an overly loud tone, her voice an octave higher than normal. At each pronouncement from her, I emerged from my stupor, nodded, and smiled.

An hour or so passed in this way, until, I spied a familiar face walking our way. I nudged Emma. It was Adola Roder and another woman from church.

"Oh my!" said Emma. "What are we to do?"

Hannah rose from the bench and waved toward the approaching duo. "Just be yourself. If she's inclined to dawdle, which I doubt, we'll tell her we were just leaving."

"Ah, Liese, I thought I recognized you," Adola said as she paused next to our bench. "Enjoying the fine weather?" Adola eyed each of us and I wondered if she detected something amiss.

"Yes, we are." My voice faltered with even these three words. I didn't think I could continue.

"Liese hasn't been feeling well," Hannah picked up for me.

"We decided to take her out for a ride, get some fresh air," Emma said.

"I am sorry to hear that. Is there anything I can do?"

"No ma'am," the three of us said in almost perfect unison. We turned to look at each other and somehow managed to laugh.

Adola failed to see the humor, the lines between her brows deepened. "We'll be on our way then. Please give my regards to Pastor Tom and your mother. I hope you'll be feeling better soon."

"I'm fine."

"We were just saying the same thing," Hannah said. She'd managed to find her normal voice.

When the two women continued on their way, we breathed a collective sigh of relief.

"Thank you both so much," I said. "Not just for covering for me now, but...for everything today. I could not have done this alone."

"You would have done the same for us, Liese." Hannah said. "Now, I think we'd better go, before we see anyone else."

Hannah stopped the car in front of my house. When the two moved to accompany me inside, I held up my hand and shook my head.

"No, I can do this. You've done enough."

"Just to the porch, Liese," Emma said.

I relented, but once we were in front of the door, I gave Emma a stern look and told her to go. The two friends drove away. As the car rounded the corner at the end of the block, Emma reached her hand through the open window and waved.

No one was home. I breathed a sigh of relief and made my way inside. Left on my own, I realized how weak I was and inched my way up the staircase and to bed. As I closed my eyes, I whispered a prayer for Jack's unborn child and then one for Jack.

Part Five: Oscar

Chapter 13

Patience and Persistence

I used to wonder what my life would have been like had Jack lived. I suppose I would have married him and moved to the country. I imagine I would have had three or four children who ran underfoot in our small house, scampered up the hillside among the goats and cows and horses, and, later, helped with the harvest. I imagine I would have learned to love him and that I would have been happy.

Instead, Oscar Wolf came back into my life. He reappeared bearing the news of Jack's death. I blamed him for that. It was the first of many things I blamed him for in the years to come.

But he brought more than the news of Jack's death. He brought a plan. He always had a plan, even if he rarely shared it or his thoughts with me. He was always a step ahead and dragging me with him on his journey. I suppose I have to blame myself to some degree. I never asked what he was thinking. I was vulnerable the second time we met; I let him take and shape my life.

* * *

I'd come from an afternoon visit with Hannah and had rounded the corner of First Avenue to find a man in uniform on our porch. He turned to leave, but stopped when he saw me approach.

"Ah, Anneliese Stephens."

"Yes?"

"You don't remember me, do you?"

"I don't think I do. I'm sorry. Should I?" I'd seen him somewhere before, but could not remember when or where. He was about my age. A son of a member of my father's congregation, I thought.

"Perhaps not. It's been almost two years since we met. And, I wasn't in uniform then." A crimp circled the hay-colored hair when he removed his hat. "I'm Oscar Wolf. Lieutenant Oscar Wolf now." He smiled. A half smile.

"Oh, yes, I do remember you. The church."

"Yes."

We stood for a moment, neither of us moving or saying a word. A long uncomfortable moment.

"Your mother, that is,...I just spoke to your mother. She told me you were out and didn't know when you'd return. I was just leaving. I didn't expect to see you."

"Yes, well, I'm here now. Oh, excuse my manners. Did you want to come in?"

"That won't be necessary. Perhaps I could just speak with you for a few minutes."

"Let's sit," I motioned toward the porch.

Oscar followed me to the right side of the porch. I cleared a basket holding swatches of fabric and threads from one of the chairs to a nearby table and signaled to Oscar to take a seat. Before he did, he leaned over and placed his hand on the back of the remaining chair. He waited for me to sit, then took his chair and scooted it around to face me.

"Earlier this week, I went to Plainfield to visit Mrs. Linger. Jack's mother." He softened his voice when he said Jack's name.

Something cold ran down my spine. I felt as though someone had taken the muscles in my body, wound them into a knot, and pulled them tight. I gasped for air and thought my lungs had collapsed.

Oscar waited a moment then continued, "I don't know if you know, she lost one son, Victor, in the war. Last July. One of my duties is to inform the next of kin of the loss of their husbands, their brothers, or fathers, or sons." A humming sound came from somewhere behind me, it grew louder, it reverberated like an engine and split the air as it approached, and crashed on top of me. His lips moved. I could see them move. I could not hear the words for the humming in my head, but I knew what he said. "Jack was killed." His lips formed those words. "I have a piece of paper here for you. It's a copy of the one I gave Mrs. Linger."

Oscar fumbled with the button on the flap that closed over the pocket on his uniform. He reached inside and withdrew a folded piece of paper. His hand twisted, extended, approached, all the while the white paper sat perched between the tips of his fingers. It was an illusion, I thought, like the magician I'd seen turn a white handkerchief into a dove. One minute it sat in his hand, a piece of white cloth. Then, he tossed the cloth in the air and a dove fluttered its wings and flew away. I stared at the piece of white paper that was not a handkerchief, not a dove. I did not take it from him. I looked away, convinced that if I could not hear him, could not see him, and did not accept the white square, the words would not be true.

Oscar drew the paper back. He unfolded it and looked down. His lips moved again. Then he stopped, looked at me, and waited for me to say something.

I wanted to cover my face. I wanted to hide from him and from the world but my hands lay in my lap, limp, unresponsive as if they belonged to someone else. I let another moment pass.

Oscar refolded the paper, creased its edge, then leaned over and placed it in my lap. I suppose he feared it would blow away or I would drop it. He lifted one of my hands and placed it over the note to secure it in my lap. Then he stood, set his hat on his head and left.

I don't know how long I remained there, alone, my eyes fixed on a spot on the wall where the paint had cracked around a rusted nail. The air had cooled. The shadows had crawled across the porch and now the stripes of the banister's spindles lay across my ankles. I unfolded the paper in my lap and read.

"We deeply regret to inform you" followed by a space into which the name was inserted, "Jack K. Linger, C Company, 120th Infantry, 30th Division". It continued, "was" and another space into which "killed in action" and then "on" and the final space into which "September 29, 1918, Somme, France" had been printed.

I rose, crossed the porch, and steadied myself against the door-jamb before I continued into the house. I commanded my legs to obey and climbed the stairs one at a time. Halfway up, I paused to let the shapes and figures that swirled in my head subside. My grandfather bellowed something from the dark below. I ignored his call. When I reached my room, I closed the door behind me.

The veins in my head throbbed against my temples as I turned to the dresser against the far wall. I opened the top-most draw-er and groped inside with my fingertips. I removed the doll-sized cardboard box and balanced it in the palm of my hand as I hobbled to my bed. With one hand clenched around the acorn-shaped iron finial on the headboard for support, I lowered myself to the edge of the mattress. I sat and stared straight ahead at nothing.

From somewhere outside, a hinge creaked. My bed sat be-tween two tall windows, covered with sheer lace curtains through which I could see outside without being seen. I looked through them to the street. Oscar Wolf had not left after all. He had passed through the front gate, closed the gate behind him, but paused there. I watched as he lit his pipe. A cluster of gray puffs rose above his head into the air. Each tiny cloud obscured his features for a moment then floated away. Instead of moving on, though, he tilted his head back and scanned the windows on the second floor. As he drew a breath through his pipe, he rested his hand on my gate.

I wanted him to go. I closed my eyes and willed him to go. I prayed for him to go, but he remained in the same position, head back, and a hand on my gate. I glared at him, though I knew he could not see me. Finally, Oscar turned and walked away.

When he had been gone several minutes, I drew back the nearest panel of curtains and peered out the window over the row of houses facing mine and the trees beyond, until I found the patch of the river visible in the distance. Ripples in the water danced, they sparkled as they rose and fell and sent rays of brightly colored light in all directions, as if a thousand mirrors had been shattered and strewn across the water.

For the better part of an hour, I sat on the edge of my bed, the reflections in the water refused to let me go, until at last my eyes grew weary. My arm tingled. It had grown numb as I held the curtains aside. I let the curtains fall, bowed my head, and prayed silently.

"Amen," I said aloud.

I turned to the box in my lap. I untied the bow that criss-crossed the top, and turned it on its side. The contents fell to the bed. A tiny dried flower pressed flat between two pages of vellum, a strand of ivy leaves on a white cloth, my first piece of embroidery, a flat grey stone, smooth and cool to the touch. I'd found the stone where Will's body had fallen by the river years ago and carried it home in the pocket of my apron. My one letter from Jack in its mutilated envelope and the kerchief he had given me. I spread the kerchief on the bed. The silk fabric, too delicate to support its own weight, sank into the curves and creases of the coverlet underneath. My fingers fluttered over the words "The Farewell", across the couple in their permanent embrace, and along the lace border. I picked up the letter, removed the single page from its envelope and re-read his words. By the time I reached the end, tears streamed down my cheeks. A single tear fell to the page, bled into the ink, and blurred one of his words.

I wiped my eyes with the back of my hand, returned the letter to its envelope, and refolded the handkerchief. The words "I promise you, we will not be parted again" rang in my head, over and over, as if the needle on a turntable had locked in place over a scratch on a recording. I returned the mementos to the box, and tied a blue satin bow around it, then carefully aligned the ends.

I secreted the box in my dresser and went downstairs. I had to finish baking before my parents returned.

Oscar lost no time in finding an excuse to come to the house again. Within a week, he was back on the porch. He rapped on the glass panes in the door. From behind the curtains in my bedroom, I'd watched him come up the walk and had heard the knock on the door. I had known he would come again and had told my father as much the night before.

"You may remember, Oscar Wolf," I said. I hoped my voice had an air of indifference. "I think he may call tomorrow and would appreciate if you told him I was not here. Or not able to see him." With another gentleman at the door, another gentleman not of the church, I knew he'd happily oblige. I offered no further explanation and my father asked no questions.

I listened as the door swung open. My father had answered but had said nothing, or at least nothing I could hear. I imagined his eyes peered over his glasses to assess Oscar, from head to toe. For a man who spent so much time greeting members of his congregation, my father was uncharacteristically rude.

Oscar broke the long, uncomfortable silence. "Good morning, Pastor Stephens." He nearly lilted his words. But, more silence followed. Perhaps my father had nodded.

"It's such a beautiful day. I thought since I was passing by that I'd see if Anneliese might like to take a walk with me." Oscar spoke the words louder than necessary. He intended them to reach me upstairs where he knew I sat. Where he knew I mourned.

He did not introduce himself and offered nothing further.

"I'm afraid Liese is not feeling well today."

"Ah, well then, I'll just call again another time. Perhaps next week. She might be feeling better then. Please let her know I came by."

I imagined another nod or a grunt before my father closed the door and returned to read his paper or work on his sermon.

Oscar returned to my house on First Avenue each of the next two Saturdays at exactly ten o'clock in the morning, as I suspected he would. Each time, I found a reason to retreat to the kitchen or my bedroom. Each time, from the snatches of conversation I could overhear, the same scene replayed at the front door. After supper on Friday of the third week, my father said, "Liese, I imagine that Wolf fellow will be coming by in the morning." His disapproval evident in the way he pronounced Oscar's name, he extended the *o* and the sound of the *f* for a fraction of a second longer than necessary. "You'll have to answer the door yourself this time. Your mother and I will be out. Besides, you must take charge of your responsibilities. Either tell him not to call again or whatever else you wish. I will not do that for you."

"I will, Father," I said. "When and if he comes again."

My mother spoke. "I don't think there's any if about it. My guess is he'll be at the door at ten o'clock sharp, just as he has the last...how many weeks has it been now? Four or five?"

"Three."

"Isn't he with the railroad? That may be where he gets his fondness for punctuality," she continued.

Like me, they had seen through Oscar's thinly disguised plan. By appearing at exactly the same time each week, at exactly ten o'clock, he knew I'd begin to expect him to call and I'd anticipate him. He was right. Last Wednesday, his lilting greeting played in my mind while I rolled out a piecrust. Last Friday, his face loomed in the shadows of my bedroom before I slept. And, last Saturday morning, long before ten o'clock, I thought of him. I'd watched for him, anticipated his arrival, and stood upstairs where I could see him reach the corner of First Avenue and Franklin a few minutes ahead of the hour. He checked his pocket watch, paused with his head bent over its face as if he counted the ticks of the second hand until it reached a designated point on the dial. Then, he pulled his shoulders back, lifted his head, and sauntered toward our gate. Once there, he paused again, made a show of removing his pocket watch, flipping open the cover, and checking the time once more before he cleared the gate. I checked my own watch. At the top of the hour, his knuckles rapped sharply on the glass. Twice.

Now, on the fourth Saturday, I waited for him in the front room, my book in my lap. Five minutes earlier, I had abandoned my pretense at reading. I'd turned only a single page over the course of the last half hour. I rubbed my hands together. I pushed the sleeves of my blouse above my elbows, then pulled them down again.

I would tell him to go and not call again, I thought. Then I rose and stood for a moment in front of the hall mirror. If that were my decision, why had I dusted my cheekbones with powder and tied my hair behind my head with a satin ribbon. I swung the door wide before Oscar had a chance to knock.

He blinked. His mouth opened. He'd expected my father to answer the door again. "Anneliese, what a pleasure." Oscar recovered quickly. "I'm glad you're up and about this morning. Your father , ah,...Pastor Tom said you weren't well when I came by last week. Are you feeling better today?"

He gave me no time to answer. I opened my mouth to say something, still unsure what it would be, but he continued with his pleasantries without so much as a small breath. He gave me no choice. I touched my hand to my hair and fumbled at the scatter of curls on my forehead, though I'd done the same only moments ago.

"Please come in, Oscar. Yes, I'm feeling better now. I must apologize for not being more polite the last time we spoke."

"Thank you, Anneliese, there's no cause for worry. My last visit was not on the most favorable of terms. I thought I might get used to that responsibility, but I don't suppose I ever will. Never mind that, let's talk of something else. That's why I came today. I consider it my duty to cheer you up a bit. Would you walk to the river with me? It's really quite pleasant out."

I accepted. Outside in the open air, I thought would be more comfortable than inside, next to him, alone in our parlor. "Let me grab a wrap and let my grandfather know I'll be out for a short bit." I emphasized the last two words, I hoped Oscar would understand my insinuation—I'd only agreed to go for a short walk.

Grandfather scowled when I told him I'd be away. But, I didn't care. I offered no explanation, only that I would return shortly. With that, I closed his door, grabbed my coat, gloves, and a woolen scarf from the hall tree, then let the front door slam behind me.

Oscar had exited and waited along the front walk. He looked over my shoulder toward the door as I approached but said nothing.

We strolled two blocks south to the river, then along the boardwalk the town had installed the previous summer. Though well frequented in good weather, today, besides the two of us, only a woman with a young boy several yards ahead had ventured out along the path.

Not accustomed to idle walks or small talk, I was at a loss for a topic that might interest Oscar. I discarded embroidery with its chain stitches, satin stitches, French knots, and buttonholes, and sewing, whether measuring, cutting, basting, or hemming, and of course, baking pies, cakes, cookies, strudels, or tarts. My interests, the things that consumed my days, were subjects of interest only to other women. Think, think, I told myself. Farming. It was the only experience I could imagine might interest a man. The thought of discussing the things I learned from Jack, planting corn and harvesting vegetables, milking cows, and making butter or cheese, forced a lump in my throat and trapped the words in my head.

Oscar filled in the silence. I hardly needed to do more than nod every sentence or two. Jack had not been one to chat idly. I remembered how he strained to find words the first time we met. He felt no urgency to fill the silence and, instead, let the sights and sounds of nature speak for him. Oscar, in comparison, had a limitless list of topics, fit for any occasion. For women or men. The weather, events in town, the railroad, cities he'd seen or wanted to visit. He paused. I imagined he ticked down a list he carried in his head to search for something he'd not already covered.

"Are you still playing the piano? I haven't been to Stallman's for quite a while. Not since last spring, come to think of it."

"Yes, I am, but only at services. I haven't been to Stallman's either...since last spring."

"I see. Yes, I hadn't forgotten that you played for the church. That was where we first met. A private concert, in a manner of speaking. I was very impressed."

"I remember it, too. It seems like such a long time ago."

"I suppose, then, I'll have to attend services at Zion to hear you play again."

"I suppose." Yet another man in the last pew at the back of the church, I thought. Like Jack, he would wait to greet my father, but my father would dismiss Oscar as he had dismissed Jack.

We'd reached the end of the boardwalk. As we turned to go back, Oscar switched sides and, from the corner of my eye, I saw he offered his arm. But I couldn't take his arm. I couldn't touch him. I couldn't allow myself that crumb of intimacy. I pretended not to notice the courtesy and reached for my hair, I shoved aside a few strands of hair, dampened by a fine mist that blew in our faces. I gathered the ends of my shawl together, and continued down the walk. I hoped he'd not taken offense.

"I also play, though not as well as you," he continued without hesitation.

"I didn't know that. What do you play?"

"The trombone. In fact, I'm playing at a concert in a few weeks at the armory. Would you care to attend? Of course, it's mostly patriotic tunes."

"I would enjoy that. Yes." Instantly, I regretted my statement. First, I'd accepted his offer to take a stroll down the boardwalk, now I'd agreed to attend a concert with him. If I hadn't wanted to do these things, why had I so readily acquiesced.

The wind gusted over the river. Oscar pulled a handkerchief from his breast pocket and wiped his dampened cheeks. "The weather's turning," he said. Now that we're walking into the wind, it's a lot less comfortable. Luckily we're almost back."

When we reached the gate to my house, Oscar stepped aside and removed his hat. "Thank you, for joining me, today, Anneliese. I'll let you know the time for the concert."

"Thank you. I enjoyed your company, Oscar, but I must go now. Grandfather will be needing me."

Oscar tipped his head, replaced his hat, and touched the tips of his fingers to the brim.

A short time later, on another, similar stroll, when offered, I did take Oscar's arm. Then weeks later, I'd allowed him to take my hand, but I refrained from a response in kind to the gentle pressure of his hand around mine.

CHAPTER 14

Death and Rebirth

In late December, my grandfather took ill, though the most recent malady was more a matter of degree than a new ailment. Every year after his accident, his health had become worse than the year prior. His illness defied the doctors and their medical tests. They did not know what I knew. They prescribed an assortment of treatments, salves, and pills, all of which my mother tried. They could not see or hear what I saw, and that it was untreatable. The decay was deep inside. It ate its way out; its tentacles wended their way from the darkest reaches of his heart and mind.

Now, the simplest acts of existence, a breath, a swallow, were enormously difficult. At this stage of his health, my mother attended to him all hours of the day. I relieved her late in the day, spelled from time to time by my father. She dreaded being out of earshot, upstairs, or even down the hall should he call for something. Near the end, she insisted someone be by his side at all times, even throughout the night. Although I feared watching over the old man at night, I had deeper concerns about the toll such a vigil would exact on my mother's health. I set aside my discomfort and took my turn each night without a single complaint. Fortunately, he slept most of the time. I distracted myself. When the house fell silent, I read or created new recipes to try the next day. I'd take a much needed nap on the couch in the front room, but I left the door to his room ajar to hear him should he wake.

As his condition worsened, Mother became more frantic. "Please don't leave him alone in the dark tonight. Not even for a minute. Call me if you need to."

I consented, but planned to nap in one of the chairs in his room. I prayed the old man would sleep through the night. I shooed Mother from the room when it came time and pulled a chair close to the nightstand. I edged it only as close as necessary to read under the dim light from the lamp on the nightstand. All week, no matter how dark we made the room, he complained the light hurt his eyes. During the day, Mother kept the shades drawn, at night, she covered the lamp with a scarf. The old man's complaints were, to my mind, just another means to garner attention. I was tempted to throw open the blinds during the day or tear away the scarf at night.

The light proved too dim for me to read comfortably. I glanced toward my grandfather, asleep on his back, the shadow of his profile a jagged mountain range on the wall. I leaned forward and folded back one edge of the scarf. I waited, prepared for a wail of complaint from him. He shifted in the bed but did not wake.

Despite the added light, I still had to squint to read. The clock in the hall chimed twice. I closed my book and let the scarf fall back in place. I sat silently in the darkened room and stared at the outline of the figure in the bed. His irregular, heavy breathing filled the room. His lungs struggled for oxygen, they rattled as he inhaled. Several times, he paused between breaths for what seemed minutes before he exhaled.

After another half hour of the torture, despite my promise, I tiptoed from the room to find a more comfortable and better-lit seat in the front room. Every half hour, I rose and went to his room but found him as before, on his back, the struggle with life still reverberating in his chest. At three in the morning, with a dry cloth Mother had placed beside the bed, I dabbed at the beads of sweat on the old man's forehead. He woke, or at least his eyes opened.

He glared at me, standing over him, observing him, dabbing his forehead. I dropped the cloth on his chest.

"*Liebling*," he said. "*Ist dass sie Liebling*? I am frightened."

I picked up the cloth with only the tips of my fingers, like tongs, careful not to come in contact with any part of him, and dropped the cloth on the nightstand. I stood erect beside the bed and met his gaze, my face as blank and emotionless as I could make it. I turned on my heels and left the room.

Our vigil lasted three days. On Wednesday morning, in the middle of the night, a scream pierced the quiet house. Instinctively, I grabbed for the side of my bed, but found only a cushion of the sofa in my fingers. My father's footsteps pounded the floor above me and then the stairs. A second scream cleared my momentary disorientation. I ran to the back of the house, to my grandfather's room. My mother lay across the motionless body in the bed. "He's dead," she said. "Oh my dear God." She wailed again. "He's gone."

My mother, who had woken in the night, must have come down the steps, across the dark living room, toward the soft glow in the open doorway, to find her father dead. I glanced around the room, the bedstead, a blanket tossed over its iron heart, the rocker empty, the Bible fallen to the floor open, face down, the scarf on the lamp barely clinging to the shade, all of the objects askew and unfamiliar.

Were it not for her grief, my mother would have certainly realized I had abandoned him and broken my promise to her. I looked at the old man. The light from the lamp radiated across his face. His eyes, dry, their dark centers fixed on something above him, glaring, unblinking, his mouth, open wide but frozen in time as if his last act had been to call out.

My panic subsided.

My father, in his pajamas without a robe, his hair spiked at all angles from his head, reached over my mother. He placed his fingers on the old man's eyes and drew his eyelids closed. Then, without a word, he pulled my mother from the bed. He knelt and took both of us by the hand. He brought us to the floor to kneel with him at the side of the bed. We bowed our heads and my father offered a prayer. "Amen," we said in unison. "Amen," I repeated.

The war was nearing its end. Evansville celebrated with parades, concerts, and speeches from local dignitaries, then turned its attention to the promise of more prosperous times ahead. My family continued much the same as we had throughout the war. My father buried himself in his weekly rituals of preparing and delivering his sermons, my mother, when she could, in accompanying him on visits to members of the congregation, and me in housework. I assumed more of my mother's daily chores not that my primary chore of caring for my grandfather in a never-ending cycle of waking, bathing, dressing, eating, and undressing, had ended .

Oscar's Saturday morning visits had become a regular feature of our household. He had more free time now. If I wasn't on walks with Oscar, I was in the kitchen. I baked endless numbers of cookies and pies for members of the congregation who, too, were in a celebratory mood.

Sweet yeast coffee cakes, oatmeal cookies, peach and blueberry cobblers, and coconut-almond cakes, the delicate white cream and beat sugar laced topping piled high, billowing, light as air, light as hope.

After services one Sunday, Mr. and Mrs. Thomas complimented me on my playing. Usually I held back and left the task of thanking the members for coming to services to my father. But that day, the Thomas's made a point of coming to thank me after the service.

"It's so good to hear a hymn with a celebratory note," Mr. Thomas said. Please tell your father to add more of these."

"And, by the way," Mrs. Thomas said, "I hear you make a wonderful apple pie, do you think you could give me your recipe or, I shouldn't ask this, bake one for me. My son's coming home. I wouldn't ask otherwise. I'd be happy to pay you."

"Oh, nonsense," I said. "Mrs. Thomas, I'd be happy to bake you one. I was going to make a few this week anyway. One more won't be a bother.'

The following week, it was the Blackstones.

"Liese, dear, how well you look today. We had dinner with the Thomas's last week and they shared a piece of one of your wonderful apple pies. You wouldn't consider baking one for us would you, dear?

"Just let me know what to pay you."

And then it was the Walkers and the Blakes.

"Baking another pie, Liese?" Oscar said when he came by my house. He'd plucked a few crumbs of piecrust from my hair and held them in front of me. "I'm absolutely going to have to schedule another concert or something to occupy your time and give you something to do other than bake."

"What is wrong with baking?"

"Oh, no. I didn't mean there was anything wrong with it, but you must be interested in something else, too."

"I don't know. I haven't given it much thought. I embroider. I play piano...and I garden."

"Yes, but haven't you ever wanted to do something you've not done before. To see someplace new maybe?"

"Well..."

"I haven't told you this before, but when I enlisted in the Army, I had hoped they'd send me to Europe straight away. I know the fighting was a terrible thing, but I thought I could help my country and see the world at the same time."

"I don't think many young men considered the war seeing the world," I said, wishing we could change the subject.

"I didn't mean it in that sense. Plenty of the boys I know thought it would be an adventure. But, the last thing I wanted to do was stay home."

"What happened? Why didn't the Army send you?"

"I was the perfect candidate for the war. I didn't have any family and, I wanted a break from the drudgery of the railroad. Most days all I did was process forms, mountains and mountains of forms. I'd been with the railroad for five years. Hired on as a local freight agent. Later, I was promoted to freight supervisor, one of three in the Evansville office. I signed up the same day the Army's enlistment office opened here.

"I ignored the sergeant's questions about my job with the railroad. I didn't think anything of them at the time. After completing training, while we were waiting for our orders to come in, I got nervous. I started thinking the Army might want to use my talents here at home."

"And they did."

"Yes." Oscar frowned. "The logistics of moving men and equipment across the country was a complex operation, one that they knew I could help with. I protested, even tried going over the sergeant's head."

"You didn't!"

"I did. I didn't care if it got me in trouble. I wanted to go. But, I found out pretty quickly that the Army had made its decision and wasn't going to reconsider."

"Well, things worked out."

"Yes, I suppose so. They didn't miss a thing. They actually read my comments on the enlistment form where I wrote something about playing the trombone. So, bam! I was drafted into the Army band."

"Aha! So, that's why you were playing at the concert."

"Yes. Better that than playing trumped up happy tunes for sending off soldiers, like I did at first. By the way," he continued, "we're going to play in Indianapolis next week. Could you consider going with me to hear us play? It'll be a great time. There'll be bands competing from all across Indiana."

"Oh, I don't think I could possibly come."

"Sure you could. I could arrange for tickets. You can't say no."

"I'll consider it. But, I don't think my mother could do without me right now."

"It would just be for the day. We could go up early in the morning and be back by evening the same day.

"I'll think about it."

I did indeed give it some thought. I tossed as I considered what a grand adventure it would be to travel by train to Indianapolis, to see the sights. A march played in my mind all night.

CHAPTER 15
White Roses

In late April, my father performed our simple, brief wedding ceremony. Despite my repeated protests that I could handle the details myself, Emma and Hannah became regular fixtures in my home, helping me prepare. Emma had an endless supply of "do's" and "don'ts." She'd married Paul Strahan, the last of a string of beaus who courted her after George Hausman disappeared from her life. Her March wedding was a frantic occasion with a large crowd of revelers. I baked her wedding cake, served as bridesmaid, and played the piano for the service. Near the end, I was as exhausted and eager for the festivities to conclude as I imagined the bride and groom were.

For my own wedding, Oscar encouraged me to have as many guests as I liked. He invited only Edgar Burns who would serve as his best man. Edgar was the Army band's tuba player and his closest friend. Oscar had no relatives in Evansville and none with whom he'd kept in contact from Indianapolis, where he'd been born. Determined not to repeat Emma's fiasco, I culled and re-culled my parent's long list of members of the congregation until I settled on three guests besides my immediate family, Emma and Paul, and unmarried Hannah.

On the Monday preceding the event, I decided to embroider a simple floral pattern on the cap of each sleeve of my dress. I had intended to stop there, but when I held the garment in front of me, I rethreaded my needle and added a few pearl-shaped beads to the design. Then, as if I needed something to occupy my time, my head, and my hands, I stitched stems and leaves in matching white thread until they trailed the length of each of the arms. I added more beadwork across the bodice. I could not stop. I worked early each morning, continued after lunch and then after dinner until my eyes rebelled and the crease in my forehead threatened to become permanent.

"It's fine," Emma said on Thursday when she saw the dress. Liese, it's fine."

"I think I can add a few petals."

"Liese, you've done enough for two wedding dresses. Stop."

She was right, I had. One for my wedding to Jack and one for my wedding to Oscar.

On the morning of the day my wedding was to take place, I rose early to frost the coconut-almond cake I'd baked the day before. In the kitchen, I beat the eggs with cream and sugar until my wrists were weak. I piped and swirled the white concoction over the cake's three layers until it gleamed like a crust of ice on a pond in winter. I added a flourish of extra icing, a fondant rose bud nestled in a crown of leaves in the center of the top layer.

Hannah arrived to help me dress at ten, two hours before the ceremony. Near exhaustion, I yielded to her insistence to handle the last minute preparations. We gathered in my bedroom on the second floor, Hannah, my mother, and me. Mother sat to the side in a wingback chair that enveloped her shrunken body. It left little but her dark eyes and fluttering hands to remind me she was there. "Liese, I've never seen you look more beautiful," she said. Astonished at her rare words of praise, I thought there was hope she might even have come to accept Oscar.

After Hannah slipped the last button through its loop, she stood back and admired her efforts and my handiwork. "You can take a look now," she said.

I spun slowly and caught my reflection in the mirror. Though from a distance, the everyday white cotton fabric was plain, up close it resembled an ivory-frosted confection, a petit four sprinkled with dots of hard candy, the intricate white-on-white, bead-studded embroidery, on the shoulders, sleeves, and neck-line, spilled down the bodice into a point just above the waistline.

Hannah gathered my hair behind my back and secured it with a white satin band.

At a twitter from the recesses of the winged chair, we both turned. My mother opened her hand to reveal three tiny white rose buds she must have picked from our garden that morning. Hannah plucked the flowers from her palm and fastened them to the band behind my head.

Only one black thought marred the otherwise perfect day. Rather than move to Oscar's rooms across town, we'd agreed he would move into my parent's home on First Avenue. At first, I thought my father would object to have Oscar, with whom he rarely ex-changed words, so close. I supposed he had decided to endure that offense if it meant I would remain at home.

"It's certainly large enough to accommodate all of us," he'd said. "You and Liese will have the entire downstairs, better than your present accommodations, I dare say." He'd never seen Os-car's apartment, of course, but would have come to the same conclusion had he been there. Perhaps he would have been even more adamant. Oscar lived in a sparsely furnished room in a boarding house on the other side of town.

"I don't spend that much time here," he argued. The concern must have shown on my face when I entered the door to his two-room dwelling at the back of the boarding house. "I'm either at work or away from town. It's just a place to sleep."

I had resigned myself to a life in the tiny set of rooms, even if only for a short period. My deepest regret was the rooms had limited access to a kitchen.

"It's just until we can afford something of our own."

"We'll manage, Oscar," I said. I made a second brief tour of the rooms, the well-worn table and two chairs, the bare walls, and the oval rug, its braid coiled like a snake asleep aside the bed.

I opened the closet door, looked out the window, then fanned my face in the close air.

He'd caught me off guard when he accepted my father's offer. On the other hand, when I thought about their relationship, if I could call it that, my father's indifference never seemed to concern Oscar. Oscar ignored my father. He talked past him as he talked past almost everyone, at times even me.

"I've saved as much as I could, but I'm still a tad short of enough for a home of our own. We'll accept your offer, but only temporarily. We'll look for a suitable place of our own by the fall."

My mother was delighted when she learned of our arrangement. Over the last few weeks, as the wedding day neared, the day I would leave home, she'd shown signs of what my father referred to as "nerves". I'd often enter a room to find her in tears or with a handkerchief at her eyes. If I asked what troubled her, she'd deny there was anything causing her worry, even as she wrung her hands ferociously in circles at her waist. When she learned of Oscar's acceptance of my father's offer, her eyes cleared, her shoulders lifted, and her fingers slowed their dance.

I extracted several conditions for accepting the offer. I insisted the "old Bauer" room, my grandfather's room, the room we would inhabit, be altered from top to bottom. I wanted the room to be unrecognizable as any of its earlier incarnations.

Mother gazed at the chest of drawers, rocker, and chairs. She pursed her lips. The tiny wrinkles that circled her mouth came to a point. "But they've been here for such a long time." Her fingers worried over each object and then the left hand found the right hand and they worried each other.

I stood my ground. My father and mother exchanged glances, then acquiesced to my demands. I think they feared I'd change my mind if they pushed the point further.

We donated the old furniture to a member of the congregation. I found an excuse to be absent when the new owner arrived to remove the iron bed frame and the other artifacts of my grandfather's existence. A workman my father had hired stripped the old cracked and faded paper from the walls and then painted them a bright white. Mother had suggested a light pink, or blue. I chose white. Pure white, naked white. White empty of sin. We sewed and hung new draperies. We purchased new furniture. Other pieces arrived as gifts from members of the congregation.

Oscar brought from his apartment one suitcase of clothes and his trombone in its case.

Despite having agreed to the arrangement, I learned Oscar had found a way to delay the inevitable, even if only for a few days. "Since we're going to be here with your parents for the foreseeable future," he said, "at least, we can have a honeymoon away from them, away from Evansville."

I'd not given any thought to a honeymoon. I had never ventured further than the family's home in the country, Uncle Paul's farm, and of course Jack's place. All within a radius of twenty miles or so from town. Oscar, as I knew, had traveled to a number of cities along the Louisville and Nashville Railroad's route. Although he never said more than a few words in passing about his earlier life, he'd said enough to let me know he'd traversed the country more than once, he'd seen the Rocky Mountains and the Pacific Ocean, and he'd been to several cities across the South.

Courtesy of the railroad, he acquired two passes to St. Louis for our honeymoon. We were to be gone for three days.

Once the ceremonies were over, I accepted the congratulations of my guests, pocketed their tokens, and received their kisses, one on each cheek. Oscar fidgeted. One minute he was by my side, the next he was gone. He returned, stood beside me. Then, exasperated, he'd shift from one foot to the other or consult his pocket watch, though he'd done the same only minutes before. He refused to eat anything more than a bite of our cake.

Once the last guest left, he hustled our suitcases out the front door and into my father's car. I said goodbye to mother, her eyes glassy, her chin nearly on her chest. When I looked back at her from the car, her head was lowered, her hands circled in front of her, shaping a small ball over and over.

At the station, Oscar jumped out of the car and put a hand on my father's door before the pastor could step down. I faced saying goodbye to my father from the curb. I offered him my hand through the open window. I looked into his eyes and for the first time in my life saw beyond his expressionless features, his clear forehead, his lips drawn together in two thin bands of flesh. Behind his spectacles, his eyes bled with raw emotion. I imagined once I was out of sight, he'd reach for his pocket square and dab two tears away.

Oscar tugged at my elbow. I squeezed my father's shoulder and scurried away. With my husband.

He navigated the familiar territory—the station, the platform, the cars, the seating—as only someone with years of experience could. Oscar insisted I take the seat nearest the window. Once I was seated, he slid the distance of the blood-red leather covered bench to sit close beside me. He took my hand and, for nearly the entire three-hour journey, he held it in his, relinquishing it only when necessary to call my attention to a sight he thought of interest.

Initially the scenery changed little from the Evansville countryside I knew, fields stretched away from both sides of the track, and in the distance gave way to forests. Then we crossed a large expanse of open country. In minutes, we reached and passed Mt. Vernon, my furthest point of reference. The train lumbered on until it reached Carmi, then Enfield, then Drivers. The conductor announced the next stop would be Ashley. Grass, trees, and hills sped by in one long blur outside my window. The foreign terrain piqued my curiosity and intimidated me at the same time.

"Are you happy, Anneliese?" Oscar asked, as we traversed western Illinois.

I turned to face him and smiled. I was always amused that he used my given name, which he said he preferred to Liese.

"Tell me."

I answered without giving his question any more thought. "Yes, Oscar. Of course."

Only moments ago, I had asked myself the same question. I remembered Hannah's words from earlier in the day. We were alone for a brief moment in the crowded house, when she said, "At least you have a husband. Be glad for that. I keep looking for mine, but I can't say as I see any likely prospects on the horizon."

I didn't know what to say. Until that moment, I hadn't stopped to think about Hannah's situation. She lived at home with her parents, like me, like most other single women. And, though she'd always been the one to offer a smile or a word of encouragement, I realized she'd never had a serious gentleman call on her. She'd never before complained or expressed any discontent with her life that I could remember. Perhaps I'd not listened. Her confession saddened me on both accounts.

Once, I had thought the same fate awaited me after Jack's death. Then, Oscar had called and taken me for a stroll on the boardwalk. I thought, too, how Oscar had taken me for more than a stroll. He had taken charge of my life from that moment, engineered our relationship, my future, and never let me have a minute to think of any other outcome. But, I had willingly relinquished my life to him.

As I turned back to stare out the window, I asked myself again, was I happy. Did I even know what being happy meant. If pressed, I could say so far only that I was thankful, relieved the first ritual of the day was over. I counted relief as happiness. I looked down at my hand in Oscar's and sat back into the crook of his arm around my shoulder. I counted comfort, even if it clung too closely around me, as happiness.

The air in the car warmed under the late afternoon sun. I turned to Oscar. "I'm going to walk over to the door. I think I need some fresh air. It's awfully close in here."

"Of course, Anneliese. I'll go with you."

We stepped into the doorway together. Oscar reached over my shoulder and tugged at the lever until the upper half of the window yielded. I leaned forward, my hand pressed against my head to keep my hat in place. A blast of fresh, clean air filled the compartment. I closed my eyes. The air stung my cheeks and the clatter of the wheels on the rails rang in my ears. I counted stinging air and clattering steel as happiness. I wanted that moment to last.

CHAPTER 16
White Caps

When the train halted at the platform in Saint Louis, Oscar, who had moments earlier removed his pocket watch, flipped the cover open with his thumb. He glanced down. "Right on the dot." he said. "We have just enough time to find our hotel and enjoy the last bit of daylight before dinner."

He had booked a room for three days at the Jefferson Hotel, where he said he'd stayed once before on railroad business. "I don't usually stay at such extravagant places, but on that trip, I arrived late and couldn't find anywhere else to stay. One day, I thought I might have a special reason to stay there again. And, now I do."

We hailed a taxi, a new experience for me, and rode the short distance to the Jefferson.

"I've booked a room overlooking the Mississippi River. The manager said it was the last one available."

I smiled.

"As I remember, there's a boardwalk alongside the hotel. Just like at home." He craned his neck to look out the taxi's window and take stock of the weather. "A few clouds, but, if our luck holds, we'll be able to take a stroll before dinner."

"I'd like that."

On our arrival, Oscar attended to the luggage with the bell-man while I climbed the few stairs to the entrance and passed through the large double doors to the lobby. A grand stairway loomed in front of me. Its white marble stairs bounded on all sides by silver-flecked faux-marble paper, rose, divided, turned, rose to the next level, and from there, I guessed, spiraled in one continuous loop to the top floor. A mural of a tropical forest covered the walls of the lobby and spread across the ceiling in one uninterrupted display. Cherry-hued wood, polished slick, accented the arched doorways and ceiling moldings. Gilded planters held towering palms on either side of doorways that lead to other rooms, filled, I imagined, with more delights. To my Evansville-dulled eyes, the lobby sparkled like a Christmas ornament. Grand enough, I thought, for royalty. President Woodrow Wilson himself had stayed at the Jefferson on one of his trips through the Midwest, so said Oscar.

I turned to see him behind me, his hands on his hips, his head tossed back. He laughed a full-throated laugh. I supposed the sight of me with my head cocked back, in the middle of the lobby, my eyes locked on the ceiling, was amusing. Until he laughed, I'd not realized, nor cared that I'd made a spectacle of myself. I had never imagined anything quite so extraordinary. Oscar laughed again. I couldn't tell whether he enjoyed showing me things I'd never experienced or whether he found amusement at the depths of my naiveté.

The bellman scurried over with our suitcases, one in each of his hands. He nodded his head toward the elevator. Once he unlocked our door and stood aside, I crossed to the room's window. I wanted to look at the view. I wanted to look outside. I wanted to look at anything other than the large bed in the center of the wall to my right. I blushed at the thought of the bed I'd share with Oscar. I avoided looking anywhere near the bellman.

I cracked the window for a better view. The river, splotched by the clouds overhead, ran parallel to the hotel, beneath and alongside our window. The wind gusted hard from the west. White caps studded the gray, swift water. We would not stroll along the boardwalk tonight.

"Anneliese, Oscar interrupted my sightseeing, "the man at the front desk said we should hurry to dinner if we intend to eat here in the hotel."

I turned. The bellman had gone. We were alone. "Yes, of course. We can unpack later. It doesn't look like we'll be going out anyway."

Without a second thought, Oscar tossed his hat on the bed then straightened his tie.

With the aid of the large oval mirror above the dresser, I removed the hatpins and hung my hat on the hook next to the dresser. I turned it around so the chocolate-colored satin bow rested on top. I paused and took stock of my reflection. My travel outfit would have to do for dinner. I ran my hands down the front of the knee-length jacket and the matching mid-calf skirt beneath and smoothed the wrinkles that had developed from the afternoon on the train.

I looked in the mirror again. Oscar's reflection smiled over my shoulder. In three long strides, he came behind me. "Anneliese, or should I say, Mrs. Wolf, you are truly more beautiful today than ever."

By the time we reached the dining room, guests had claimed nearly every table. My eyes darted from one detail to the next in the elegant Washington Room, a mirror of the elegance in the lobby. Light jade-colored panels lined the walls. Gleaming white moldings outlined each panel. Brass brackets along the wall held candle-filled sconces. More light fell from overhead chandeliers dripping with crystals. I counted over a dozen arrayed across the fifteen-foot high ceiling.

Oscar cleared his throat. He held the back of a chair for me. I could not say how long he'd been standing there.

The waiter must have placed a menu on the table, though I had been unaware of his coming and going. I'd not finished my survey of the opulent surroundings. Light bounced off the silverware and empty glasses on the table. Star-like shapes and prisms gleamed in the air. I ran my fingertips across the table and felt the luxurious heft of the pressed linen. I stole a glance at the other tables, velvet green capped sleeves over a woman's ivory skin, feather-trimmed wraps hung on the backs of chairs, and inky black bowties, sleek as otters graced the necks of most of the gentlemen.

"Mrs. Wolf," Oscar said, "perhaps you'd like to look at the menu."

"Yes. I'm sorry. There's so much to look at."

I realized I was famished. I'd not eaten anything since breakfast. We ordered identical items from the menu, carrot soup and roast breast of chicken. After the meal, Oscar indulged in a rich bread pudding. As I thought what the end of the meal portended, my appetite waned. I declined dessert.

After Oscar swallowed the last of his pudding, he dabbed his lips with his napkin and motioned for the waiter.

"Let's have a glass of champagne to celebrate the day."

"Oh, none, for me. I'm content as is." I waved my hand in protest.

"You have no idea what you're missing," Oscar said. When he raised two fingers in the air, the waiter nodded and returned in a few minutes with two glasses and a bottle on a tray. The waiter poured the champagne then melted back into the crowd of diners.

Oscar raised his glass. I lifted mine in response then returned it to the table. My father's face loomed from the empty chair on my right, a disapproving frown above his glasses. I'd never had a sip, not during those evenings at Stallman's with its stash from Evansville's breweries, not at Emma's wedding party, not on any other occasion. I watched as Oscar drained his glass and then looked inquisitively at me. I took a deep breath, the vows of obedience I'd sworn earlier in the day rang in my head. I raised the glass and took a sip. He grinned.

I turned to watch as a few couples joined a throng already on the dance floor at the front of the room. A five-piece band played familiar tunes; a few were ones I'd played at Stallman's, a lifetime ago, others Emma had played for Hannah and me on her Victrola. Although I'd persuaded father to purchase a player, the only recordings we owned contained hymns.

The bandleader announced they would play one last tune before the dining room closed for the evening. "Mrs. Wolf, will you dance with me?" Oscar asked. He had risen from the table and stood before me with his hand out, palm up, waiting for mine.

My heart sank. "Oscar, I don't dance. I...I can't dance," I said. A furtive glance around to the other tables ensured no one noticed me still seated in front of Oscar.

"Nonsense, Anneliese. You've just never tried."

It wasn't true. I'd tried. Many times. In the privacy of my room, when no one but my grandfather was home, I'd hummed a tune, softly so he would not hear, and attempted what I thought was dancing. I darted across the floor between my bed and my dresser. I took one long step with my right foot, then another to bring my left foot forward to meet the right. Right foot again, then the left. I collided with the bed's footboard. My left foot slammed to the floor and arrested my fall. I waited. I listened for any telltale sounds my grandfather might have heard. I feared he'd report the commotion to my parents. I persisted though, and, with repeated attempts aided later by visions of being in Jack's arms, I managed to perform my version of a waltz.

"I insist. Please, trust me," Oscar said, his left hand hovered in mid-air in front of my face. The new wedding band on his finger gleamed in the soft light. A few heads at nearby tables turned to look at the man with an outstretched arm, who'd stood for some time in front of his table. Their stares made me uncomfortable. I rose from my chair. As I did, the heads turned back to resume whatever the conversation they'd halted.

At least, I thought, we'll only have time for one. The bandleader had said the tune would be the last. Fortunately, too, he had chosen to end with a slower paced melody than many of those he'd played earlier.

I kept my head bowed as I followed Oscar to the dance floor. I imagined all eyes were on me. Oscar held me close, supporting me with his arm at my waist. We joined the other couples who circled in their own orbits across the floor. Oscar moved with a grace that I lacked. He stepped lightly and turned effortlessly in the direction he intended me to follow. He no doubt had danced with other women in a more carefree and exuberant manner; but he kept his steps short for me and refrained from sudden turns.

"See, Anneliese, that wasn't so bad," he said when we returned to the safety of our table. The band busied themselves with packing away their instruments.

"Everyone was looking."

"You have a vivid imagination, my dear. No one was paying any attention to us. They were enjoying their own last dance. Come. Let's have one more glass before retiring."

"Oh no, I think I'd better not. I'm already light headed."

"Come, come. We have a lot to celebrate."

Oscar signaled to the waiter, raising his fingers again but this time, he turned them down toward the empty glasses on the table. The waiter nodded and promptly brought an open bottle and filled our glasses. The second glass tasted smoother, more to my liking than the first. The now familiar bubbles burst on my tongue and tingled my throat.

CHAPTER 17
The Great Wheel

Light streamed through the glass in the window. Shades of peach, gold, and orange bathed the back of my eyelids. I opened my eyes. My body jolted at the light. I needed a moment to make sense of the surroundings. A man stood at the window gazing out, one arm extended, propped on the window frame. Oscar. I groped about, my hands found only unfamiliar sheets on an unfamiliar bed. He turned.

"Aha. So you are awake, Mrs. Wolf! Good morning. My, how you slept!"

"What time is it?"

"Nearly nine."

I shook my head. It felt swollen, clouded, as if I had contracted a cold. I reached to sweep the hair back from my eyes. My bare arm glistened in the morning light. I was naked under the sheets. Instead of fixing my hair, I tugged at the sheet, then the blanket. I stretched them, nearly pulling the other end from the mattress as I covered my breasts.

"I tried to help you into your night gown last night, Anneliese. I'm afraid I didn't do a very good job. No matter. Are you hungry? Ready for breakfast? A walk by the river? It's a spectacular day!"

"I...I'll take a bath first."

"And some breakfast no doubt."

"Yes. I could use some coffee."

"I imagine so. I'll go down and arrange for a table. I'll wait for you in the dining room." As he approached the bed, I scrunched my shoulders to retreat further beneath the bed covers, like a tortoise seeking refuge in its shell. He leaned over and kissed me on the top of my head.

"Don't be long." It was that singsong way he had of speaking. He smiled then pulled the door closed behind him.

For several minutes after he left, I dared not move. I could not move. I lay mummified, the sheet and blanket drawn tightly around me while I tried to sort through the events of the night before.

Step by step. In chronological order, I thought. The station, the taxi, the hotel, checking in, the dining room. I remembered dinner, the herbed chicken, Oscar's dessert, bread pudding, then...yes, then champagne. My father looked down from his pulpit at me. I had danced with Oscar. My mother scowled beside the kitchen sink. More champagne. Had it been two or three glasses. There were stairs. One flight, then another, the topmost step ended in fog. The trail of memories ended in fog.

I tried again, the station, the taxi, the hotel. Again, the memory of our wedding night faded somewhere on the stairs, like a wartime newsreel that faded to black between scenes.

The loss of awareness frightened and embarrassed me. I hoped Oscar would not ask any details. A bath. Yes, that would do it. A good hot soak would somehow bring my memory back. I cocked an ear toward the door and the hallway beyond. No one passed by, no guest, no bellman, no maid. I stood and, as I did so, dragged the sheet from the bed to cover myself. I took only two strides before I stopped and let the soiled sheet fall to the floor in a heap. I grabbed the light blanket from the bed and draped it over my shoulders. Then, in a single, awkward dash, I pulled the curtains closed, crossed the room, and turned the lock in the door.

As I came through the alcove into the dining room, I spotted Oscar seated at a table in the corner. His head was buried in the day's newspaper. At about the same time, he raised his head and saw me. In a second, he was by my side to walk me to the table.

"I am feeling particularly awful today. I don't think last night's champagne agreed with me."

"Some food and fresh air will do you good."

"Fresh air. Yes."

"I spoke with the manager this morning. He's found us two tickets for a riverboat dinner. It's not until late this afternoon, so you'll have plenty of time to rest and recover."

"A riverboat? Oh, I don't think so. Didn't one sink a while ago? Here in St. Louis?"

"No, not here. I think it was up in Peoria. The river's much narrower there. There's nothing to worry about."

I knew about the ships. I read how they came across logs and other debris that could rupture their hulls.

"I remember now. It was in Peoria. It was a paddle steamer, the *Columbia* I think."

Last summer even the *Evansville Courier* had reported at length on the accident. The paper described how the barge had hit a sandbar near the shore in the middle of the night. The current had dragged the ship with its broken, waterlogged hull into deep water.

"Liese, were you listening?"

"No, I'm sorry, Oscar. What were you saying?"

"I said, on Mondays, the *Goldenrod* goes from Saint Louis to Peoria. But, on Sundays, it offers a sightseeing excursion right here. You can view Saint Louis from the river." Oscar embarked on another of his discourses, which I had come to know were one-sided discussions meant to fill the air, and presumably, now, make light of my concerns. My thoughts returned to the *Columbia*.

The paper had recounted tales of survivors who told of passengers rushing the stairs. The crew had tried to keep everyone calm, but the throngs blocked the exits as they clambered to reach higher levels. Those trapped on the lower decks proved the most unfortunate. The ship lost power, throwing the whole into darkness, making the chaotic situation worse. The steamer sank into the mud of the narrow river. The final count was over one hundred casualties.

Oscar's voice rose to the surface. "...our choice of a morning or evening excursion. I told him we'd take the later trip as it included dinner. We've eaten here in the hotel already and we'll probably eat here again before we return. What do you think? Is that alright with you, dear?"

I thought for a minute. I started to say it was fine, but Oscar continued. He'd posed a question for which he expected no reply. "I thought it would be good to have a change of scenery. And to see the city from out on the water. Won't that be grand?"

At five in the afternoon, we took a car from the hotel to the dock. The spectacle there eased my earlier trepidations. The steamer sparkled from stem to stern under a fresh coat of white paint. In the river, a mirror image doubled the effect.

"It's stunning. It's so white. It must have just been painted."

"See, I told you," Oscar said. "You are really going to enjoy this."

To board, we walked up the ramp near the bow. Only a few other passengers had arrived ahead of us, some of them now walked along the balconies of the upper deck. Oscar stopped at the ticket booth to show the clerk our tickets. I had a minute to admire the ornately furnished interior. I ran my hand along the dark mahogany wainscoting that lined the ticketing room. Above the wainscoting, a cream-colored brocade-like paper. Carved, gold-colored swags and figurines studded the walls around the room. How ordinary our home and everything else about Evansville seemed in comparison.

The ticketing agent took our tickets, tore them in half, and returned the stubs to Oscar. "You may take the stairs to the left, Sir. If you like, you are welcome to visit the observation deck above the dining salon." He nodded to his right.

Oscar took my arm and led me through the set of stained-glass inlaid double doors the agent had indicated. We entered another immense room, the lobby, again lined all around with dark wood and lit by gilt sconces just above head-height. I was drunk with the details of light and gold and mahogany. The artifacts swirled in front of my eyes, a new marvel everywhere I turned, even to the ceiling with its patterned-tin painted white after the fashion of the day. Three tin medallions at even intervals across the ceiling capped three chandeliers. They matched the one I'd admired in the entryway.

"Are you pleased?"

"Yes, Oscar, it's beautiful. I'm glad we came."

We passed through the lobby toward the stern and to the stairs to the upper decks. Large windows lined the stairs and allowed an uninterrupted view of the river and the Illinois shore opposite. On the second level, an open loft formed a semicircle over the dining room. A bar stood at one side, the doors to the observation deck at the other. More cream-colored bands and gold figurines. I passed them without a second glance. I chose instead to admire a hundred miniature lights twinkling like stars through pin-sized holes cut into the deep blue ceiling.

The ship would depart the dock at half past five. We were free to wander the decks for an hour. After we located our assigned table, we exited the dining salon and climbed the stairs to the loft. From there, we watched as a steady stream of passengers wended their way to the dock and climbed aboard. Most patrons swarmed into the bar while a few, who did not care for a drink, moved on to the observation deck. Some remained inside the shelter of the glass-enclosed section while others ventured out into the open air. We moved to the enclosed salon. Although several couples and a few families with children already lined the deck, the salon was less crowded than the bar. Oscar spied a small opening on the quayside.

"Let's watch from over there," he said, pointing to a vacant spot in front of two large windows.

We took our places between a well-dressed elderly couple and a lone young man in a hideous plaid overcoat. Oscar tipped his hat at the couple who moved a step to the right to make room for us. I stepped aside to allow Oscar a view just as the wake of another ship or perhaps a gust of wind forced the *Goldenrod* against the dock. The sudden motion jostled everyone on the deck. I bumped against the lone passenger on my left.

"Oh, excuse me," I said.

The young man turned toward me and, though he looked at me, his eyes settled on an object directly behind me, or I thought, through me, as if I weren't there. He said nothing. Then, he merely stopped looking at whatever he had seen, turned around, and resumed his position peering out over the dock.

From our vantage point, we watched the last group of passengers come aboard. Two crewmen followed close behind them as a single, long blast from the ship's horn signaled our departure. The dockhands jumped into action. They removed the mooring lines from the bollards at the front and back positions and tossed the lines to the crew already on board. I'd pointed the men out to Oscar.

"They're called "fore" and "aft", not front and back."

I frowned at him. "It's not like I'm going to take up sailing."

Hidden from view, directly below us, other hands tucked away the boarding ramp. Moments later, the stern-mounted wheel turned. It creaked and groaned as it inched forward. As the ship gained speed, the groan became stronger, more protracted until it settled at last into a rhythmic hum that vibrated the deck under my feet. I grabbed the handrail that ran the length of the observation windows. The young man did the same. The knuckles of his hands were white. I hardly noticed the ship separate from the dock. We were underway. I relaxed my grip. The young man did not.

The ship's wheel picked up speed and drove the ship into the river's current. I watched the water cascade from the heavy steel paddles as they rose then turned to cut through the darker water near the hull on their return trip to the underside of the wheel.

"Before it gets too cool, let's take a look at the city from out-side," Oscar said. He motioned to the door that led from the enclosed area to the open deck. I fastened my jacket and secured my hat to my head. I followed Oscar out the door and took his outstretched hand. The closer we came to the wheel, the more imposing it became. I held my hands over my ears to dampen the noise, but the wheel roared through my fingers as water cascaded from its blades, and slapped into the river in sheets. Behind the ship, the water churned as it rushed to close the furrow left in its wake.

A light breeze blew across the open deck. As I grew accus-tomed to the din, the sounds blended into the background. I lowered my hands. Soon, though, as the boat gained speed, the breeze grew stronger, the air more brisk. Oscar tapped my arm, the air too thick for me to hear him. We turned to go inside and left the deck to the only other brave soul, the young man who'd stood beside me earlier on the observation deck.

As the sun set, lights came on across the ship. The rails, strung with lights, twinkled above the water and in the *Goldenrod*'s mir-ror image below. Light from the chandeliers washed across the dining salon. I gazed out at the shore and the boardwalk along which couples, parents with children trailing behind or running ahead, men, women, boys, and girls, walked and now and then, pointed toward our vessel. I imagined it looked to them like a jeweled crown sparkling in the distance.

We wove our way through the crowd to our table at the rear corner of the dining salon. Every table had a view of something of interest, the near riverbank with the city's lights, the far shore-line with other boats plying between, or the trail of white water the wheel tossed behind. Oscar sat with his face to the bow of the boat. I had the advantage of a broader perspective both to my right toward the riverbank and back toward the churning wheel.

In the center of the room, a band played a lively melody, a tune I did not recognize. A few couples took the floor to dance.

Oscar shot a glance toward the band then back at me. Thinking I could already read his mind, I pre-empted his invitation, "Not tonight, Oscar."

He smiled. "Alright, my dear. We'll save the next dance till we're back on shore."

"No champagne, either."

We both laughed.

Dinner consisted of cream of tomato soup followed by roast beef with peas and mashed potatoes. Everything was well prepared. I marveled at how the chef managed with the limitations I supposed the floating kitchen must have. Oscar chose a creamy, rice pudding with vanilla flavoring for dessert. I again declined. "Instead of champagne," I said, "let's finish with a cup of coffee."

The room had quieted as we along with many of our fellow passengers lingered at our tables over coffee or other after-dinner drinks. The band played more softly now. They anticipated the audience's subdued mood after dinner. Oscar reached across the table and took my hand. As we listened to the music, with his thumb, he traced the surface of my new wedding band.

With a clear view of the great wheel, I was the principal witness, though not the first to scream. At the sight, I withdrew my hand from Oscar's and, in a single motion, rose. My chair teetered and nearly fell to the floor.

Others around me screamed. Oscar, whose back had been to the window, looked at me, puzzled. He swiveled in his seat. His eyes scanned the room, searching for the source of the panic. Oscar rose from his seat and came around to my side of the table. "What is it? What's wrong?"

By now, several other passengers had risen from their seats. The lady seated at the table next to me, though, had frozen in her seat; her outstretched arm still pointed toward the wheel. Almost everyone in the room either stood or turned to look outside. They followed the gazes and gestures of others. One gentleman rushed outside through the door at the back of the salon. A few others followed. The music stopped.

"That young man. The one in the overcoat. It was him, I'm sure."

"What? What are you saying?"

"Remember the man that was beside us earlier? The young man. The man with that awful plaid overcoat. The one standing at the rail. The same one that we left on the deck outside?"

"I think so, I'm not sure. Why? What happened?

"He fell. He fell into the wheel or into the water. I saw something. Someone...something fell. Plaid. I think it was him. He fell into the water beside the wheel."

"Well, maybe it was just his coat. Someone will check."

The ship's engine slowed which drew the attention of those who had somehow not noticed the earlier fracas. Crew rushed up the stairs and through the dining salon to the stern. The tramp of feet thundered above us on the observation deck. A few of the musicians, instruments in hand, stood with the passengers to watch the commotion from the dining salon.

While the crew worked outside under the glow of light thrown off by the lights strung on the handrails, the boat drifted in the current. Finally, someone switched on several overhead lamps, flooding the open deck with light as bright as the middle of the day. Standing where we were, closest to the aft windows, we watched the wheel slow to a crawl. Crew waited to one side. At last, one paddle rose from the water, bearing the broken form of a human figure. Water gushed over the dark gash that creased the back of the man's head. Water trickled down his neck, and dripped onto the sodden plaid overcoat. One of the man's arms lay wedged between the edge of the paddle and the side of the wheel. The wheel advanced, raised the body all the way up, then down again, the legs lifeless as a ragdoll, flopping with the whim of the wheel. I could not bear to watch, yet I could not tear my eyes away. Oscar placed an arm around me and urged me to sit, to look away. I sat, but I watched.

The crew waited until the body surfaced again. The wheel stopped. They grabbed hold where they could. One clawed at the overcoat, another grabbed an arm, and a third reached for the man's foot.

Two crewmen untangled the limp corpse and wrestled it to the deck. One of the crewmen shouted something though his words were inaudible to us inside the dining salon. His lips moved and the crowd of onlookers, mostly male passengers, retreated a few feet. One of the crewmen removed his jacket and draped it over the motionless figure lying in a pool of water threaded with scarlet. The jacket covered only the head and upper part of the twisted body.

From my chair, the body appeared and disappeared between the legs and torsos of those on the deck as they shuffled back and forth. The crowd parted again. This time, caught in the light, the drenched but discernible plaid of the overcoat lay flattened against the young man's body. Oscar moved to place himself between the window and me.

The Captain came into the salon and took the microphone from the bandleader. Stammering as he spoke, he announced to the gathered diners that, due to an accident aboard, he would return to shore immediately. He offered his apologies.

When the boat docked, we disembarked and hurried back to our hotel. I did not say a word all the way back to the hotel. Nor did Oscar. I climbed in the bed, our bed, though I didn't waste a minute thinking of it in those terms. I pulled the sheets and blankets around me. Oscar sat on the side of the bed. He stroked my hair until I fell asleep.

I woke in the middle of the night, confused and dazed. I wondered for a moment where I was, then, I felt the unfamiliar sheets and heard the deep breath of the body next to me. I tried to sleep. Each time I thought it was just one more breath away, the plaid coat fell into the wheel and the broken body rose to the surface again. The sight would not leave me.

We returned to Evansville the next morning. We chose to forego the final day of our honeymoon, or perhaps it was only I who wanted to leave, nevertheless, Oscar consented to my wishes. My parents met us at the station. They had brought the car to carry our suitcases back to the house. Though they peppered us with questions about the events of the weekend and the sights of Saint Louis, we said little in response. Oscar did most of the talking. He mentioned the weather, it was good but cloudy; the walks along the boardwalk, we'd managed to take one on Sunday; the fine meals we'd enjoyed, we'd had dinner in the hotel's Washington Room; the music. Thankfully, he did not elaborate on the music. Neither one of us spoke of the riverboat or the unfortunate accident.

My father stopped the car in front of the house and mentioned, awkwardly I thought, that he had an appointment to attend to. "We'll be back in a few hours," he said. "In time for dinner."

We carried our suitcases to the front porch and watched as they drove away. Oscar took a deep breath then opened the front door. I stepped inside but held back as Oscar carried our suitcases down the hall and into our room. I remained in the alcove between the front room and the hallway, between my old life, I thought, and my new one. I closed my eyes and murmured a quick prayer under my breath.

When I entered our room, Oscar had already emptied the contents of the two suitcases onto the bed. He looked around, surveying his surroundings, his new home. I walked the perimeter of the room, touching the walls, the bed, the chest of drawers, and the chairs. All of these were new and unfamiliar. Just as I had wanted them to be.

Despite the freshly painted walls and the new furnishings, the all too familiar scent of old paper, liniments, and spice hung in the room. If he noticed the odor, Oscar did not say. He had the advantage, I thought. In time he'd become accustomed to the scent. In a few weeks or months, he would no longer notice. He'd live amid the tang of old liniment and salve, oblivious that I smelled the odors that clung to my clothes, my skin, and the hair on my body. They were part of me but I'd never become accustomed to them.

Oscar put his hands on my shoulders. "Anneliese, we'll have a place of our own one day soon, I promise," he said. He only half understood my dread.

We had no way of knowing at the time, but within a year, my father and mother would both have died, my mother in August just four months after the wedding. She had contracted pneumonia but ignored the signs and even accompanied my father on his rounds, until the week before her death.

My father survived for seven more months. He'd been in reasonably good health; his death was an accident, the result of a fall. After patching a section of the roof of his church, he'd slipped on the rung of his ladder and lay on the ground for several hours before Samuel found him. Samuel Walker was the church's handyman. While he had not planned to work that Friday, Samuel had come to retrieve a saw he said he had left behind. When he arrived, he noticed the ladder propped against the west wall of the building. Samuel, certain he had not left it there the previous day, went to investigate and found the pastor splayed on the ground next to the ladder. His hip was broken.

The fall left my father bedridden. Oscar and I moved from our newly renovated room into my parent's former room upstairs.

"We wouldn't think of you sleeping on the couch in the front room," I said. You simply must stay in here. Just until you're well."

Having made a gift of the new room to us, my father at first refused to accept the change. He agreed only after prolonged arguments with Oscar and me and on condition that once he was able to climb stairs again, we would switch places. With Father confined to his bed downstairs, I resumed a familiar role, carrying dinner trays to the Bauer room. Despite the change in appearance, the new furnishings, the new colors, the memories persisted. Midway down the hall to my father's room, I'd stop to listen. I swear, had I wanted or dared to tell someone, that I heard steps behind me.

If I closed my eyes, I imagined a young girl who inched her way down a hall, counted her steps, and scuffed her heels in the dark. She carried a tray for her grandfather, a man everyone considered a bit daft but benign. I saw the young girl put food in the old man's mouth. I felt the young girl cringe at his touch. I heard the young girl stand in the hall and scream though no sound came from her lips. She had two blue buttons for eyes and a single red button for a mouth.

Dr. Elias Morgan, who had come to set Tom's leg after the accident, instructed me on my father's care. A member of the church, the doctor had ministered to the family in medical matters for as long as I could recall. He'd attended Grandfather Bauer and even presided over my birth, so my mother had said.

On one of his weekly visits, Dr. Morgan unbuttoned the pastor's cotton shirt to expose his chest and listen to my father's heart and lungs with his stethoscope. I saw how frail he had become; his collarbone pressed against the paper-thin parchment-like skin. His ribs rippled across his chest like waves across a pond.

"Everything sounds fine, Tom. What you need is rest and good care. You have a fine nurse in Liese here. I'll see you next week."

Dr. Morgan, concerned that my father might hear, said nothing more until we reached the front door. "I see no physical reason your father's not getting better. His hip is healing well, better than I expected, quite frankly. He's not in any pain. In a few days we'll see if he can put some weight on his leg." He tipped his head to put his hat on as he stepped outside.

"Thank you for coming."

He turned again to me. "He'll likely need a cane to walk, if he does walk again. Even so, I think he's just lost the will to go on."

"I agree, Doctor. He's heard the church has brought in Pastor Norton, even if they said it would be temporary. And, of course, without Mother..."

My father died in March 1920. Oscar and I were alone in the house on First Avenue for the first time.

"Alone," Oscar said, "at last."

Part Six:
Ellie

CHAPTER 18
Two Perfect Feet

I'd buried my first pregnancy with its unfortunate end so deep in my past that I thought it had happened to someone else, Hannah or Emma by chance. I denied the new pregnancy for two months; I hoped I was wrong, in part because I was unprepared to be a mother but mostly because I thought only a malformed creature could find its way from my ravaged womb.

When Ellie emerged, I believed again in the possibility of good things to come, but as she grew, she frightened me. She had much more of Oscar in her than me. Perhaps I was right, my womb had been scraped clean and there was nothing for her to be but Oscar.

* * *

The new pastor's wife, Amelia, had taken me under her wing. She visited me in the house next door, whenever she accompanied her husband to the church. Confident and caring, she was in every way my mother's opposite and determined to take up where my mother had left off. When I reached the eighth month of my pregnancy, Amelia had even gone so far as to arrange for a midwife. At the mention of Edith Becker's name, I blanched and reached behind me for the back of a chair.

"Oh, my dear. Liese, are you feeling faint?"

"No, I...I'll be alright. I was just dizzy for a moment."

"You have nothing to worry about."

"I know. But, I would like to find someone else."

"Mrs. Becker is extremely competent."

"I don't care, Amelia." When I saw the shock of my abrupt refusal on Amelia's face, I softened my objection. "I'm sorry, I know you mean well, and I thank you for all you've done in the last few weeks. But, Hannah has already found someone." I marveled at how easily I found I could now lie. I did not fear years in purgatory or hell for a few necessary accommodations.

"Oh, who?"

"Ah, well...she didn't say who when she called."

The next morning, I sent Hannah on a quest. She found Gerta Fields through a friend, a member of the congregation. I did not want to delay any further. I agreed immediately though neither Hannah nor her friend had anything to offer by way of personal experience with Gerta.

"She's old enough to be my grandmother, Hannah," I said after I had met Gerta. "And, fairly rotund, don't you think? I don't know how she'll manage to do everything I need."

"Liese, you know I'll be here and Emma, too. Don't worry."

Gerta visited me several times over the next few weeks. She made me promise to let her know when my water broke. On Friday, Emma, who'd taken her turn to sit with me, rang for Gerta. "It's starting. Oh, please come quickly."

"Calm down, Mrs. Strahan," Gerta said. "You'll get Liese excited. It's her first so we should have plenty of time, but I'll be there shortly."

With each stab of pain, I winced. Emma responded with a flinch then set her jaw. "You'll see," she said, "after all this waiting and waiting it will all be over in just a few hours."

"Hours?" I moaned.

"Maybe not that long now," Emma said.

I'd worried every waking hour from the first moment I knew I was pregnant. I'd assumed after my prior terminated pregnancy—the only way I could refer to my abortion—I could not conceive. I'd not breathed a word to Oscar and hoped he would accept that we were just another of those unfortunate couples who could not have children. When he'd asked about my concerns, I told him of my mother's two miscarriages but nothing of the damage done to my body and, at least as far as I was concerned, what the effect might be on the child.

"Oh, my," I moaned and surrendered to the gnarled and twisted fingers of pain that wracked my body. "I'm so afraid," I said to Hannah, who had come at Emma's call. She'd arrived ahead of the midwife.

"Nonsense," she said. "You have nothing to worry about."

My delirium prevented me from determining what qualified either Hannah or Emma to speak about childbirth. Hannah, of course, had never married and Emma, though married for over a year had not become pregnant. We avoided the topic.

"Besides," Hannah said, "we'll be right here the whole time."

"I just want...I just want the baby to live and to be healthy."

"I for one don't think you have anything to worry about. I'm sure the baby will be fine. Perfect in fact," Hannah said.

"I don't know. I just don't know," I said. I turned away from the two women who sat alongside the bed.

Hannah ran a cool hand across my forehead and stroked my hair. She loosened a few strands from behind my neck and spread them across the starched white pillowslip.

"We can say a prayer," Emma offered.

"I've prayed and prayed till I don't think I can pray any more. You'll let me know as soon as you see, won't you? I can't bear to look. Please remember, let me know first, before anyone tells Oscar."

"We will. We will. Stop worrying," Emma said. She and Hannah both nodded.

Another stab of pain shot through my pelvis and up my spine. I arched my back. I grabbed Emma's hand, clenched it in my fist, and shoved it against the mattress.

Emma winced, though she said, "Good, Liese, good. Hannah, go find out what's keeping Gerta. I think we're getting close."

Hannah walked to the door. She called from the top of the stairs. "Gerta. Gerta! I think we're...I think Liese's ready."

"I'm coming. I'm coming. My goodness, if I didn't know better, I would have said you are all giving birth." Gerta panted audibly as she struggled up the stairs.

"I told you we should have done this down stairs," Emma said. "Gerta will be forever getting up and down those stairs."

I refused to rehash the subject I had exhausted earlier in the week. I would not have the baby in my grandfather's room. I did not want to tempt fate any more than I had.

Gerta appeared in the doorway, a large basin of hot water in her hands.

"Here, let me help you," Emma said, rushing to the midwife's side. She took the bowl from Gerta but remained near the door where she set the basin on a table. She gave Hannah a furtive, worried look, one I was sure she'd not meant me to see. She must have her own doubts I thought. Her eyes were cast toward her feet. Her lips moved. She prayed.

The women paced the room, carried pails of hot water and fresh towels for two hours. They held my hand and encouraged me to push then suggested I rest to regain strength for the next round. In another few minutes, the ordeal ended. Gerta bundled the newborn infant in one of the towels piled at the foot of the bed while I collapsed on to the pillow soaked with my sweat. Exhausted, I was unable to expend any further effort, unable even to ask.

Hannah and Emma remained at their positions, near the head of my bed, one on each side. They'd not released their hold of my hands. They'd not looked. They too waited for Gerta. Afraid too, I thought, despite their assurances. Gerta worked silently, busy with her trade and the tasks that now fell to her. She wiped the baby, tended to the afterbirth, and cut the umbilical cord.

A wail from the baby woke me, and I realized I'd allowed my eyes to close. They sprang wide at the sound. A second wail brought Oscar to the stairs. He clattered up the first few steps. I heard him stop, hesitate, and then take a few more steps. "Tell me. Quick," I said. "Tell me."

Gerta carried the squirming baby to me. "See for yourself, Mrs. Wolf, a perfect baby girl." She passed the bundle to me, her knuckles, chapped and red from years of work in water, stood in marked contrast to the pale pink blanket Emma had crocheted for the occasion.

I exhaled at last, every muscle in my body relaxed for the first time in many months. I let myself sink deep into the cushion of the bed before I raised my arms for the baby. With Emma and Hannah peering over my shoulders, I pulled back the blanket to expose two eyes, a nose, a mouth, two tiny, perfectly formed hands, two tiny, perfectly formed feet.

For days, even weeks after Ellie's birth, I examined every inch of the little body a thousand times. No one could dissuade me. I checked and rechecked Ellie. I put my ear to her tiny mouth and listened to her breathe. I touched her chest and felt for the beat of her heart. I looked for signs she was turning blue, but her cheeks only glowed a pale rose. Each time I left her room, I halted at the door, held my breath, and listened for hers. Then, I would run to the kitchen, or the bathroom, or the front door and sprint back to check again.

I listened closely to what others said when they held the baby in their arms, my hopes hung on their every word. To a person, they assured me as to her health, and her beauty. I took their words with a grain of salt. Did they just say the things they said to every new mother?

Oscar, on the other hand, never had concerns about the possibility of Ellie being born anything other than perfect. He had tried, without success, to convince me of the same. He never understood my concerns. I'd never given him a reason to do so.

I gave thanks repeatedly, twice as much as I had prayed in advance of the birth for nothing to be wrong. Finally, I stopped checking, though I tucked away in the back of my mind the thought that somehow a flaw did exist but would refuse to reveal its ugly self until the time were right.

CHAPTER 19
Mother and Daughter

We doted on Ellie. Except when she slept, we did not leave her side. Each day when Oscar came home from work, he brought something for Ellie, a flower, a feather, a bow, something to catch her eye, to delight her.

Oscar's attention though did eventually come full circle, to me. He had been solicitous of me through the long months of my pregnancy and, even after Ellie had been born, accepted my decision to sleep downstairs, in the white room, as I referred to it for the still fresh white paint on its walls.

"The white room? "You mean the old Bauer room?"

"Yes, the white room."

"Call it whatever you want." He didn't understand that it needed this name, that I needed it to have a name, a new name, not one associated with its past. "Why do you want to sleep there?"

"It'll save me from having to climb the stairs," I said. "Just these last few weeks."

I knew I'd have to return to our room upstairs eventually. For four or five weeks after her birth, each evening as he turned to go up the stairs, Oscar would look at me and say, "Coming?"

"I think it's best if I stay here another night with Ellie, downstairs. You'll sleep better without her crying in your ear."

He was anxious to resume our roles as husband and wife, or, more precisely, man and woman. Oscar purchased a crib and a chest of drawers and set them in what had been my room as a child, upstairs. A few days later, Oscar surprised me with a rocker for the room.

"It looks just like—"

"It is," he said. "It's Adam's old rocker. I refinished it. For you."

I swallowed hard. I realized how hard he had worked, sanding and painting it to match the other furnishings; I said nothing and forced a smile to my lips. I put the rocker in a corner of the room, as far from the crib as I could. I would never use it.

I returned to bed in our room, but insisted on having Ellie near us. After considerable badgering, Oscar yielded to me with regard to things a newborn might need. He allowed me to move the crib into our bedroom on my side of the bed.

"But only for one more week," he said.

"Agreed. Thank you."

Even after Ellie slept through the night, I would slip out of bed to watch her as she slept in her crib, her little chest rising and falling with each breath. I marveled at how smooth and round her cheeks were, how tiny yet well formed the little fingers and toes were, how perfect. The most wonderful object in the world.

Sometimes, she coughed or stirred noisily and woke Oscar. He would call my name and argue with me in a hushed tone. Our voices shuttled back and forth over the crib. Other times, while Oscar slept, I would pick up Ellie, carry her across the hall to her room, and sit with her beside her crib. The rocker looked on from across the room.

"Anneliese, you must come to bed. You're not getting enough sleep," Oscar would say when he found us there. "The child will be fine. You're wearing yourself out."

"I'm fine," I said, though earlier that afternoon, I had caught a glimpse of myself in the mirror. Dark circles framed my eyes. My clothes hung on my frame. My hair fell loose around my shoulders.

Oscar became less patient as the weeks wore on. He never raised his voice, but he'd sigh, turn on his heels and grab his hat to go outside when I would not give in to his demands. He wanted his old life back. Our life, however, would not return to what it was before. Our daily routine, or at least mine, included preparing baby food, feeding, bathing, dressing, undressing, changing, and at the end of the day putting the baby to sleep.

One day, three months after her birth, when I returned from a stroll with Ellie and carried her upstairs for a nap, I was surprised to find the crib was not in our room. A commotion across the hall caught my attention. Oscar was on the floor, smoothing the rug underneath my wingback chair.

"What in the world are you doing, Oscar?"

"I just moved the rug so that the crib would fit snug against the wall."

And there it was. Just as he said. The crib sat against the wall to the right.

"Come look." He beamed as he unveiled how he had moved the other furniture to situate the crib away from the window and any possible draft, closer to the door where we could easily hear Ellie if she cried. I said nothing, but held Ellie in my arms and bounced her gently.

That night, I took far longer than usual to put the child in the crib. As I crossed the hall to our bedroom, I paused two or three times and cocked my head back toward the open door. I listened for a whimper or a cry, but she slept silently. When I entered our room, a pencil-thin line of white light cast by the rising moon outlined the shape of Oscar's body on our bed. He lay on the far side, his hand rested on the covers he'd drawn back on my side. I climbed in and tugged on the sheet and blanket until they covered my shoulders. Though my head lay on the pillow, it barely rested there. I begged my heart not to beat so loudly. I could not hear Ellie breathing. Oscar touched me on the shoulder and tugged lightly to bring me closer to him. I bent to the warmth of his fingertips and yielded. I turned to him. I returned his kiss, touched his cheek with my hand, then rolled back on my side, away from him, to sleep. To listen.

Except for the few weeks surrounding Ellie's birth, we never missed Sunday services at Zion Evangelical Church. We brought our daughter with us. It was important that Ellie be there, at least it was important to me. I wanted her to know the simple, clapboard church of her grandfather, even if another pastor preached there.

Augustus Norton's brand of preaching did not appeal to me. He spoke of a far too generous and forgiving Christ, and of reaching heaven without the fervor and sacrifice my father had demanded.

He showed little interest in the hymns and left the selection of them to me. Augustus failed to see how they could add meaning and substance to his message. In his church, the hymns had no mystery or magic. They were just hymns. Try as I might, even playing my best, I could do nothing to enhance his flat, passionless sermons.

While I played the piano, Oscar minded Ellie in his favorite spot in the last pew.

I also insisted that Ellie learn to speak German. I sang her lullabies in my ancestors; tongue as my mother had done for me, or at least as I remember her saying she had done.

At seven, I thought Ellie was old enough to help in the kitchen, I taught her to cook in German, accomplishing two tasks in one, I thought.

"One cup of sugar, *eine tasse zucker*" I said. I provided both the English and the German equivalent. When I needed something we had rehearsed before, I omitted the English phrase and asked in German alone for ingredients or for her to cut, or mix, or pour.

"Say it again, Ellie. Think first, then speak."

She pulled her lips together, drew her delicate eyebrows down, and narrowed her eyes as she thought, her smooth, unblemished face now wrinkled and twisted into a knot as she pondered the phrase. Ellie knew from experience she would have to repeat it again and again until she managed to say the phrase without hesitation.

"Mischen sie zwei tassen zucker mit einer tasse butter."

"Gut, sehr gut". I beamed when she remembered the words, though a Midwest accent laced her German. I kissed the top of her head.

My cookbooks, some in English others in German, lined the shelf in the kitchen, but I rarely consulted them. I baked from recipes I knew by heart or had learned by feel. This confounded Ellie.

"I don't understand. How do you know what to put in and when, unless you look it up?"

"Practice, Ellie. Practice and pleasure. Once you've done this a hundred times, you'll understand."

"A hundred times?" She frowned again. Worry darkened her face. "That's an awful lot."

"You'll know what to do by how firm or how soft the batter is, how warm or cool it is. You won't find that in a book. You have to touch and taste as you go. Some things go together. Some things don't."

"Are you still talking about baking or something else?"

"I suppose you could say baking and something else. Baking is a lot like other things in life. If you try to do something...to do something really well, because you love it with all your heart, like baking not because you need to eat, or sewing not because a shirt might need a button, you'll understand."

"Um." She paused. "But wouldn't it be easier to write it down?"

"Maybe. But it isn't always about making it easy. You'll see. People can tell when you're just following a recipe. What's more, you'll know."

Ellie's eyebrows knit together. I thought how different she was than me. How little she liked being in the kitchen. I'd begged my mother to let me help. Perhaps it had been more of a refuge for me. Ellie had no need to escape the life around her. She waited for me to order the next ingredient or followed along in a cookbook, or more often, the stained cards in my mother's recipe box. They would have been difficult to read even without the Crisco smudges and dried splatters of vanilla or milk. The longhand of a generation or more ago had its own peculiar flourishes, an elongated *t* slashed through words above and below, an *i* lacked its dot. The abbreviations were a code to which Ellie lacked the key.

"Think, Ellie, think," I said. I urged her to learn the next step or ingredient and not resort to the card. "Close your eyes. Think about how sweet the sugar tastes, imagine it dissolving on your tongue? Now, keep your eyes closed." She shut them tightly. "Open your mouth. Taste it. See?"

Ellie chewed, swallowed the piece of oatmeal cookie and grinned. "See what?"

If I kept her in the kitchen too long, she'd squirm in her chair and talk of going outside. She only came alive near the end when the aroma of whatever I baked was near its peak or after I pulled a layer of cake from the oven and frosted it with a Crisco-laden icing. While I cleaned the used pots and pans, she'd spin the cake around on its plate, examine it from all sides, then, with a clean knife, she'd create patterns in the icing. She'd swirl the still warm frosting into a set of tiny concentric circles then add a flourish to the innermost circle. Or she'd carve wave-like ripples, up one side, across the top, and down the other. If the object of her attention were one of my highly acclaimed apple pies, Ellie'd remake my traditional latticework crust. Before she allowed me to put the pie in the oven, she cut small shapes from the left-over dough, leaves, or stars, or tulips, whatever shape came to her mind. She'd scatter the butter-laden designs across the lattice. Sometimes she'd do this when I turned away, and I would discover her handiwork only after I slid the pie from the oven. Crisp, brown, and festooned with the child's art.

CHAPTER 20

Oscar and Ellie

Oscar made few demands of Ellie. He spent his time with her playing, reading, telling stories, or taking her for walks, whatever she wanted to do. Oscar was like a child around her, sitting on the floor, skipping along the walk, or sitting beside her in her bed as he read a bedtime story.

At nine, Ellie entered an inquisitive stage. No matter what the topic of conversation, she asked why. She questioned everything, especially the things that concerned her father. He was a mystery to her, whereas I was a known thing. Where did he go when he left the house in the morning? What did he do during the day? Ellie had difficulty fathoming a manager's job at the railroad. She understood what an engineer did; she'd seen one at the controls of a locomotive as it pulled through a crossing. She'd seen the ticket vendor and the Pullman. Those were simple, concrete jobs with obvious responsibilities. The concept of an office manager defied her imagination. Ellie was determined to understand it.

"You'll just have to come see for yourself one day," Oscar said, though I doubted he meant it. Even he was growing tired of Ellie's fixation, which I knew would wane as soon as another unfamiliar object took its place.

For the time being, though, Ellie reminded Oscar every day after he came home that he had promised to take her with him to the station one day. Finally, when school recessed for the summer, Oscar relented. I think he wanted to show her off anyway. We'd introduced Ellie to a few of his coworkers after services at church. Most, I suspected, had only seen the ever-expanding array of photos that Oscar had framed for his desk. Ellie in a christening outfit, a puzzled, perhaps fearful expression on her face as she sat propped in a wicker chair in the photographer's studio. Ellie atop a pony at Uncle Paul's farm. Ellie on her eighth birthday, surrounded by a group of relatives in front of the immense Santa Claus statue in Santa Claus, Indiana where we had taken her one weekend. Ellie beamed from the photo, the center of attention, but somehow alone despite the crowd. I remember remarking after seeing the photo for the first time how it revealed the woman she would be. There was something adult-like in her smile, a coyness in the way she eyed the camera, a bravado in her full-shouldered stance.

"I just think she looks beautiful," Oscar said.

"I know, but, there's something more. I just can't put my finger on it." I looked again at the bobbed hair, the color of ink. It reflected the light as it brushed her neckline. Thin, like me, but less angular, soft and round in places—the last vestiges of the childhood. They would fall away, far too soon.

The morning of her trip to Oscar's office, I helped Ellie dress and gave in to her demand to try on several dresses. She settled at last on what she deemed the perfect one, a dark green dress with cream trim. She liked contrasts, dark against light, and broad, simple washes of color. Together, we came down the stairs to where Oscar paced by the door. He had his pocket watch in his hand.

"You look lovely, Ellie. Very grown up." Ellie pivoted slowly, showing off all sides, making sure that Oscar saw the matching bow I had tied in the back. "Yes, yes, I see. You will be a big hit today."

Oscar pecked me on the cheek. I smiled after the pair as they reached the street and turned toward the station. Ellie skipped, tugging against Oscar's hand. Then, I turned to go to the kitchen alone.

German chocolate! That is what I would do. I would bake Ellie's favorite cake. She would want a reward after all day in an office with nothing to do but watch Oscar work. He'd find out how difficult a task it was to keep her engaged.

I imagined Ellie seated in a hard wooden chair across from Oscar's desk. She'd listen to him place phone calls, sit quietly as he made sums of long columns of figures, watch him write reports, and hear his pen scratch the page. I knew how tiresome that could be, but I also knew that Oscar would indulge her. He might, in fact, accomplish nothing at work while he let her swing her legs as she sat, rearrange the furniture to create a play space, or chatter on about an idea that had caught her fancy.

Ellie would charm them all. I pictured Oscar as he introduced her around, showed her off to everyone, Mrs. Waters, Oscar's secretary, even Henry Asner, his boss. Ellie would have a word, or several, for everyone. Mrs. Waters would exclaim, "How sweet." Mr. Asner would complement Ellie, "What a very pretty girl. A charmer. Just as you described her, Oscar."

Ellie would bask in the attention. Oscar would beam.

To my surprise, they returned by mid-afternoon. Ellie's singsong chatter betrayed her long before she came through the door. She laughed. Then, by the quick pattern of her steps, I knew she was running up the walk to the house.

"Mother, Mother! We're home from work. Mother!"

Ellie ran into my arms. I knelt to hug her.

"Look what I have." Ellie held a piece of stationery for me to see. She, or someone, had typed a few words on the page, and she had signed her name at the bottom, the loops of the *l*'s and the *e*'s in wide curves. "It's a letter. Mrs. Waters taught me how to type on the typewriters."

"Can you read it, Mother?" she said. She gestured to the words Ellie Wolf at the bottom. "I signed it right there."

"Yes, yes I can read it."

"She said I could come back any time I wanted. Isn't that right, Father?"

Oscar dropped his briefcase on the table. "Yes, that's right, Ellie. But, I think you have some more school to attend to before you can go to work."

"Home so early?" I said.

"I underestimated how quickly she might tire of the office. Thank goodness for Mrs. Waters. She entertained her most of the day."

"Ellie," I said, noticing she was still enamored with her typing handiwork, "You might want to check in the kitchen. There's a surprise waiting for you."

"Ooh. I'll bet it's German Chocolate." She ran to the kitchen. I followed behind and left Oscar in the front room where he could finish his work.

Ellie sliced into the cake.

"Here, let me help you. It's three layers. Very special, no?"

"Yes. It looks very good."

"Tomorrow, I'm going to bake a pie for the church bazaar. Won't that be fun? We can start early. You can help."

"But, Mother, I promised Marcy, I'd go see her," Ellie said as she took a seat at the kitchen table to eat her cake. Marcy was Ellie's best friend from school. "Remember?"

"Yes, of course. Well, maybe Saturday." I turned to put the cake under a tin.

"Maybe."

I glanced back at her over my shoulder. Ellie had a mouthful of cake, her face a blank slate.

A few days before Ellie's fifteenth birthday, Oscar arrived home before Ellie. Unlike in her earlier years when Ellie rushed home to share what she'd learned, Ellie now took her time making it home. Sometimes, she did not reach the house until three thirty, sometimes four. She'd linger to chat with her group of friends, boys and girls, who took the same route.

Oscar placed his things in the entryway. "Anneliese? Where are you?" He always called out my name, though he knew quite well I would be in the kitchen.

"In here, Oscar. In the kitchen," I said, the same as I did each time. "You're early. Is everything alright at the station?" I ran water over a handful of green beans fresh from the garden. Of late, he had an unending list of reasons to arrive home early. I wondered if the railroad had enough work for him. Times were better than they had been for years; so-called experts claimed the economic downturn, what everyone called the Great Depression, was over.

Oscar had sloughed off any mention of trouble through the darkest days while everyone else I knew worried about the security of their jobs. In the mornings, once Oscar left for the day, I'd read the newspaper he left behind. I knew some people had no work. But, in the past few weeks, the papers held glimmers of better times ahead. If there were even a hint of good news, it blared from the headlines. Even Oscar had said the railroad had managed through the latest difficulties. No one had lost their job.

Like most of the other families in town, we'd endured lean days, but we had never wanted for food or shelter. Even Ellie had understood the times. She made thrift a game. She reused scraps of spare cloth to create a new outfit, turned an old red coat that had become too short into a jacket and piped it with a length of red and black checkered trim I'd salvaged from a worn jacket of my own.

I dropped the beans into a colander to drain and turned off the faucet. I heard Oscar's steps and looked up from where I stood at the sink. As I did, the series of marks on the doorjamb caught my eye. Ellie had grown close to two inches in the last year.

Oscar came into the kitchen. He fingered the edge of an envelope in his vest pocket. "Hello, Anneliese. Yes, everything's fine. I wanted to beat Ellie home so that we could talk about her birthday." He removed the envelope and placed it on the counter, the L&N insignia clearly visible.

"What's this?"

"It's a surprise, for Ellie. I wanted to share it with you before she got home."

I dried my hands on my apron and picked up the envelope.

"Go ahead, open it."

Inside were three railroad tickets. Destination: St. Louis.

"What are these for?" I asked, though the answer was obvious. Ellie's birthday was a week away.

"Ellie's fifteenth birthday. You know, it won't be long before she grows up. Before she'd rather spend time with her friends. This might be one of the last chances we have to celebrate together."

"I think we have plenty of time. She's not going anywhere."

"Maybe so. I just thought we might surprise her with a trip. Just the three of us. What do you say?"

"I'm not sure." I pursed my lips and looked again at the words, St. Louis. I'd lost my ability to hide my feelings. Perhaps, I wanted them to show. The smile on Oscar's face faded as my eyebrows pulled close and forced a premature worry line on my forehead to deepen. Over the last few years, I'd seen the creases multiply in my mirror. "It's rather short notice."

"Short notice? Shucks Anneliese, we have a week. Besides, it's only to Saint Louis. We're not talking about going across the country. I want to tell her tonight at dinner, that's why I came home early. To let you know. So that we can tell her together. It's a gift from the two of us. To her." As my cool reception dampened his spirits, his words sputtered.

"I don't know."

"It will be fun. Remember our own trip to Saint Louis?"

The muscles in my jaw tightened.

"It's been so long since we've done something fun together. We've scrimped so much; I think it's high time we celebrate. We'll go to the zoo, the riverfront, and the art museums, and we'll take her shopping."

He was speaking more quickly than usual. Nervous, I thought. The list of activities he'd rattled off was a list of things I knew he'd wanted to do and see so many years before.

"You could have picked another destination."

"They were a gift from Henry. I wasn't about to complain."

"Well, I'll think about it. I've already invited Emma and Hannah to have dinner here with us."

"Yes, I know, but I thought we could do something Ellie'd like, something livelier. Let her experience something new. She can spend time with Emma and Hannah anytime."

"I'll think about it."

"My God, Liese." It was the tipping point. When he used the shortened version of my name, his patience had run out. He turned on his heels and left the room. I braced myself against the counter where I'd returned the envelope. The front door opened and then closed abruptly. He had not slammed the door, merely closed it firmly behind him.

I regretted not showing more enthusiasm. I hated surprises. Oscar knew that. It was one thing to surprise Ellie, another to do the same to me. It had not been a spur of the moment decision. He must have mentioned it days or weeks ago to Henry. Now, he'd accepted the tickets without thinking to ask me.

"Hello. Hello. I'm home." Ellie's voice practically sang from the front of the house. I placed a cookbook over Oscar's envelope.

Ellie came into the kitchen and crossed to the sink where I stood. I held out my cheek for her to give me a kiss as she did every time she came home. "Is there anything you need me to do now? If not, I'm going to my room to study."

"No, Ellie," I said, "that's fine, you can go. Supper will be ready at five."

Ellie turned to go and nearly collided into Oscar who'd returned quietly. "I'm going up to change, too," Oscar said. Without even a glance toward me, he grabbed Ellie around the shoulder and gave her a hug. The two linked arms and strode down the hall together.

I pulled a knife from the drawer and chopped the vegetables. I set aside the withered ends and sections damaged by insects, their brown-ringed holes pocked the beans here and there. The lid rattled over the pot of boiling water on the stove and drowned the jumble of words and laughter that echoed from the stairs. I lifted the lid and dropped the sliced beans into the pot.

Ellie pushed her chair back from the table. She reached across the table and stacked a few of the dishes. Oscar reached out and caught her by the arm, "Sit a minute more, dear."

Ellie took her seat again and eyed him suspiciously.

"You know you have a birthday coming up soon."

I put my fork and knife down on my empty plate. I could not look at Oscar or Ellie. I looked down at my lap.

"Of course I do. One more week. I've reminded you about it every day so you won't forget."

"We wouldn't dare forget," he said. "In fact, your mother and I wanted to surprise you. We're going to take you on a trip."

I knew what would come next. Ellie would burst with joy and Oscar would do everything he could to leverage her excitement, to persuade me to do what he wanted.

"A trip! Oh, my goodness! That would be wonderful. Where? When?"

I raised my head to watch the show. Ellie's mouth opened wide. She wanted to ask so many questions she didn't know where to start. She glanced back and forth, first at her father then at me.

Oscar pulled the envelope from his shirt pocket. He handed it to Ellie, who tore it open to reveal the three L&N tickets. She spread the tickets on the table in front of her. She squinted as she scanned the tiny print for the destination and departure date. "Saint Louis! Next weekend. Oh my. Oh won't Marcy be jealous. This is fabulous."

"Thank you, thank you, thank you," Ellie jumped up from the table. She spun around. Her skirt billowed out about her knees then fluttered back to cloak her slim legs. She circled the table, put her arms around my shoulders, and pecked me on the cheek, then ran around the table to do the same to Oscar. "Oh, my. I've got to think what I have to wear. I'll have to go see!"

"Clear the dishes, Ellie," I said, "Then you can go upstairs."

"Oh, yes. Sorry. I almost forgot."

Once she had disappeared into the kitchen, Oscar turned to me, "See how happy she is. I told you this would be a good thing to do."

"Well, I have plenty to do between now and then, if we're going to be ready."

"Everything will be fine. Don't go get all worked up. I'll help with whatever you need to do."

The packed suitcases sat side by side near the door on Thursday evening, ready for an early start on Friday. Ellie crouched near hers, scooting it from the line to the center of the floor as I watched from the parlor. She opened it and sorted through the neatly folded skirts, blouses, jackets. Two pairs of shoes were wedged along one side, toe to heel, to occupy the least space and leave room for more outfits.

"What are you doing now?" Oscar asked as he came down the stairs.

"I thought I would take my blue jacket instead of the gray one." Ellie removed the gray jacket, folded the blue one, and laid it in the suitcase. She ran her hands over the tops of the clothes again until they were smooth.

"Ellie, stop fussing, you have plenty of clothes in there already," I said. "We'll only be gone two days."

"I know. I know. But, I just can't make my mind up."

I rose from my chair. I couldn't bear to watch. On my right side, just above the waist, a muscle twinged. A sharp pain shot across my back. I grabbed my side. I took a step, paused to take a deep breath, and then took another. As I passed through the foyer, Ellie looked up from where she knelt. I turned away, but not before she'd had a chance to see the grimace on my face. I'd not made much attempt to disguise how I felt.

"Mother, you don't look very well. Are you sick? Are you coming down with something?"

"I don't know. I'm going upstairs to lie down."

"Oh, Mother, you can't be sick. We're leaving in the morning. Early in the morning. Let me help you. Maybe if you go to bed now...if you get a good night's sleep, you'll be fine in the morning."

"Maybe."

Ellie cupped my elbow in her hand as I climbed the stairs. She helped me find the side of the bed.

"It's alright, you go ahead now," I said.

I could not sleep and managed only to doze for an hour or so during the night. As the first rays of sun snuck through the blinds, the springs in Ellie's bed squeaked. Minutes later, I heard her tiptoe down the stairs. She tried, unsuccessfully, to muffle the click of latch on her suitcase as it snapped open. I guessed she was adding another item to her wardrobe for the weekend. The latched closed, softly.

She moved to the kitchen and soon the aroma of steaming coffee wound its way up the stairs. Oscar stirred in the bed beside me. He rose, dressed, and went downstairs. I did not move.

A few words of conversation flitted between them in the kitchen. "Happy birthday, Ellie. The coffee smells great."

"I'm so excited."

"Watch out, Father, you'll mess my hair."

Moments later, Ellie stood at the door to my bedroom. "Mother, you're not up yet! You've got to hurry or we'll be late." Ellie entered with a cup of coffee in her hand. She took delicate, ballerina like steps across the room, keeping her eye on the cup so as not to spill a drop.

"Thank you, Ellie. Put it on the nightstand, please. I don't think I can drink it right now."

"You must. You have to get up."

"I don't think so. I feel much worse than last night. I don't think I can even move."

"But, Mother..."

Ellie ran from the room. Her shoes clattered down the stairs. She called for her father, panic evident in her voice.

Oscar's heavier steps echoed up the stairwell. His steps were measured, evenly timed, methodical. I didn't turn toward him or lift the hand that shaded my eyes from the light. He'd stopped at the doorway and paused. A moment later, his steps clicked on the stairs.

Their voices were clear. I imagined they stood in the entryway below the stairs.

"I'm afraid your mother can't go with us. She's not feeling well. I told her I would not want to spoil your birthday so we'll go ahead. Just you and me."

"Oh, no. I'll go upstairs. I'll see if I can convince her to come. I'm sure she will, if I ask her."

"No, Ellie. She's probably already back asleep by now. It'll be better if she gets some rest."

"Will she be alright?"

"Yes, she'll be fine."

The discomfort in my side had bothered me several times over the last few months. I could not explain it and had not been to see a doctor, despite Oscar's repeated pleas. The pain left me nearly immobile for a day or two. Then it would disappear as quickly as it had come. Oscar accused me once of fabricating the spells, of using them to manipulate circumstances that were not going my way. Blessed with a marvelous constitution, he could not fathom my condition.

"Your mother said she would call Hannah if she needed something." Then, he added, with a particularly cheerful tone, "She said she wanted you to go ahead and go and have the best birthday ever. And not to worry. Come. Let's get our luggage."

"Well, we'll bring her something, a souvenir," Ellie said, her mood sounding brighter already. They exited the house and closed the door behind them. My lone suitcase remained behind, standing upright just inside the door.

I propped myself up in bed and watched as Oscar and Ellie walked from the house, a suitcase in each of their hands. Perched atop Ellie's head was the tiniest of felt hats, a light gray that accentuated her dark hair. Her handbag and shoes bore the exact same shade of gray. Impeccably dressed, as always.

I sank back onto the bed.

In the two days they were gone, I left my bed only long enough to take a hot bath or warm a bowl of soup. The pain subsided on Sunday. I dressed and made my way downstairs, determined to greet them with a smile when they returned. I vowed to ask a hundred questions about the trip.

Ellie bounded through the doorway at five o'clock. Oscar trailed behind, the suitcases in his hands.

"Mother, look. Look. What do you notice?"

"I notice that you are now older. Fifteen, I'd say." I took her in my arms and hugged her close.

Ellie pulled away. "No, not that. Look. Closer." She tilted her head in my direction and raised both hands beside her head with a flourish.

"I suppose that's a new hat?" The pale blue cloche sat at a jaunty angle on her head. It covered her hair but allowed her dark eyes to peer from below its brim. How modern it looked, how mature an appearance it lent her.

"Yes, Father let me buy it. It was a present for my birthday. And, from one of the grandest of shops."

Oscar entered. He paused a moment, glanced at the two of us as we chatted about Ellie's latest clothing acquisition, then continued up the stairs with his suitcase.

Ellie paused, looked quizzically at his back as he disappeared and then at me.

"So, what did you see? Tell me," I drew her attention away from the vacuum of his greeting.

"Gosh, I don't know where to start. We took the streetcar. We went to an exhibit at the art museum. Best of all, we saw a baseball game. The St. Louis Cardinal's in Sportsman's Park...."

She recounted the events in detail. I paid attention enough to confirm they'd not taken a riverboat cruise—the one promise I had extracted from Oscar when I'd agreed to the trip. Oscar returned in a few minutes. He held a small box covered in gold paper in his outstretched hand.

"For you, Anneliese," he said. "You are feeling better, I hope."

"I am now, thank you." I nodded and took the gold box of chocolates from him. Oscar bent close and kissed me on the cheek.

We fell back into our routine quickly. Monday, Ellie went back to school, Oscar to work, and me to my housework. Not until the following Friday, when I put away the laundry did I discover a second box of chocolates at the back of one of the drawers in Oscar's highboy, the topmost.

·

CHAPTER 21
Affairs of the Head and Heart

I don't think Oscar had planned to be unfaithful. Initially, in fact, I think he had gone out of his way to avoid contact with Louisa. Miss Louisa Barnes had come to Evansville from New York. She came with high recommendations. The Evansville School System hired her to teach music to students in the ninth through twelfth grades but had had to acquiesce to Louisa's demand to institute a formal, comprehensive arts program at Central High School and to allow her to oversee the program.

Louisa, schooled in dance, had once performed in a professional dance troop in New York. She had the body of a ballerina, slim and petite, no taller than Ellie, even though Louisa was now in her mid-thirties. Word of her arrival in Evansville wound along its circuitous, mouth-to-mouth route, as it would have in any small town.

No one, though, knew the whole of Louisa's story.

Members of my quilting circle speculated on the single woman's past at nearly every meeting. One afternoon, Emma said, "I heard that Miss Barnes was sent off to live with her grandmother in New York before she was even five years old. No one seems to know why since her mother and father stayed behind here in Evansville."

Molly, always with an ear to the ground, continued, "I heard she performed on stage in Vaudeville. And, what's more, that she managed to get there through her connections, not her talent." Molly raised an eyebrow and paused before and after the word "connections".

"They say she married the owner of a theater in New York," someone else twittered.

Other rumors made the rounds, each one building on the last. Depending on who did the telling, the embellishments grew more fantastic, more romantic, or more squalid. The details were murky. In one version, she had left her husband, in another, he had left her. Whether there had been a divorce or not, no one knew. Some said she returned to Evansville to care for her widowed mother who died within six months of Louisa's return. The more charitable of the women who indulged in speculation about Louisa insisted she'd come back to bring a much needed bit of culture to Evansville.

Ellie had attended Miss Barnes' music classes since the start of the school year in 1935 when she had entered the ninth grade. She learned later that Miss Barnes also taught classes in art and theater after hours on an invitation only basis. They required special permission. Miss Barnes had extended an invitation to Ellie, though how our daughter's interests in these arts had come to the woman's attention, we could only guess. Even we had not known of her penchant for the theater.

Oscar and I met with Louisa to give our permission for Ellie's participation in the program.

"Ellie has a natural gift for the arts, especially painting. Does someone else in the family paint or perhaps sing or dance?" Louisa asked.

Oscar did not wait for me to volunteer. He knew I would not mention my musical abilities, or, if I did, that I would make light of them.

"Ah ha, I thought so. There usually is an obvious source for the talent. I do hope you encourage Ellie to pursue her interests, whichever of the arts she chooses." Louisa smiled and looked at both of us for concurrence.

We nodded.

"If you agree, I would like to extend an invitation to her to attend my evening classes. I tutor a group of girls about her age. Only the more serious students, of course. Those with promise."

We nodded again.

"I think Ellie could benefit from the personal instruction."

We'd already discussed the demands the classes would place on Ellie. Now, we assured Miss Barnes that Ellie could manage the additional work. We gave our permission. We committed Ellie to a roster of evening classes at Louisa's home for the remainder of the school year.

When Ellie returned from the first class, and after almost every one that followed, she recounted highlights of the session throughout dinner. Invariably, she added details about Louisa. "Louisa did this," or "Louisa said that". Ellie had acquired a nearly inexhaustible list of Louisa doings and sayings. She would talk of nothing else for days. Though we were delighted with the interest she expressed, every day we reminded Ellie to pay as much attention to her in-school courses as her evening arts classes.

Oscar and I also saw Miss Barnes a number of other times during the school year. We participated in the school's fundraiser for the arts—one that Louisa chaired—and later attended a few musical performances she orchestrated. I don't remember Oscar ever seeing her without me during that time.

In the late fall, with its shorter days, the evening classes concluded well after dark. Although Louisa lived less than a mile away, I did not like the thought of Ellie, even now at fifteen years old, walking home alone. We agreed to share the responsibility to meet Ellie after class and escort her home. I handled the task whenever Oscar's work kept him late or away from home.

One evening in mid-February 1936, I'd thought I had made it clear to Oscar that I would pass by Miss Barnes home to escort Ellie. As I rounded the corner to Louisa's home, Oscar stood on the porch at the door to her home, his hat in his hand. I thought I'd join him so the three of us could walk home together. I rushed ahead a few steps. As I opened my mouth to call out to Oscar, the door opened a crack. A woman's arm emerged, a bare arm, pale under the porch light. With the grace of a dancer, the arm reached for Oscar's elbow and, in a single fluid motion, pulled him into the house.

The blood drained from my head. My own arm, raised as it had been when I'd thought to call out, remained frozen in place, awkwardly. I imagined I bore a striking resemblance to the commemorative sculpture of an American doughboy calling to his comrades in Evansville's town center. My feet, like his, were leaden and locked to the sidewalk. I remained in that position and watched the two through the window of the softly lit parlor. As Oscar's arms encircled Louisa's waist, she turned and drew the curtains.

I lowered my arm and ambled slowly back home. I'd walked those blocks numerous times, but tonight, after I'd come about halfway back, I found I'd made a few wrong turns, leaving me several blocks east of our home. Dazed, I searched up and down the block for a familiar home, a familiar street sign. Oak Street the sign at the end of the block read. I'd come four blocks from where I should have turned for home. I covered them rapidly now, eager to see familiar things, familiar faces, desperate to be safe at home.

Ellie and Oscar arrived a half hour later. She carried a plate of cookies with her. "Miss Barnes baked these for us. There were so many left and she said, seeing how much Daddy likes them, I should take them home."

"That was very kind of her," I said. I took the plate of sweets into the kitchen. "I'll be sure to return the dish next week."

On Thursday morning, before Oscar and Ellie came downstairs I discarded the last three coconut macaroons into the waste bin and cleaned the plate.

Later, at breakfast, I said, "Oscar, I'll meet Ellie after class today. I can thank Louisa for the cookies and return her plate." I forced myself to maintain a matter of fact tone, with a slightly cheerful note.

"It's really no trouble," Oscar said. "I can swing by on my way home. I won't be late."

"That's quite alright. I can use a few minutes of fresh air. I'll do it."

I was determined to see that Oscar had as few chances to do whatever he did with Miss Barnes. For two days, the image of Oscar and Louisa had played continuously in my head. It invaded every moment of my day and would not leave me in peace. Each time, I'd forced myself to say it was nothing. After all, Ellie and the other students were there, even if they might be in the studio at the back of the house.

After Ellie had left for school and Oscar for work, I gathered the courage to satisfy my suspicions. I searched Oscar's dresser, the topmost drawer—the one I needed a footstool to access. I probed the back of the drawer with my fingertips. It held nothing more than his socks, rolled into neat bundles, arranged in rows as straight as railroad tracks. The second box of gold-wrapped chocolates was not there. Nor was it in any of the other drawers.

Months later, Ellie arrived home from school with an uncharacteristic frown on her face. She flopped into the chair in the kitchen.

I ignored her. Ellie was always more forthcoming if not prodded. "Um, good," I said. I dipped a large wooden spoon into the pot of chicken noodle soup on the stove. I drew out another spoonful. "Here, taste this."

"I don't want any."

"It's delicious, look how golden—why, Ellie, what's wrong?" Tears welled in Ellie's eyes.

"It's Miss Barnes."

I turned my back to her and poured the unwanted spoonful of soup back into the pot. "What about Miss Barnes?"

"She told us she's leaving. Leaving Evansville."

"Really? Why would she do that? She hasn't been here a whole year. When is she going?"

"I don't know why. She just said she would finish out the year and then she would be going. Back to New York, I think."

"I'm sorry to hear that," I said. I didn't bother to add a hint of regret in my voice.

Oscar arrived. As he did every day, he pinched Ellie's cheek as he entered the room.

"Why so glum, sweetheart?"

"Ellie's just been telling me her bad news," I said. I stopped short of explaining. I wanted Ellie to deliver the news. I wanted to be free to observe Oscar's reaction.

"It's Miss Barnes. She's going to leave at the end of the year."

"Ah, yes, so I heard," Oscar said without hesitation.

"You had?" I said. "Wherever would you have heard that? I had no idea until just now when Ellie mentioned it."

"I don't know. I just heard it. What does it matter?"

CHAPTER 22

Girls, Boys, and Nature

Floods were a frequent occurrence in the Midwest, home to both the Ohio and the Missouri rivers. Earlier in the century, a disastrous storm had ravaged Indiana, earning its aftermath the moniker "The Great Flood". Most of the damage, though, had occurred in mid-state, near Indianapolis, long before our daughter and her friend Marcy had been born.

The extreme cold that blanketed Evansville over the winter of 1936 abated in mid-January 1937. Temperatures rose into the thirties, almost a cause for celebration, until it began to rain. It rained for days. Everyone was confined indoors, which to me was hardly an inconvenience. I filled the hours reading, sewing, or baking. Ellie, however, could not sit in one place for long. She rambled from room to room, unable to find anything to occupy her. She paced around the front room. One circuit, she passed my chair and sighed. Two circuits. Oscar set the newspaper aside and left the room. Three. Four. Accustomed to Ellie's restlessness, I ignored her for as long as I could. On her next circuit of the room, I put my embroidery aside. Ellie's frustration had exhausted my patience.

"Ellie, I know it's still raining, but…" I pulled the curtains aside and peered at the steady stream of drops that fell from the edge of the roof, "do you think you could run an errand for me? The rain may have let up a little." It hadn't.

She'd sped to the hallway to find her rain gear, a "Yes, Yes" floated in the air behind her.

I could have managed a few more days without the sundries, but it would give Ellie something to do. I rose and went to the kitchen. From the second shelf of the cupboard, I grabbed the glass jar where I kept spare change. I counted out three dollars in fifty-cent pieces and quarters. More than enough for eggs and butter. I expected her to spend the extra cash on something for herself.

Ellie stuffed my short list and the handful of coins into one of the pockets of her raincoat. "Is it alright if I go by Marcy's and see if she wants to go with me? It will only be a few extra blocks. I can still be back in an hour."

"Of course, just be careful."

She hadn't gone two blocks from home when thunder cracked overhead. The rain pounded against the roof. Instantly, I regretted having let her go.

Four hours passed with no sign of Ellie. I took up her earlier agitation. I paced back and forth across the front room and hallway.

"Maybe, I should go after her?" I mused aloud. "Where is she?"

"Anneliese, the girl is almost seventeen. She'll be fine. Call the Blake's if you like. I'm sure the girls are there. I'll wager they've forgotten all about your groceries."

Then, as I passed the front window again, she was there, skipping up the walk. Unconcerned about the rain, she splashed in the water pooled in the low spot in the front walk.

I met her at the door. "Where have you been, I was so worried?"

"Oh, Mother. I'm sorry. Marcy and I went by the movie theater on the way back from the grocer. We wanted to see what was playing. And, well...we ran into Clark."

"Clark?"

"He's a friend from school. He works there on the weekends."

"Well you should have let me know. You said you'd only be gone an hour."

"I know. I'm sorry. But, you won't believe it—since there was no one at the theater, Clark let us come in and watch him set up for the afternoon show. We got to go inside the projector room. It was so interesting." She drew out the "so" for emphasis.

"A fine thing that is. You gallivanting around with a young man."

"I wasn't gallivanting around. Besides Marcy was with me. We just stopped by for a few minutes." Ellie handed me the package of groceries and then hung her wet coat in the hallway.

"Harrumph," I said. The paper sack, crumpled and wet, sagged in my hand. It was only minutes from spilling its contents.

When I emptied the sack on the kitchen counter, I found a magazine along with my eggs and butter. I unrolled Ellie's purchase on the counter. Wallis Simpson's face stared at me from the cover, her head perched on her hands, her long fingers tipped with dark polish.

Ellie padded into the kitchen in her bare feet. "I almost forgot my magazine," she said as she plucked it from the counter. I looked around in time to see her scoot out the door, a Wallis Simpson-like scarlet polish on her fingers and toes.

As I stowed the eggs and butter in the icebox, Ellie popped her head back in through the door. "Oh, yes. I forgot. Mrs. Smith said to tell you there's a flood warning. If the rain doesn't let up, she said the Ohio is supposed to come out of its banks by tomorrow."

The flood of 1937 superseded all earlier records.

The snow had come earlier than usual, the first flurries in October. And then, since the onset of winter, a heavier than normal snowfall contributed to the extreme conditions. Plows worked overtime throughout December and January to keep the streets passable. In some parts of the city, mountains of snow stood as high as eight feet. In the outskirts, drifts of a heavy mix of snow and mud clogged the roads. Travel was perilous, if not impossible.

We waited for the temperatures to moderate, as they did each winter about this time. This year, however, during the hiatus in the cold, it rained without stopping for twenty-four days. Some days, we had a light mist, others a deluge as intense as a monsoon, or what I believed a monsoon must be, never having been to India or wherever I'd read they had monsoons.

The Green River, emanating from Kentucky grew in force until it crossed over into the Ohio and flooded the lower reaches of the center of Evansville. The grade of the main road south of town deflected and spread the water across a broad expanse. It muted the current's force, for a while.

Everyone had something to say about the weather; it made the headlines of the *Evansville Courier* daily. At first, no one expressed any undue alarm. Evansville had had its share of floods before. The riverbanks provided a measure of protection, rising steadily from the river basin to the higher ground in the center of town. Wanting to do even more to protect its citizens, years ago, the city had taken additional precautions, raising the banks to protect the most flood-prone areas.

During the last, but much less severe, flood five years earlier, we'd taken in Uncle Paul and Aunt Dora for a period. We were not alone then or now. Almost every one of our neighbors had relatives from the rural areas with them, whether cousins, aunts, uncles, sisters, or brothers. Evansville's population swelled. Paul and Dora brought their two grandchildren to stay with us on First Avenue. The adults moved into the spare room downstairs and the two young girls, Margaret and Bess, several years younger than Ellie, slept on makeshift beds in Ellie's room. Mina and Nathan, their parents, elected to stay at the farm unless conditions worsened. The farmhouse sat on a slight rise. It was habitable for the shortfall.

"We've got a lot of work to do," Mina had said. "We've rolled up the carpets and set our belongings on top of the dining room table. Just in case."

Oscar had volunteered to help, but Nathan said they had things in hand. "We can manage the things around the house. There's nothing we can do for the livestock. Just hope and pray."

Oscar and I had checked on a few friends outside town earlier in the week. To our astonishment, the barren fields were unrecognizable; low-lying expanses had become ponds. When we had started out, the roads looked like nothing more than two long canals where there had been tire ruts for as far as I could see. On our way home, though we had not been gone for long, on several bypasses, the canals had disappeared. They'd merged and engulfed the road in one uninterrupted expanse of water between the banks of snow along the roadside.

After several days in the crowded house, Ellie offered to stay with Marcy's family. "Mother, if I go stay with her, there'll be more room for everyone. And, I can help the Blakes."

"Oh, I don't know if that is such a good idea, Ellie. You've got your school work and..."

"Marcy said the whole first floor of the main building is covered with water." Central High sat on a city block in one of the lower lying sections of town. "School is canceled, for next week anyway." She grinned. "It won't be—"

A child's scream punctured the air. Bess ran through the room. In a second, her sister Margaret followed.

"Shush, Bess, shush. Stop running." Dora tried to quiet the two when they skidded into the kitchen.

"Alright," I said, relenting. I wondered how much more of the chaos I could endure. "Just until Saturday evening." Crowded together, chock-a-block, for the last week, I thought we'd all benefit from a bit of added breathing room.

"Before dinner time on Saturday," Oscar said, "I'll come get you at the Blakes to walk you home."

Ellie sprang to life and bounced up the stairs. "I'll go put some things together then. Thank you, thank you."

"If there's any trouble, Oscar will come fetch you. Do not walk home alone," I called after her.

"Yes, ma'am. I won't. I promise." Ellie's voice disappeared above me.

Saturday, I stopped to count. Three days and two nights.

On Friday, the water rose again. This time it flooded the entire downtown. The water rushed over the riverfront, the lowest part of town, and then washed into the lower lying districts south of the center of town, a ten by five block area. The area contained numerous commercial buildings, the library, a bank, countless shops, the theater, and the high school.

Oscar came in from a walk around the area to check on the damage. I met him at the front door. He tipped his hat and drained a cup of water from the brim before he came inside.

"Everything west of here is flooded," he said.

"What about the Blake's," I asked.

"I didn't get over there, but they're on high ground. I think they're out of danger for the moment. Nothing's for sure though."

We read the warnings of the potential for additional flooding in the paper the next day. The city's original forecasts were for the river to crest at ten feet above flood stage. The water surpassed that level by Friday evening.

At noon on Saturday, though dense gray clouds covered the sky, the rain stopped. I learned later from Mrs. Blake that Marcy and Ellie took advantage of the break in the weather to explore the waterlogged streets. Mrs. Blake let them go, an act I could never forgive.

"I insisted they take raincoats as a precaution," she said. "Their own coats were still damp from being out earlier, so I scoured my closet for dry ones. Marcy took a gray coat and Ellie a green and blue plaid." She paused and looked at the corner of the room as if she saw something or someone there. "I remember Ellie saying the blue in the plaid matched the skirt she wore."

I had ventured out as well that Saturday morning. Only minutes from the house, a number of neighbors joined me. They emerged from their houses, one by one, and blinked in the sunlight that broke through the clouds.

The girls had stopped at Hollingsworth Drugs, Clark told us later. He and Victor, another of Ellie's friends from Central High, had been freeing a boat underneath Hollingworth's crawlspace when the girls spotted them. "It was really just a dinghy. We put it in the water down by Westchester where the water was deep enough to float. I should have known better. When all four of us were aboard, it sat pretty low in the water."

Ellie had mentioned Clark's name several times over the days and weeks before the flood. I imagined the girls couldn't resist joining the young boys, following them on their adventure.

At half past three in the afternoon, the roadbed of US 41 South, that had until that point held back the bulk of the water, disintegrated. The collapse allowed a torrent of water to flow into areas that had so far escaped the flood. The event caused a wave of rushing water to speed through the eastern arm of the crescent that defined Evansville. Water gushed along the top of the horseshoe-shaped bend and into the city center.

The front of the one hundred-yard wide wave collided against the sides of the buildings in its path. It forced windows or doors that had withstood earlier flooding to give way. Later, the authorities estimated that the water had peaked at sixty and in some places eighty or more feet above normal.

These details came later. First, there were young people howling in the street.

By early afternoon on Saturday, Oscar and I had collapsed into two chairs in the kitchen. We'd forgotten how active young children were and we'd expended all our energy corralling Margaret and Bess as they careened through the house.

"What's that?" Dora said. She heard the commotion in the street before anyone else heard a thing.

CHAPTER 23

Ten Perfect Toes

It was raining again, nearly sideways this time. Drops pinged against the kitchen window.

"Mrs. Wolf, Mrs. Wolf!" A boy's voice. Out in the street. "Help. Help!"

By the time I reached the front door, neighbors had gathered outside along the street. They watched as the two young friends stumbled to my gate. Through the glass panes in the door, I recognized Marcy, despite the fact she looked like a wet seal, more animal than human. Her hair lay slick, plastered against her head, her clothes a tangle of matted fabric.

I backed away. I retreated to the alcove.

Dora came from the kitchen, circled around me to open the door. "No," I said. "No." I did not want her to open the door. I did not want to let the young people in. I did want the words they carried with them into my house.

Marcy and Victor tumbled into the foyer, breathless. Victor doubled over, placed his hands on his knees, and tried to catch his breath. Marcy rubbed her hands up and down her arms to absorb the warmth of the house. She did not look at me.

The commotion brought the shy Stephens children, Margaret and Bess, out of the kitchen. They stood half-hidden, one blonde head above the other peered around the arch of the alcove.

In the kitchen, something fell. A thwack from a chair back as it hit the floor. A crash of china splintered, perhaps with the remains of a cup of cocoa spreading across the rug. Paul and Oscar appeared, at once, side by side. Oscar wiped a stain in his pants. Splotches of brown, muddy water dotted the white napkin in his hand.

"Marcy," Victor said. "Tell them..."

"Mrs. Wolf. It's Ellie." Marcy gasped for another breath then continued. "She's gone. She's gone. We looked everywhere for her." The words tumbled from her mouth.

"Slow down, Marcy. What's going on? What's happened?" Oscar asked, his tone even. His words came slowly, measured, as if he unwound them from a spool.

As the foyer filled with people, the confusion multiplied. Dora understood and retreated. She took the two young children by the shoulders and herded them back into the front room. Oscar took a position between Victor and Marcy, one hand on Victor's shoulder, the other on Marcy's.

I remained in the alcove between the two rooms. My hands gripped the molding for support, my knuckles as white as the paint on the trim. Oscar raised his head and looked at me. I shook my head; I refused to come closer. I refused to take part in the scene in the foyer. I refused to make sense of the words Marcy repeated. My own voice stuck in my throat. My own words sank back into my heart.

"Slow down," Oscar said. "Take a breath." He wanted to hear. He didn't know what I knew. "Tell us what happened. How did you get so wet? Where is Ellie? Why isn't she with you?"

"Mr. Wolf," Victor said, "let me explain. Marcy and Ellie...and Clark...We took Mr. Hollingsworth's boat to see the flood. It was calm when we started out. It wasn't even raining. We thought... we didn't think it would—"

"It tipped over and we all fell into the water," Marcy interrupted. "We looked and looked." Marcy sobbed again and could not continue.

"A huge rush of water came at us just as we were coming back," Victor said, picking up from Marcy. "It tipped the boat. Marcy said Ellie couldn't swim. She just disappeared. Clark went to the police to get help."

Oscar knew now. He didn't wait for Victor to finish. Instead, he launched into a frenzy of motion, grabbed his hat and coat from the hallstand, found a wool scarf to wrap around his neck, and picked up a pair of boots. He took charge, organizing his resources and issuing instructions to the group. "Okay, Anneliese, Dora, you take care of Marcy. Get her into some dry clothes and then walk her home. Paul, can you come with me? We may need all the help we can find."

Paul hurried back to the spare room to grab his coat. When he returned, he and Oscar slipped on waterproof boots. Oscar glanced at me. He opened his mouth. I didn't know whether he wanted to offer some words of comfort, hollow words as he and I both knew, or whether he wanted to issue another instruction. He must have thought better of it as he stopped and tugged on his boots.

"Victor," Oscar said, "grab a dry coat. You'll have to take us back to where you were."

The three left the house on a run. Victor led the way.

Dora shut the door after them and took Marcy back to the kitchen. I heard a chair scrape across the floor as my aunt righted whatever Oscar must have toppled. Dora told Marcy to remove her wet clothes.

"I'll fetch some dry things from Ellie's room. Then, we'll walk you home. This is just dreadful, but I'm sure that Oscar and Paul will find her safe and sound."

"Oh no, Mrs. Stephens," Marcy said. "She's gone. I know it." Her sobs surfaced again.

"Now there, you sit here a moment. I'll go get a towel so you can dry off and I'll get some dry clothes. I'll be right back. Don't move."

Dora called my name when she saw me in the alcove. "Liese?" I didn't answer and she continued up the stairs.

Though my eyes were open, fixed on a spot a few feet in front of me, I saw nothing. My hands clutched the doorframe. They hurt from being in one place so long. They were numb. My lips were dry, my throat parched. There had been a commotion earlier, but now silence cloaked the house. To clear the thoughts cartwheeling in my head, I took in a long, deep breath, then another. I straightened my back and lifted my head.

Dora called my name.

"I'll be alright, Dora. Please tend to Marcy for me, will you?" I loosened my grip on the doorframe.

"Of course. I was just going to give her these dry things. Then I'll walk her home. I'll take the children with me. They could use some air." I nodded slowly, my head bobbed up then down, then up again. I wondered if I had the will to stop.

As soon as Marcy and the children were ready, Dora herded them quietly out the front door. "Margaret," she said to her eldest grandchild, "you take Bessie's hand and go along in front." As she closed the door, Dora glanced at me through the crack. I looked away. I waited until the door had closed and she had gone down the walk and turned toward Marcy's home.

Alone. If everyone left me alone, I thought, I could sort things out. I could make sense of what had happened. I could think through what I had heard and put the pieces together, like a jigsaw puzzle. When I completed the picture, everything would be as it should have been.

My twin eyed me from the hall mirror. I saw a lock of gray hair had escaped from the tortoise shell clasp behind her ear. I said to her, "You should get going. You should bake something."

"How about a warm apple pie to welcome her home?"

"That's it. I'll surprise Ellie. Of course, it won't be a surprise for long, she'll know as soon as she opens the door and smells the apples in the oven."

I went to the kitchen, leaving my twin in the hallway. I filled the house with sound. Cabinet doors clattered. *Creak*. One opened. *Bang*. One shut. *Clang*. One pan collided with another on the counter. *Ching*. A mixing spoon chimed as I tossed it into the sink. The house breathed life and drowned out the silence. I welcomed the rush of warm air that filled the room as I checked the oven's temperature. I pulled spice tins from the shelf. I inhaled the scent of cinnamon and tasted the salt of unshed tears. I filled the metal sifter with flour, added a pinch of sugar, then cranked the handle, around and around.

The pie had cooled completely. Dusk had fallen but I had not turned on any lights. I'd set three plates and three forks on the table and sat down to wait for Oscar and Ellie.

When the door opened, I counted the steps. I judged the number of pairs of footfalls. Oscar entered the kitchen. He took a seat. Water ran down the rain-soaked coat and dripped onto the floor. He did not move. The drops on the floor grew into small pools.

I did not take my eyes off his face. His emotions played out, sorrow, anger, regret, resolution, but not acceptance. Not yet. Then, he removed his hat and dropped it on the table. I rose and went behind his chair to help him with his coat. Rather than carry the coat back to the hallway, I laid the coat across the chair next to him. I did not want to leave him alone. He might say something about what had happened whether or not anyone listened.

"We could not find her."

He stopped. A few minutes passed, or perhaps it was only seconds. I didn't want to ask him for more. I feared on the one hand he would say nothing, on the other that he would tell me everything. Things I might not want to know.

"Sheriff Allen said they had rescued two other people already this morning. He said we would be able to find her. He, Deputy Elmer, Clark and I took two boats and paddled out to the high school. The water is deepest there. Clark said they'd taken their boat in through the main doorway on Court Street and when they were coming back out a wave of water pushed their boat against the wall. They tipped over. Only Victor managed to stay in the boat.

"The whole first floor was flooded. Easily seven or eight feet deep."

"Maybe Ellie made it to the second floor?"

"I looked. We called her name. A dozen times. More. She couldn't have heard us though. The water was sloshing around. There was lots of debris, broken bits of furniture, other things. Sheriff Allen steered our boat to the staircase in the center of the building and I jumped out. I went upstairs. I called again, but there was no answer, no one there. I checked all the classrooms."

"Well, maybe the library down the block. Maybe the..."

"You don't understand," he said. "There aren't blocks any more. There aren't streets. It's just one huge river. It's too dark now. We have to wait."

"We can't wait. We have to go try again."

"I'm telling you, Liese, it's no use now." At that, Oscar rose from the table, grabbed his raincoat, and disappeared down the hall.

Two weeks elapsed before the floodwaters receded to levels where streets became recognizable again, even if layers of mud and debris now coated them instead of rushing water. I walked into town to see what remained of the familiar landscape. In places, the river had taken every manmade item with it and left only a muddy expanse, rippled by the receding water. Elsewhere, whether kinder or not, it had left shells of buildings devoid of belongings that had not been secured in upper stories or shielded by interior walls.

On the outskirts of town, livestock meandered across fenceless fields. Some scoured the pavement or unfamiliar snow and mud covered ground for food. They nosed at the few strands of grass, flattened but still clinging to life. Others drowned. Bloated with water, they lay on their sides. They decomposed in the mud. Sheriff Allen, his deputy, and teams of volunteers spent days rounding up the animals. They moved them to fenced pastures the river had spared to wait until some semblance of normality returned.

Day after day, Oscar rose early and joined Paul, Clark, and Victor, together with Sheriff Allen or Deputy Elmer when they could spare the time to check the area near the school. They slogged through the mud as they searched the area surrounding the school. Several teams had shoveled mud from around the buildings at the center of town. They had started with the public facilities, and then made their way from the hospital, to the post office, to the schools.

I'd go to the edge of Central High every morning where the volunteers cleared away the mud. I watched them shovel. My eyes could detect the slightest change in the activity. I knew when they found something. They would gather in one place. Their motions would slow. I'd hold my breath. Then, they'd toss a broken chair leg, or a book, or the lid of a desk onto a pile of debris. Other volunteers worked the debris pile. They filled wheelbarrows and carts then carried the debris away, to where I didn't know. I'd take another breath and wait for another sign.

It was Clark who found Ellie. She had eluded them until the work neared completion. When she'd fallen into the water, the current had grabbed hold of her and swept her behind one of the school's massive wooden doors. In the ensuing days, there, in the space behind the door, the river had deposited a pocket of black mud four feet deep. Clark said he and another volunteer, Ben Adler, had just freed the door when he caught sight of a patch of plaid in the mud.

Ben yelled for help. Several volunteers rushed to where the boys stood. The commotion caught my attention and beckoned me closer. I stumbled over mounds of sodden dirt and debris. I did not care that my shoes sank in the mud or that my coat dragged in the mud as I picked my way forward.

Ben dropped to the ground beside Clark. He clawed the mud with his hands.

"Careful, careful," Clark said, his voice cracking, barely audible. Then, he made a sound, not a cry, not a scream, just a sound. His hands went to his face. He sat back on his heels.

I pushed my way to the side of the doorway and looked into the pile of dark sludge. Ellie's black hair still tied behind her head but matted with mud was easily identifiable, as was her slender body. No matter how careful they were now, nothing could undo the damage. They resumed digging, more slowly now, gently. They caressed the earth around her as they freed her from its grasp. When her body lay exposed, Clark covered her upper torso with his jacket then slumped forward and held his head in his hands.

Ellie's legs and feet lay before me. The river had taken her shoes and left her feet bare. The skin around her ankles was swollen and splotched, even black in places. On her toenails, chipped red polish gleamed in the sun like a string of rubies.

Part Seven:
Anneliese

CHAPTER 24

One River, Two Lives

I should not have been surprised that the river defined my life, per-
haps as much or more than Oscar did. After all, I was born within
sight of the Ohio. I believe someday, too, my life will end there, in
Evansville, on the north side of the river where, having flowed along
one side of the finger of land that juts from Kentucky into Indiana,
the Ohio makes an abrupt turn before heading back southward. Ex-
cept for that brief sojourn to Saint Louis, I've never been far from it.
I've witnessed each sunrise, breathed each breath, and walked each
step of my life along the hairpin curve in the river.

* * *

The flood spared our house on First Avenue, though it might as
well have swept it clean or carried it away. Oscar and I carried on.
We meandered through the rooms each day, along the distinct
but separate paths we claimed for ourselves as though the river
had carved a deep chasm between its halves.

The kitchen and the garden were mine. Oscar owned the front
room and the veranda where he'd read and the upstairs bedroom
where we slept, together but alone.

Whether Oscar came downstairs early or late, breakfast waited
for him on the dining room table. I would have already eaten, if I
had an appetite for anything at all. Often, once he had eaten and

put his plate in the sink, he carried his cup of coffee to the back door and stared through the panes of rippled, lead-lined glass into the garden.

Sometimes, when in the garden, whether I was planting, weeding, pruning, or harvesting fresh vegetables, depending on the season, I'd sense Oscar's presence and turn to see him through the glass of the kitchen door. He would nod then turn away. I'd find his empty cup in the sink beside the other dishes, the remains of his coffee in a brown circle at the bottom.

Today, I sat crouched near a bed of dahlias, a few I'd cut lay on the ground beside me in perfect alignment, their stems shorn of leaves. The flowers were for Ellie's room. I kept a vase of fresh flowers there, full with whatever bloomed in the garden. I took pleasure in arranging them on the nightstand beside her bed. If I had finished my other chores around the house, I might take my Bible to her room and read from it in the bright light that flooded through the upper-story windows.

In the weeks after she had drowned, I would lie down on the bed, run my hands over the coverlet, sink my nose into the pillow, and inhale the last of her scent. Until it, too, vanished.

I laid another dahlia beside the group of cut flowers, gathered the bunch in my hand and examined them from several angles. I imagined them in a vase, the one with a pattern of strands of ivy running its length. I returned them to the ground, aligned them again in a precise row, then turned to pull some weeds. I worked at a leisurely pace, whether here in the garden or in the kitchen, without concern for the time. In truth, I lost myself in whatever task I performed as if it were my only occupation, as if there were no other chore calling, as if the day would last forever. As they sometimes did.

In those first few months after Ellie's death, Oscar accompanied me to Zion Evangelical as he had nearly every Sunday since we'd married. Though Augustus' preaching style had not changed, merely being in the church, among the oiled pews and colored light that filtered from the stained glass Augustus had installed, revived my spirits. I left with a sense of calm and more accepting of our circumstances, better able to carry on with the small, commonplace, and meaningless tasks that filled my life—at least I felt that way for one or two days. Then with each day that followed over the course of the week, the clouds would roll back in, first one white cotton speck in the sky, then two or three, then a sky full, darker and more ominous.

Oscar found no solace in the church. He dealt with his loss by thrusting headlong into his work, whether it comforted him or not. Often, he stayed at the office long after the other managers, agents, and clerks had left for the day. I remarked one evening, that he should not spend so much time there alone, but he looked at me with such a puzzled expression, I did not mention it again.

When Oscar did arrive home in time for supper, we dined together, our two chairs at opposite ends of the table, mine on the side closest to the kitchen. The other chairs in the set of four rested against the wall piled with books or clean table linens. The chairs had a purpose and I could pretend they were not reminders of who should have been seated in them, whether Ellie or Ellie and Marcy or one of her other friends. Usually Oscar brought the newspaper with him to the table to catch up on any news he had missed at breakfast. News qualified as a safe topic in the household. Every once in a while, if he found an article he thought interesting, Oscar would read a passage or the headline aloud.

The only other topic we exchanged regularly related to the evening meal. Oscar complimented me on the food I'd prepared. He was not merely being polite; the meals were delicious. I experimented with new menus, new dishes, new spices. I indulged in cooking and baking. I spent hours, sometimes my whole day in the kitchen. I forced myself to read recipes and books on cooking, techniques for soufflés, brioches, and éclairs, foreign techniques with exotic names, or at least exotic to me, things that captured my attention and fended off more burdensome thoughts.

"What do we have here today?" Oscar would ask as he sat down to dinner.

Depending on the evening's menu, I'd respond, "chicken and apple dumplings," or "roast pork with tomatoes", simple home-cooked meals made from recipes passed from one generation to the next in either the Stephens or the Bauer family early in the week. More extravagant meals with foreign names and imported ingredients as the week progressed.

Oscar noticed, but never questioned my efforts. When I made one of the meals I had served for years, and reminded him of that, he admitted he might have just tasted the food for the first time. He savored the simple combination of ingredients. When the meal was something new, he would ask me to name the spices he could not name. We lingered over our dinners together. We took advantage of the one time of day we were the man and woman we had once been, me the wife he had once loved, he the husband I believed I'd loved.

Oscar spent more nights away from home, whether because his work required him to travel more frequently or because he simply volunteered for the duty more often than his cohorts did, he did not say. The L&N had promoted Oscar to the position of regional freight manager. With the change in title, he acquired responsibility for Louisville to the east, and Paducah to the southwest. The position also required he travel more often. When he could, Oscar took the morning train to one or other of the cities and returned home late the same day.

Even when he arrived home late, if he'd missed our dinner together, I would leave a plate of food for him. I would have already eaten and gone to our bedroom upstairs. During those solitary suppers, the pages of the newspaper rustled as he turned them, reading while he ate. He took his time, relishing the meal without me. When he finished he carried his plate to the kitchen then went out to the front porch. If the temperature were mild, he would sit in one of the rockers and smoke his pipe in the dark. As he rocked, one of the floor panels made a light, rhythmic creak. I kept the window by our bed cracked an inch or two. The rhythmic tone of the rocker seeped through the crack. *Creak,* pause, *creak*, pause, like the steady clatter of a railcar advancing along the track.

When he smoked, tendrils of gray rose in the night air. They snaked upward, above the porch, to the second floor, and then dissipated. A scent of tobacco drifted through the window upstairs where I lay. Awake.

Eventually, Oscar would climb the stairs to bed.

He would come to our bed, undress, and reach across in the darkened room for me. I let him touch me, let him caress my shoulder and brush his fingertips against my hips, but I said nothing and made no move toward him. I lay with my back to him, my eyes closed, and my breath even.

"Anneliese," he whispered. Then again, "Anneliese."

Always twice. Then, he'd turn in the bed and lower his head to his pillow.

I brought the vase of freshly cut dahlias into Ellie's room and placed them on the nightstand near the window. On Tuesdays, I dusted the entire house. Ellie's room was always the last on my schedule. After arranging the dahlias in the vase, I sat on the edge of the bed and peered down into the garden. From the years I'd spent in this room when it had been my parents' house, I knew that the church, the railroad station, and the river, were visible from the window. Nevertheless, I avoided so much as a glance at the slice of sparkling water that tempted and dared me to look. The sun warmed the air, its soft rays entered at a slant through the window and rested on the folds of my skirt. I closed my eyes for a few moments.

When I opened them again, minute dust particles danced in the light as they drifted through the air in front of my face. I remembered why I was here. I sighed and resumed my chore. I wiped a thin layer of dust from the nightstand then crossed to the dresser to wipe it as well. Long emptied of Ellie's clothing, I had stored a few of my own things inside, gloves, a scarf, and my keepsakes tucked away at the back of the topmost drawer. I slid the drawer open and ran my cloth over the top edge. As I pushed the drawer closed, an edge of blue ribbon caught my eye. I opened the drawer again, wider this time. I saw the bow that surrounded my keepsakes had come loose—or had been untied by someone. One of the strands lay undone, limp against the bottom of the drawer; a crease dimpled the delicate kerchief. With both hands, I removed the box and retied the bow, and aligned its edges. I did not take the time to unfold the kerchief or read the words in the letter. Had I wished to, I could have penciled an accurate representation of the scene from memory alone. I could have cited the words in the letter by heart. Instead, I returned the bundle to its place at the back of the drawer, closed the drawer, and moved on to the next.

When I finished, I returned down the stairs to the first floor and to the spare room where I kept my crochet work. I settled into the rocker—the refinished rocker I'd come to accept after thirty or forty years—and did a few rows before bed. Sometimes, when Oscar spent the night away from home, I slept there as I had during the last weeks of my pregnancy.

Oscar had been surprised the first time he arrived home late to find our bed empty. His steps echoed across the floor above my head. After checking Ellie's room, he paused, then came down the stairs. He found me downstairs, caressed my shoulder with his fingers. This time, he did not call my name. A click let me know he'd closed the door behind him.

Hannah, Emma, Molly, and I met on Wednesdays each week without fail. We'd chosen Wednesdays. It was the only day during the week that Hannah closed the hair salon she'd operated for the last fifteen years. Having never married, the salon provided her a means of support. One day away from the salon in the middle of the week was all she dared sacrifice. We spent our time together embroidering, knitting, or quilting. Our hands were never idle. Plates piled with samples of my cakes or cookies sat on the tables around us while we gossiped.

The conversation usually wandered a familiar path from baking, to sewing, to church activities. Other than when one of us asked politely after Molly's two young daughters, we avoided discussing children. Molly kept her stories of their latest escapades brief, sensitive to my loss and to Emma's. Emma and Paul had tried but failed to bear children.

Rarely did the conversation touch on business or the economy. This Wednesday, the third week of May, was an exception. Emma shared the news.

"Where did you hear that," Molly asked.

"Ouch," I said as I rubbed the tip of my finger where I had pricked it with my needle.

"Paul told me," Emma said. "He said he heard it from Loren. He swears it's true. He said the manager from Chicago would break the news next week. Liese, I'm sure you've heard the same from Oscar?"

The women turned to look at me. Preoccupied in stemming the flow of blood from the tip of my finger, I had avoided the conversation until that moment.

"Well, I don't pay too much attention to rumors, Emma. Even if they are true, we've been through hard times before. I am quite sure there'll be more in the future. You can count on that. Anyway, Oscar's not concerned."

"I hope you're right," Emma said.

I caught a glimpse of Molly studying my face. She said, "Let's talk about something more pleasant."

The conversation turned to the upcoming church bazaar. I had difficulty following the dialogue. I brought the linen hand towel closer to my face and forced myself to concentrate on the unfinished outline of the flower petal. I had just changed threads. I selected a light peach color to outline the five magenta petals. Emma's rumor, though, refused to be ignored. It hung in the air, as if it were an unpleasant odor or an annoying buzz. It surrounded the settee where I sat, hardened into a shell that drowned out the familiar patter of my friends' voices until they were nothing more than whispers in the background.

Oscar had made no mention of troubles at the railroad. He'd always preferred to keep business matters to himself. Even during the Depression, when the railroad had declared bankruptcy, I had learned the news from someone else. Now, I hoped that if Emma's rumor were correct, that layoffs were coming, the railroad would point its finger at someone else, not at Oscar. He had paid his dues. We had paid our dues. I reassured myself with the knowledge that Oscar had recently received his promotion accompanied by a small increase in salary. Someone must have recognized his value to the railroad. He'd worked into the wee hours of the morning and traveled away from home each time they had asked him. He'd never once complained. Surely, that was proof of his allegiance.

When Oscar arrived home that evening, he seemed his usual self. After he hung his hat and coat on the hall tree, he sauntered into the kitchen to let me know he'd arrived. He asked what we were having for dinner. As he turned to go upstairs to change, I asked how his day had gone.

"Fine, same as always," he answered. I detected a note of surprise. I rarely inquired after his day.

I decided I'd wait until dinner to inquire further. I wanted to gauge his mood before I posed a few questions, before I relayed Emma's news. I turned back to the sink and listened for the echo of his steps on the stairs before I ran the faucet to blanch the beans.

Throughout dinner, I observed Oscar's manner carefully. I scanned his face for signs of concern, of nervousness, of concealment. As usual, he looked through the paper while we ate and mentioned an item or two, but said and did nothing out of the ordinary. I finished ahead of Oscar. I kept my hands in my lap. I circled them over each other several times. I'd tried to catch myself when I did that. It reminded me of my mother and I feared that I had become her. I placed my hands apart on my thighs and willed them to be still. When, at last, Oscar folded the paper and set it aside, I said, "I heard there might be some difficulties at the railroad. Some new trouble, perhaps even layoffs coming."

"What are you talking about? Where did you hear that?"

"From Emma. Today. She and Hannah were here this afternoon. Of course, I have no idea where she might have heard the rumor."

"You can't believe everything you hear, especially not third or fourth hand."

"I thought the worst was over, that business was improving. Just last week, you said so."

"Yes, it has been. The latest merger should give us a boost as well."

"That's what I thought you said."

"Well, you can never be certain. New managers always think they have to make cuts. They have to show they can eke out another penny here, another penny there. It's not something you need to concern yourself with."

Oscar pushed his chair back from the table. He grabbed the paper up and took it with him to the front room, leaving me with my thoughts and little comfort from his words.

Several days passed without a mention of the railroad. I dared not ask Oscar for any news. I decided to visit his office, to see for myself, if I could. I hadn't gone to the station more than a handful of times before, but I knew the people, particularly Henry Asner, Oscar's boss and Edith Waters, his secretary. I don't know what I expected to find but I believed if I encountered either, I'd sense their outlook. I'd learn more there than I would on the lines in Oscar's face.

I'd fabricated a cover story, something to do with reminding Oscar to speak with Wallace at the hardware store on his way home. My clothes washer needed repairs. That much was true. It did need repairs, though it was something I could take care of myself, and usually did. The excuse would serve though if questioned by Edith, or Henry, or Oscar.

The administrative building sat opposite the railway station. A tall double door opened to a dark stairway with bare walls. I climbed to the second floor, my steps echoed behind me as I went. At the top, another door stood, much smaller than the one

I'd come through on the street. The hustle and bustle of activity inside the large room struck me at once. Keys slapped the carriages of four typewriters in unison. A rat-a-tat-tat spit into the air followed by an occasional zip as the four women typists sent the typewriter carriages back to their starting positions. Two or three phones rang from behind glass-enclosed offices that circled the typists. Snippets of conversation barked over the din of the typewriters. Chicago. Yes, tomorrow at noon. Yes. New York. Let me see.

No one noticed my entrance. In front of me, a dour-faced woman sat with a deep frown on her face. She squinted hard at the pages in front of her, ignoring or forgetting the eyeglasses that a chain of clear plastic beads held around her neck.

I looked past her, to the left and spotted Edith. She looked up as I approached. Edith smiled broadly, stood, and came around her desk.

"Mrs. Wolf, what a surprise. I wasn't expecting to see you."

"Hello, Edith. I was just passing by." I'd already glanced around and through the glass that separated Oscar's office from the typing pool. His office was vacant. He was nowhere to be seen anywhere else on the floor either. "I thought I might catch Oscar before he left, so that..." I let my voice trail off.

"That's too bad. He's gone. He told me he had some errands to do. Mr. Dooley from Chicago is here today and due back any minute. He's the First Vice President you know, and as I am sure Oscar told you, he called a meeting for later today. So, I'm sure Oscar will be back."

"That's quite alright, Edith. Yes, I do remember Oscar said something about a late meeting. My mistake. No matter. I'll talk to him later this evening at home."

"Certainly, Mrs. Wolf."

"I'll be going. By the way, how are Sally and Sam?" I made a half-turn to go, hoping to avoid a conversation about her two grandchildren.

"Why they're doing just fine. Thank you."

"Wonderful. Goodbye."

When I reached the house, I heard Oscar in the kitchen.

'You're home early," I said.

"Yes, I finished what I needed to do."

He made no mention of the meeting with Mr. Dooley, which he clearly had no plan to attend. What's more, he made no attempt to explain his being home at this early hour.

I tried to act as if nothing out of the ordinary had occurred. "Would you like a cup of coffee?" I asked. I reached for the tin in the cupboard.

'No. Liese," he paused, "I think you should sit down."

Besides Oscar, the railroad had also eliminated one of the other Evansville managers and two clerks. The layoff devastated Oscar. At first, he rose as he always had, bathed, and dressed as if for work. The same starched white shirt, the same gray trousers and coat, the same dark tie. He'd read the newspaper for hours whereas before it had taken him only minutes. He'd walk from room to room, until he made me dizzy. I escaped into the garden. By dinnertime, he would have changed from his work clothes to something more comfortable. He would go to bed early.

He rose later and later each day. Some days, I wondered whether he would get up at all.

We had suffered through the threat of unemployment during the Great Depression when every day had been a challenge. With the economy improving, we'd thought such trepidations were behind us. Business rebounded, though, and within six months of his furlough, Oscar returned to work. Regardless, the layoff had a lasting effect on his morale. He dressed, went to work, and returned, but never spoke of his work in quite the same way. Where before he had said the railroad needed and valued his expertise, his contacts, his ethics, even wondered if they could do without him, now he talked of the younger, hungrier men who were ready to take his place with little notice and less cost.

Years earlier, I remembered he had once compared the railroad to his family. I chose not to remind him of that statement.

CHAPTER 25

Oscar and the Hummingbird

An hour before supper, I heard Hannah call my name. She'd come around the house and into the garden. I turned, surprised to see her, surprised that she would arrive without notice. Facing the blinding light of the afternoon sun, I squinted and raised a hand to shield my eyes.

Behind Hannah, Sheriff Alvin approached the closed gate. The silhouette of his bulk unmistakable. I could not fathom why he had come with Hannah to my home.

"Liese. It's Oscar." Hannah's words were little more than a whisper.

I flinched at the words, but made no move toward or away from Hannah. Instead, I focused on Sheriff Alvin; his clumsy sausage like fingers fumbled with the latch on the gate, the sweat beaded on his forehead as he failed to open the simple clasp.

"He's gone," Hannah continued, still in a hushed tone. "There was an accident. Out on King's Road. By the river."

The breeze that had blown my apron and trapped my hand in its folds evaporated. The oppressive heat returned. The apron hung limp against my skirt. There was only a strong white light in front of me. I crumpled to the ground. The cluster of early-blooming zinnias that edged the beds of peas on the left, lettuce and cauliflower on the right, offered little to cushion my fall.

I heard Hannah gasp. Then she knelt beside me on the ground. She removed a handkerchief from my sleeve and fanned the air above my face. A whiff of lavender filled the air.

"Sheriff, please come help."

Sheriff Allen strode into the garden. He did not bother to close the gate and instead crossed to my other side and looked down at me, oblivious that he had trampled a patch of zinnias in the process. Hannah grabbed my elbow and tried to help me sit upright. Sheriff Allen shooed her aside and placed a hand around my arm. I was standing again. I flailed in the air to wave off the sheriff. I feared he would lift me off my feet and carry me into the house otherwise.

"I'll be alright. I'm fine," I said. Still, the sheriff did not release his hold on my arms. "Please. Leave me alone. I said I'm alright," my irritation at their fussing over me noticeable in my tone. Hannah stepped back one pace and then so did the sheriff.

"It's okay David," Hannah said. "I think we can manage now."

I pulled away from them and walked unaided toward the kitchen door. Once inside, I reached behind my back to undo the bow formed by the apron's ties. I held the soiled apron in front of my face and shook my head. Hannah, who had joined me at the sink, stared at the smudges of black earth where my knees had taken the brunt of the fall. I plucked a few crushed zinnia petals from the apron and dropped them on to the counter. I reached around the back of the door for another apron.

"I need to clean this before the mud sets in," I said, more to the walls than to my cousin.

"I'll take care of the apron." Hannah wrenched the garment from me. She guided me to one of the four hard-back chairs at the kitchen table. "Sit." I sat. "Just sit for a minute or two," Hannah said. She took a glass from the cupboard, filled it with fresh water, and set it in front me on the table. I stared straight ahead at the wall across the room. I could not drink. I could not raise the glass.

Hannah had never married. Over the years, though, she had comforted enough friends and relatives who had lost loved ones to consider herself experienced in these matters. What's more, she knew me almost as well as she knew herself. She knew I would refuse help, refuse to have her or anyone else stay with me, refuse to come stay at her home. Nevertheless, Hannah tried to reason with me.

"You should come spend the night with me."

"No."

"Liese. Be reasonable. If you won't come stay with me, then let me stay with you here."

"No."

I rose from my chair, walked with slow, firm steps along the short, windowless hallway to the front room. I walked as if someone or something else controlled my movements. When I reached the open Bible on the stand at the far side of the sitting room, I bent over the thick well-thumbed book and grasped the stand with one hand. I flipped back to the frontispiece, then turned forward a few pages.

A handwritten account of family births, marriages, and deaths filled the third page of the Stephens family Bible. Stephens upon Stephens, some written as Stefan or Stephan, lined the left hand side in pencil, a scatter of Bauers on the right in all manner of handwriting. At the top of the page, the entries were harder to read, the writing uneven, crowded, and faded. Near the bottom, in my own careful penmanship, I read the names of my mother and father. Above them, I read my grandfather's name in my mother's handwriting.

Using the sharpened pencil lying in the cradle carved into the stand's ledge, I added Oscar Andrew Wolf, deceased June 25, 1946 on the blank row at the bottom.

The entry filled the last line on the page.

Two weeks passed before I summoned the courage to drive to King's Crossing. I drove alone in the Ford wagon and arrived at the crossing at 9:00 am, earlier than I imagined Oscar had on that day. He would have allowed neither too little nor too much time. I put the Ford in park and shut off the engine. The unpaved, deserted crossing filled the view through the windshield. I leaned against the seatback and closed my eyes. Rays of early morning light warmed the left side of my face and the sleeve of my blouse as my arm rested on the door through the lowered window. A typical warm summer day lay ahead. The temperature would inch upward throughout the day. It would be overbearing by mid-afternoon.

A slight breeze picked up the scent of fresh mown hay and carried it through the open window on one side of the car and out the other. I took a deep breath and thought how Oscar might have done the same. I opened my eyes and noticed for the first time the fields that lined the road on either side of the car. Long, neat rows of hay lay drying in the sun. The buzz of untold numbers of insects flying over or crawling through the straw rose then fell away in unison, each one perhaps signaling their territory, alerting others to a predator, or vying for the attention of a mate.

I glanced down at the cloth covered bench seat and to the objects that lay there where Oscar had placed them, his pocket watch and key ring, a simple metal loop that held the keys to the car, our home on First Avenue, the main door at the L&N office, and the top drawer of his desk. My hand rested on the upholstery, the threads coarse and stiff against my fingertips. I cupped my hand over the key ring and touched what he would have touched in his last moments.

I imagined Oscar, sitting calmly, his shirtfront rising and falling with each breath. His heart would have beat underneath in a precise, metronome-like rhythm, neither faster nor slower than usual. He would have been wearing his timepiece in his vest pocket and would have had to slide the t-bar through the buttonhole of the dark wool vest he wore despite the temperature. Though pocket watches had gone out of fashion after the war, like many railroad men, Oscar had continued to use one. He had carried his wherever he went. I had watched him thread it into his vest countless times, struck by his meticulous positioning of the chain. Now, I picked up the watch from the seat and held the case against one ear. A reassuring tick reverberated as the balance wheel rocked and the sweep hand, hidden inside, jumped ahead from mark to mark. I pressed the latch that opened the case to the face of the pocket watch. I ran my finger over the faded picture Oscar had cut to fit inside the unadorned gold cover. Ellie on her fifth birthday, 1925. She'd been just a young child then but even a casual observer could see the beauty in her features.

I closed the cover with one hand and listened for the audible click as it snapped into place over the face. The metal cooled my moist palm. It would fill the box in my drawer, I thought, as I laid the watch beside the key ring. The links of the chain tumbled and sank into and along one row of the seams stitched at perfect intervals across the blue cloth.

I imagined Oscar would have waited until precisely 9:40. After over thirty years with the railroad, starting with the Central and Eastern Illinois, later the Louisville and Nashville Railroad, Oscar knew the routes and schedules almost by heart. He also would have known some crossings were manned at all times due to heavy use while many more, most of them in little used, remote locations, like King's Road, were unattended. He would have reached through the open window and groped along the door with his left hand to find the door handle. The interior handle had not functioned for weeks. I remembered him saying several weeks ago he would take it apart to find the problem. Then, he would have opened the door, perhaps he propped it open to allow a breath of air to penetrate while he leaned over to the passenger side and raised the window. The sheriff found the car with both windows rolled up. Oscar would have done that to prevent dust from the fields to drift inside.

I closed my eyes again. I saw Oscar pick his hat from the seat, pause with his hand in midair, the hat balanced between his thumb and forefinger. Though he had likely tilted his head to put the hat on, he'd changed his mind, returned the hat to the seat, and placed it beside the key ring and watch. Oscar might have bent forward to wipe a speck from his left shoe, perhaps a piece of dirt, perhaps a stray bit of hay that had blown in the open door. Then, he would have stepped from the car. He would have squinted as the full force of the sun struck him. The lines on his forehead would have deepened. I'd seen those creases a thousand times.

He would have stooped over, reached into the car, and picked up his coat from where it lay folded over the front seat. Despite the temperature, he had put on the jacket and then walked the few paces to the tracks.

As if from nowhere, a horn blared. The sound shattered the peaceful morning. I started in my seat, opened my eyes, and stared forward as the cars of the train sped by in one long blur of color, heat, and noise.

The *Evansville Courier* ran a story about the incident, though it did not mention Oscar by name. The article merely stated the accident had shattered the on-time record for the *Hummingbird*, the name that L&N had given to its flagship locomotive. A photograph accompanied the article and in it, embarrassing for the railroad, the engine rested awkwardly, its stack smoking, simmering while its string of cars straddled the little used King's Crossing. A delay of three hours ensued.

I learned later, from the Sheriff, they'd retrieved the mangled corpse the *Hummingbird* had carried two hundred yards along the tracks before tossing it to the ground.

CHAPTER 26
Loaves and Leaves

From behind the counter of my bakery, I glanced at the clock—ten minutes until noon, closing time on Saturdays. Only two customers more needed my help before I would be free to go. I had invited Hannah for dinner for her fifty-fifth birthday and needed the afternoon to prepare.

Julie and Elizabeth, two women I knew from church, had stopped by to purchase bread for the weekend. They had planned a special dinner and wanted my advice on which of my breads, the dark *Volkornbrot*, with a sprinkle of sunflower seeds or the lighter sourdough, perfect in its flour-dusted simplicity, would best compliment their planned meal. In the three years since I had opened my bakery, Anneliese's German American Confectionary, I had learned a great deal. Not about baking, but about marketing. Rarely did anyone leave the premises without a loaf of bread or a pastry they had not planned to purchase.

Today, however, I was anxious to close. I wanted to complete the transaction whether they left with one loaf or none. I had expounded on the merits of several alternatives. The dark, savory flavor of pumpernickel infused with ground dates—a secret ingredient I never acknowledged. The light air-filled cheddar and olive loaf, I assured them would never overpower Julie's Sunday Chicken. And now, they were torn between the *Volkornbrot* and the sourdough. Still, they hemmed and hawed.

While the two discussed their list again, I set covers over the unsold pastries atop my display case, wiped the counter, and counted the day's proceeds. I'd hoped these activities would spur them to a decision.

"We'll take the pumpernickel, Liese," Julie said.

"And the cheddar," Elizabeth added. "You know that's my favorite. I'll save it for later if we finish the pumpernickel tonight."

They left. The tin bells chimed as I closed the door behind them. I turned out the lights and then gathered my things to leave. I had my own shopping to do.

Wedging the bag of groceries between my hip and the doorframe, I unlatched the front door and pushed it open with my foot. I passed through the front room and went straight to the kitchen where I dropped the groceries on the counter. I had not looked at the clock, but now, as it chimed, I counted...three...four. Two hours before Hannah was due. I had ample time to finish Hannah's favorite meal, chicken and dumplings. I'd brought a rhubarb pie from the bakery for dessert.

I retrieved a carton of milk and three eggs from the refrigerator, and placed them on the counter beside the groceries. I eyed the eggs for a second to ensure they did not roll away. My pattern of movements around the kitchen was a marvel of efficiency—a tribute to years of baking—with one hand I could open a cabinet, reach in and extract a bowl or jar or spoon without a glance while I opened a drawer with my other hand.

The dumplings came together quickly. Most of my recipes, I could complete instinctively. I rarely referred to a recipe.

I mixed, kneaded, and rolled the silken dough. I took half, folded it over onto itself and set it aside. It would be enough for leftovers the next day. Once the dumplings were made, I let them rest and sliced the fresh, whole chicken I'd bought at the market. I put on a kettle of water to make a broth with the scraps. Soon, the soothing aroma of chicken, celery, and sage filled the kitchen.

I turned my attention to the pie. I spooned the ruby red rhubarb into the center of the dough-lined pan. As a final touch for this special event, I cut a dozen leaf shapes from the spare dough.

I never passed through an entire day without a thought of Ellie. Today was no exception. Usually insignificant, everyday tasks raised the memories, tasks like decorating a pie, or drawing a spoon from a pot of chicken soup, or turning a page in my cookbook to find where she had drawn a flower or stuffed a leaf to flatten it for some long-ago planned project. All sliced deep into my heart. They poked at the still open wound. Usually, I stopped, breathed deeply to regain my composure, then carried on.

Today, the tears welled in my eyes in spite of my attempt to focus on the pie. I tried to take a deep breath but the tears were stuck in my throat. I tried to lift one of the limp, warm leaf shapes and place it on the piecrust, but stopped. I held it in mid-air for a moment then returned it to the counter.

I wiped my eyes with the back of my hand and left a smudge of flour dust on my cheek. The tears streamed down my cheeks and made their way through the smudge of flour, then flowed unchecked down to my chin. I sobbed. I had not cried when I had buried Ellie or when I had lost Oscar. Now, my body heaved with sorrow, not just for the loss of Ellie, or Oscar, but for all my losses. Dark shapes appeared in my head, behind my closed eyes, shapes of the widows I'd visited so long ago. I remembered how, draped in black, they had mourned without reservation, without shame, acknowledging openly the depth of their loss.

From somewhere deep inside, Oscar's name clawed its way. Oscar. It grabbed at my dry throat. Oscar. It blistered the roof of my mouth, and finally, it emerged into a single long moan.

I sat at the kitchen table and let my head drop into my arms crossed on top of the table. I wept until I'd run out of tears. Drained, I raised the edge of my apron to wipe my eyes and the traces of flour from my face. On the counter, the unfinished pie begged me to finish. The six remaining leaves had grown limp in the humid air on the counter. After a few minutes, I rose, took a knife, and pressed its edge in each. I drew the point around to form a perfect circle, perhaps it was the letter *o*, perhaps it was just a circle, in the center of each leaf. Ellie would be proud, I thought. I placed the newly adorned leaves on the bare half of the pie then whisked it into the oven. I peeked into the covered pot on the stove to check on the chicken. I sampled the hot broth.

Five-thirty. The pie would need another forty-five minutes.

I washed, dried, and put away my utensils and realized a tune had crept into the back of my mind. I'd hummed a few bars, not quite knowing what the tune had been and how to continue. When I closed my eyes, it came back, a few bars at first, then more, the tune took shape, the melody rang clear.

In the living room, I crouched beside my new turntable set, an extravagance I'd allowed myself last year. Though modest, the survivors' benefits from Oscar's railroad pension covered my basic needs. The bakery had not yet turned a profit, but I thought of it as a calling, not a business anyway. I'd purchased a few recordings as a gift to myself last Christmas. The recordings stood in alphabetical order in the four divided compartments below the turntable. I could find my favorite melodies with little effort. I removed the second vinyl in the third compartment from the left and then extracted the ink-black disk from its sleeve. I wiped it gently with the hem of my skirt, following the circular grooves. When I lowered the needle onto the disk, strains of a tune I recalled from an evening long ago in St. Louis filled the room.

I took a few steps across the room toward the wingback chair, then halted in the center of the open expanse. I closed my eyes and let the music surround me. I lifted an arm and extended it to my dance partner. He took it and grasped me around the waist. I placed my free arm on his shoulder. "Why not?" I thought. Laughing aloud, I said, "Thank you. Yes, I would love to have this dance."

I stepped to the right, one step, then followed with my other foot. I leaned forward, stepped again, right, then left. I moved in a wider and wider arc across the floor. Though anyone who observed the solitary dance might have thought I stepped hesitantly, unevenly, and clumsily, in my mind's eye and my partner's, I circled the room with grace. I completed a few turns around the room and started another, my back now to the door.

Hannah shouted loud enough to be heard over the music, "Liese, what are you doing?"

I had not heard her knock. Though startled by her voice, I pushed my left foot forward in time with the music. "*Stille*," I said, "come dance with me."

Acknowledgements

Conceiving, researching, writing, editing, and publishing this story would not have been possible without the help of family members, friends, critique group members, advance readers, editors, and countless sources of information.

Particular thanks goes to my grandmother who decades ago gifted me the WWI sweetheart scarf she kept tucked away in a drawer for so many years. And, to my mother who preserved the photo of my grandmother's boyfriend in his horse-drawn carriage and the many labeled and unlabeled photos of her family and friends from Evansville. Both were in large part responsible for sending me down that long and winding path of discovery.

I am also deeply indebted to: the Willard Library in Evansville, Indiana and their online archives, whether their Postcard and Photography Galleries or their many indices to sources of information on life along the Ohio; to the Evansville Courier Press for their coverage of the 1937 Flood and other historical events; and to Ancestry.com and a thousand other websites I devoured during my research.

Finally, thanks to my husband for waiting, however patiently or not, for conversation and company on many nights until I'd pecked away at my keyboard well past a decent hour.

About the Author

 Rona Simmons grew up in a military family with its constant duty rotations denying her the luxury of establishing roots and the comfort of the familiar, but she gained the invaluable opportunity to live abroad and experience diverse cultures.

Rona was determined to pursue a business career and earned a BA in Economics from Newcomb College and later an MBA from Georgia State. She spent thirty years in corporate America where she honed her skills in analysis and research, never knowing that she'd make use of those same talents after retiring in unearthing, examining, and constructing stories from the smallest kernel of information.

Her previous works include a ghostwritten biography of a prominent Atlanta businessman, a collection of short stories compiled from interviews of family and friends from the early to mid 1900s, articles for a local Atlanta magazine and a horticultural journal, and flash fiction broadcast on internet radio.

Rona lives with her husband and (she swears) the last member of a passel of cats outside Atlanta, Georgia on eight pine-studded acres. Though still fascinated by her German-Midwest American heritage, Rona is busy exploring her father's side of the family for a new novel set in Boston, Massachusetts.

Her website is www.ronasimmons.com where she has posted photographs and other information relevant to Liese's story.

Discussion

1. In her opening words, Liese recalls the scents of cinnamon, sugar cookies, and chicken and dumplings, all warm, comforting smells we attribute to her mother baking in the nearby kitchen. She also recalls other, less pleasant odors associated with her mother's scrubbing, rubbing, beating, and polishing as she cleans the home, perhaps obsessively. Once, when she stands close to Will, she wonders, even worries, what her own scent is. How would you describe Liese's scent? What other scents are mentioned in the story? What scents can you recall from your early years and what memories do they evoke, whether pleasant or unpleasant?

2. Liese learns how to behave, not only by threat of punishment, but also by example. After visiting a recently widowed member of the congregation, she observes her father make a note in what may be nothing more than a pocket calendar. Liese interprets this act as the means to manage the loss of something dear and begins to write down her own losses. How does this ritual influence, consciously or subconsciously, her means of handling losses later in life? Is there a custom or belief that you learned by observation only to later find that you were misled?

3. The abuse that Liese suffers at the hands of her grandfather is one of the many causes of Liese's stunted emotional develop-

ment. Is Liese the only emotionally challenged character in the book? Do you feel more connected with Liese after she shares her story of abuse? What other revelations provide an emotional bond with the characters?

4. When Liese receives a parting gift from Jack, she places it in a box at the back of a drawer in her bedroom and mentions she does not look at it again for six months. Later we learn she also collected a stone from the riverbank where Will died and put this object into the box. Are the items in the box keepsakes to preserve the memory or memorials to those gone, or simply elements of a ritual that she executes? Is Liese avoiding dealing with her losses in the way she handles the objects? Do you collect things and if so, what sorts of things are they and what do you do with them?

5. References to water occur throughout the story, from the opening chapter that establishes Liese's hometown to be on the banks of the Ohio, to the stream by which the hunting accident occurs, to the slice of river that Liese can see from her upstairs window, and to the figurative river that carves her home in two near the end. What is the significance of these references? How do they unite the story?

6. Besides sorrow from the death of those near and dear to Liese, she suffers from neglect, abuse, shame, fear, hate, and unfaithfulness, situations that would test even the most virtuous, god-fearing individual. How do each of Liese's trials affect her and how does she respond? How could she have done things differently? For what outcome is she to blame?

7. In the book, there are numerous examples of obedience, including Liese's obedience to the dictates of her father's church and preaching, her mother's requests for help, and her grandfather's demands. During her honeymoon, Liese considers the vows she took earlier in the day, including to love, cherish and

obey, the last of which is often eliminated in contemporary wedding ceremonies. How does obedience play into each of Liese's relationships?

8. Liese reaches adulthood stunted emotionally as a result of her upbringing. In her story, she singles out the four men in her life and her daughter, all people she should be able to love. Does she truly love any one of them? Do any of them truly love her?

9. The ending is deliberately vague, though there are hints of Liese's state of mind. What do you think the future holds for her? Has she or will she find happiness, peace, love?